TRUST ISSUES

TRUST ISSUES

/ A NOVEL /

Elizabeth McCullough Keenan and Greg Wands

DUTTON

DUTTON

An imprint of Penguin Random House LLC

penguinrandomhouse.com

DUTTON and the D colophon are registered trademarks of Penguin Random House LLC.

LIBRARY OF CONGRESS CATALOGING-IN-PUBLICATION DATA
has been applied for.

ISBN 9780593474204 (hardcover)
ISBN 9780593474228 (ebook)

Printed in the United States of America
1st Printing

BOOK DESIGN BY LAURA K. CORLESS

For Christopher

You're all players, Sonny. You get high on the action.

—Caroline Crockett, *Miami Vice*

PART
I

PROLOGUE

The ground slips out from beneath her feet.

She's over the low wall, stomach in her throat as a hand shoots up desperately to try to grasp the edge of the weathered stone. Panic swells as fingers swipe the cold, hard slab to no avail, her body tumbling in a heap, knocking helplessly against the rocky surface, bright bursts of pain reducing her vision to a blinding flash of white, tensed muscles going limp from the sudden shock.

Her body clears the wall and continues its descent, the sheer terror of helplessness giving way for a blessed second to the complete freedom of weightlessness. She thinks of Hazel. She thinks of Kagan. She thinks of Perry. There is the briefest burst of love, of regret, of rage, of grief, of acceptance.

And then, there is nothing.

CHAPTER 1

Perry watches as the doorman retrieves his suitcase from the trunk of the parked sedan. He offers Perry a tentative smile, teeth clenched. "Good evening, Mr. Walters. How was your trip?"

"As well as could be hoped for, Theo." Perry shuts the door behind him and taps the roof of the car, sending it off.

"You have visitors waiting." Theo lowers his voice a shade. "A couple of detectives, from the NYPD."

As Perry picks up on the look of unease the young doorman is doing his best to mask, a hollow feeling creeps into the pit of his stomach. Distracted by the sensation in his gut, he's suddenly transported back to childhood, to an interaction with his mother.

When his older sister, Constance, abruptly left home, Perry began splitting his time between the one-screen movie house in his small town and the children's nook of the public library. He first encountered the expression "pit of the stomach" in one of the storybooks he read while working his way through the contents of the towering shelves.

When Perry returned home that particular day, he asked his mother about the meaning behind the phrase. She mumbled something unintelligible in response, her voice thick with booze, before sucking down a long pull off her Pall Mall.

The sight of the duo awaiting him in the lobby snaps Perry back into the present, and he shakes off a chill that can't be blamed on the warm spring weather. He smooths his rumpled shirtfront with flat palms as a smartly dressed woman and a sinewy man with a neatly manicured goatee stand up from a pair of chairs. They both appear impossibly youthful for their job titles.

"Perry Walters?" asks the woman.

"Yes, that's me."

"Detective Gina Calabrese, with the NYPD. This is my partner, Detective Woodson." The young woman extends a hand, which Perry takes with his own. Her hair is collected in a bun, and her fresh face is devoid of all but a hint of makeup. There's a trace of Long Island in her voice. She's doing a fine job of keeping her expression neutral, but he can sense unease at the edge of her gaze. Her partner, meanwhile, offers a polite but solemn nod. "Mind if we have a word with you in private?"

"Is everything okay?" asks Perry, the churn in his gut ramping up. "Did something happen?"

"Mr. Walters," says Calabrese, her gaze shifting subtly toward the doorman. "It would be better if we spoke elsewhere."

"Of course." Perry leads Detective Calabrese toward the elevator as Detective Woodson takes Perry's suitcase and follows them down the hall. They step into the elevator and head upstairs.

"You've been traveling, sir?" asks Calabrese as she eyes the luggage.

"Yes, I was down in South Carolina these past few days, handling some family matters."

"I see," she says, and the detectives exchange a glance. A stilted silence ensues, until they arrive on the tenth floor and step out of the elevator. Perry leads the partners down the hall and opens the apartment door.

He studies the detectives as Calabrese subtly takes in the interior of the space—the extravagant artwork on the walls, the antique furniture, the Restoration Hardware light fixture above the long table, all courtesy of his wife Janice's deep pocketbook—while a deferential Woodson sets the suitcase in a corner and watches his partner closely for cues. After a moment, the young woman turns to Perry with a look of concern.

"Is there somewhere we can have a seat and talk, Mr. Walters?"

"Please, call me Perry." He points the detectives to the living room, then nods in the direction of the walnut-and-leather lounge chairs at either end of the coffee table. They take their seats as he lowers himself onto the sofa. Calabrese's eyes sweep across the floor-to-ceiling bookshelves built into the wall before landing uneasily on Perry. "You're the emergency contact for a Janice Thornhill?"

"Yes, she's my wife." He sets a hand on the arm of the sofa to steady himself. "Oh, God, is everything okay?"

"When's the last time you spoke with your wife, sir?"

"I called her as soon as I landed, but it went to voicemail."

Detective Calabrese blinks for a long second, as if trying to ward off the news she and her partner have come here to break. "I'm afraid there's been an accident."

Perry digs the heel of his other hand into the sofa cushion beside him. "What sort of . . . accident?"

"Your wife was found late this afternoon. I'm very sorry."

"Very sorry, sir," echoes Woodson.

"No." Perry tries desperately to suck air into his lungs as a sob erupts. He rocks back and forth, folding further into himself with each sway. "No, no, no." Oh, Janice. "This can't be."

The detectives say nothing as they allow Perry time to work through the horrific shock of the news. After a few long, agonizing moments, he straightens up, wipes the tears from his eyes with the sleeve of his oxford shirt, and squares his attention on Calabrese.

"Tell me what happened to her."

"Well, that's what we're trying to figure out, sir. Can you share a bit about your wife's typical routine?"

"Certainly." Perry clears his throat. "Janice spent most days working as a docent at the Cloisters, up near Inwood."

"A *docent*, you said?"

"Yes, sort of like a museum tour guide. It's a voluntary position. Mostly retired people, like us."

"I see." Detective Calabrese jots something in a notepad she's plucked from her jacket pocket. "So you're retired as well, Mr. Walters?"

"I am. I worked as a corporate accountant for many years."

"Uh-huh. And your wife was interested in art, I take it?"

"She was. Janice studied art history during undergrad. She's been an avid collector for years, and the museum position was the perfect fit."

"Right. And do you have a sense of what her postwork routine normally entailed?"

"On nice days, like today, she'd usually take a walk around the grounds after the museum closed at five, to have a look at the scenery. Then she'd get a car home. I'd often be coming back from birdwatching in Central Park, and so we'd discuss our time in nature with each other. It was one of our favorite parts of the day." Perry's voice cracks, and he takes a moment to compose himself. "I'm sorry, I'm just . . ."

"Nothing to apologize for. Please, take all the time you need."

He looks at the ceiling as he blinks away tears, then turns back to Calabrese and nods.

"Are you okay to go on?"

"Yes. Thank you."

"Of course. Now, were you concerned when your wife failed to pick up her phone earlier?"

"Not particularly. Janice doesn't always answer. Neither of us is very tech savvy. And to be honest with you, I was still a bit distracted from the visit with my sister."

"In South Carolina."

"That's right."

"I see." Calabrese adds to her notes. "And I'm assuming your sister can confirm this?"

"I . . . well, I hope so, yes."

She catches Woodson's glance before cocking her head to the side and reassessing Perry. "You *hope* so?"

"My sister's memory is slipping. Considerably, I'm afraid. Part of the reason I went for a visit was to see what sort of shape she was in." He clears his throat. "I may have to set up other arrangements for her soon." Constance's current condition jarred Perry. It seemed these days that every time he showed up at the neglected old house on Hilton Head, his sister had slid further toward the abyss. The condition of the place, along with the woman's failing health, served as an unsettling reminder of impending mortality.

"I see. I'm sorry to hear that. Do you have any other family you can reach out to?"

"Well, I *had* a daughter." Perry stares off mournfully. "Once upon a time."

"Oh." Calabrese is quiet for a moment. "Again, I'm sorry."

"That's kind of you to say. Thank you." He returns his focus to her. "In any case, I'm sure I can provide you with the ticket stubs from my flights, and the car receipts." He offers both detectives a grim look. "I realize you have a job to do."

"That would be appreciated." There's a trace of bashfulness in the detective's expression. "Now, I just want to pivot back for a moment, Mr. Walters. Would you say your wife got along with her work colleagues, as far as you were aware?"

"I believe so, yes. There was a lot of competition around landing that position, if you can believe it. Lots of lobbying, getting the right recommendation, that sort of thing. There's a certain cachet to being a docent, and I know Janice engendered some animosity at first." He studies Calabrese's eyes as he assesses her question and finds in them a look of morbid curiosity. *What exactly is this young detective angling at?* "Why are you asking about this? Didn't you say that her death was accidental?"

Detective Calabrese straightens up nearly imperceptibly in the chair, and her partner unconsciously mirrors the movement. "Sir," she says, "your wife was discovered at the bottom of a steep incline near the base of a stone wall surrounding one of the lookout points in the park. It's entirely possible that she simply lost her balance and tumbled over the wall, but the trajectory of the fall suggests there may have been foul play involved."

"Foul play?" Perry's stomach clenches up all over again.

"Yes, sir. We think it's possible someone may have pushed her over that wall."

A fog of silence fills the space as Perry grapples with the thought. "But who in the hell would have . . ."

"That's what I was hoping you might be able to help us answer.

You don't think it's possible anyone at work was harboring a big enough grudge to do this sort of thing?"

"It's a museum job, for Christ's sake!" Perry catches the emotion in his voice and takes a long, slow breath. "I'm sorry, Detective."

"Completely understandable." She marks something down in the notepad. "And you'd describe your wife as a happy person overall?"

"Happy? Yes, I mean, all in all. Why do you ask?"

Calabrese swallows nervously. "I don't mean to be indelicate, Mr. Walters, but I just need to rule out all . . . *possibilities* here."

Perry laughs in spite of himself. "Detective, I can't tell you with any certainty what happened to Janice, but I can absolutely assure you that my wife did not take her own life. In addition to being a person of devout faith, she was the most positive human being I've ever known. The thought would never have crossed her mind."

"I see."

"This was a woman who truly looked at every day as a gift filled with the possibility of infinite surprise. And not in that sunny affirmation, self-help way. She really felt the truth of it, as hokey as that might sound. There was a passage from Corinthians that she liked to quote, about God's temple being holy, and each one of us being that temple." Perry swipes away a looming tear. "No, Detective, you can go ahead and take that idea right off the table."

"Okay, Mr. Walters. I hear what you're saying." She makes a note. "Which brings us back to my previous question. Is there anyone *else* you can think of, outside her job, who may have had an issue with your wife?"

Perry's focus fuzzes out for a stretch before landing squarely back on Calabrese. His jaw tightens as the lids over his eyes narrow. "You know what, Detective? I think there just might be."

CHAPTER 2

Hazel knows she's pushing too hard, but she can't control herself. If she doesn't find Adam, she's going to lose it. This isn't like him, and she's starting to think she should call the police. The only thing stopping her is the possibility that he is fine; maybe his phone died or he had an emergency that has kept him from returning her many, many calls and texts. How would that look to him? Like she's taking their relationship a lot more seriously than he is. They haven't been together long enough to merit a call to the authorities. No, she can't go there yet.

Hazel trembles as she taps Adam's number on her phone. She hasn't slept more than an hour the entire night, tossing and turning, waiting for some message letting her know that he's okay. The voicemail prompt comes on after two rings, and she screams into her room and disconnects. This is the same result she's gotten for the past twenty-four hours since he failed to show up for their date yesterday. She can't leave another message.

Hazel tries everything she can think of to no avail. She's already gone by his place on the Upper East Side and buzzed his apartment, but nothing. She has an irking feeling that something terrible has happened. He wouldn't just disappear off the face of the earth like this.

She recalls their conversations earlier this week, trying to mine her memories for some missed comment or clue that would explain things. She tenses thinking about their argument last week, when Adam criticized her for being too distracted. She was the one to pick a fight, accusing him of being secretive and aloof lately, and he turned it back on her instantly. He'd been more or less supportive of her online persona and social media platforms, if not apathetic. Hazel assumed it was because he felt a little jealous about her admirers, who she explained were necessary to her only for their monetary validation. They'd started dating around the time she'd hit her stride with the MeTube channel she'd built up, and initially, he'd been amused, then aloof. Last week, he was judgmental.

"The social media stuff has completely consumed you," he said disapprovingly. They'd just had sex, and as soon as he got up to shower, she got on her laptop and started filming her next video.

"You sound like my mother," she replied.

"She's a smart woman, then."

"Is this about my stalker?" she asked, wondering if her most ardent fan, JanArt54, who'd liked and commented on every single post she'd ever made, actually bothered him. Hazel had mentioned this follower more than once to spur Adam's jealousy, which may have worked.

"Your followers are wing nuts. And honestly, your channel is unhinged."

Adam didn't spend the night and didn't call or message her for two days. She was raw and pissed off, but she was proud of herself for not calling him or sending any fishing texts. Her unavailability worked, and Adam suggested lunch and a walk in the park, which she happily accepted. But his comments rooted in Hazel's body like a splinter.

Adam's job as a project manager for Habitat for Humanity had appealed to Hazel's desire to surround herself with more selfless people, or more honestly, appear more altruistic when she described what her partner did. What his actual job required aside from traveling on short notice often was still unclear. But Hazel had thought that Janice, her mother, would approve, which was a plus. She needed to return to her mother's good graces for several reasons, and a well-rounded, kindhearted man would be a good start.

In the six months they'd been dating, Hazel had started to really love Adam. Her older brother, Kagan, referred to the relationship as her "latest infatuation," which stung. But she knew there was a kernel of truth in that statement. Hazel tended to fall hard for the people she was seeing, especially if they were elusive. Which Adam was at times.

But this disappearing act differed from his occasional days of spotty communication or moodiness. For the most part, he was a sweet guy on the quieter side and a good listener who wasn't afraid of having a deep conversation. And she was increasingly attracted to him the more time she spent with him. At first glance, she'd written him off as a dime-a-dozen white guy in a striped button-down and dark jeans with a decent haircut. His brown hair, brown eyes, and straight teeth weren't remarkable, yet he had a magnetism that she couldn't pinpoint.

When Hazel left her apartment to meet Adam yesterday, she'd decided to tell him she loved him. He hadn't said it yet, but his understated personality made her think he wasn't the type to say it first. She'd also persuaded herself to ask him to meet her mother. He'd been very open to meeting Kagan, who hadn't been himself since his divorce started. Adam had tried, asking Kagan many thoughtful questions about their childhood without much reciprocation from her brother. Hazel expected that telling Adam she loved him would help along the natural evolution of this relationship. Having a partner who met her mother's expectations would be helpful in smoothing things over with Janice. Everyone would win.

Hazel was mentally composing the email to her mother on her way to the planned meeting spot with Adam in Fort Tryon Park, a five-minute walk from her apartment. He never showed.

She feels like falling into bed and crying for the remainder of the day, but Hazel refuses to let this slow her down. She prepares her face to take her mind off Adam and curb her crying. Once she's made up, she won't want to let anyone screw up her hard work.

Hazel smooths her foundation in front of the vanity in her bedroom, mechanically applying the contouring shading that makes her look flawlessly filtered. She's mastered transforming her straight brown hair, hazel eyes, and light freckles into a social media goddess: perfectly shaped eyebrows, tarantula eyelashes, smoky eyes, and velvety bee-stung lips. Some of her commenters have called her a real-life anime character, while others have likened her look to "porn star." Her followers are fans of both and are very different from her original audience of tween girls who came for her makeup tutorials. It's a toss-up which audience's comments are more critical, but the older male audience's follow and like numbers are much higher, and they pay. Even so, Hazel really needs to earn more.

Her iPhone comes alive again, spawning a stomach flutter. Hazel's hope pivots to annoyance when she sees the incoming call from Kagan. Hazel doesn't feel like talking to him and sends it to voicemail. He calls back seconds later. She forwards him again, but a text chimes in all caps. Kagan's written, 911 EMERGENCY. Before she can press to call him, his name pops up again.

"Jesus, what? Who died?" Hazel deadpans.

"Mom," Kagan says without a glimmer of irony.

"Right," she scoffs. The siblings have done this dead-mom routine before, but her mood is too low even for gallows humor.

"I'm serious, Hazel." Kagan's voice trembles slightly. "She's dead."

His tone communicates a realness not often traceable in either sibling. Hazel feels her legs weaken. "Jesus, Kagan." Her mouth is suddenly bone dry. She struggles to get her words out. "*This* is how you're telling me that our mother is dead?"

Hazel's stomach churns, and she is overwhelmed by a chilling sense that something truly terrible is about to happen.

"I would have come in person, but I've been stuck downtown all morning. I didn't want you to hear it from anyone else."

"What was more important than this?" Hazel shrieks.

"Court."

She flinches in response to forgetting her brother's court appearance and failing to reach out last night, let alone show up today for moral support. She'd promised him that she would be there. Hazel's been so engrossed in creating new content. Kagan hadn't been in touch for a few days or appeared supine on her couch, unannounced, as was his usual practice. But rationalizing her apparent "out of sight, out of mind" mentality right now doesn't feel appropriate. The devastating reality that she is the only family that Kagan has left, and vice versa, brings her to her knees.

"When? How did you find out? *What* happened?" she asks.

"I got a voicemail from Perry."

Hearing Perry's name stirs old resentments in Hazel. "What did he say?"

"He sounded like he was in shock, wanted you to hear the news from me," Kagan says.

"Kagan! What happened to *Mom?*"

"She fell."

"She fell? Like in the shower?" Hazel asks tearfully.

"In Fort Tryon Park."

The coincidence sends Hazel into dizzying confusion.

"How did she fall? I don't get it. She died from a fall?" Strangled emotion chokes each question.

"Perry just said she tumbled over a wall and fell down the embankment. They don't think she suffered," he replies morosely.

"Is that supposed to make us feel better? How would he even know if she suffered or not?" Hazel is surprised by the emotional spin cycle overtaking her. Her short-fused fury dissolves into desperation. "What was she doing there?"

"Apparently, she was working at the Cloisters."

Hazel lets this hang between them as she sniffles.

"I was right there," she sobs.

"Haze, there wasn't anything you could have done. You haven't spoken to each other for almost two years. Why would yesterday be any different?"

CHAPTER 3

The moment Kagan steps into his friend's apartment, he flings his cell phone onto the overstuffed chair situated at the far end of the coffee table. The device has delivered him nothing but bad news lately, and it's starting to feel like more of a liability the longer it stays in his palm. He yanks off his suit jacket and tie and flops down onto the sofa with the sensation that he's being overtaken by an avalanche.

Court was a disaster. Bethany wants nothing to do with him. Kagan's plan to catch his estranged wife before the hearing and plead his case for a second chance fell on indifferent ears, even with the revelation of his mother's death. Only a couple of months into their separation, and his ex has made up her mind. Concretely. She's had enough of his "willful delinquency," whatever the hell that means. Seems relieved to be rid of the problem. And if that weren't enough of a knife twist, his sister—probably the closest person Kagan has in this life—appears to be at the end of her patience with him too. And now their mother is gone.

The first, reflexive thought he had upon hearing the news about Janice was to call Bethany. Seek comfort amid the shock and emerging grief. But even in more harmonious times, she'd never been the most effusive person in his life. Not the one to commiserate over that kind of loss. His sister enjoyed that particular distinction, but there's so much unresolved friction between Hazel and their mother that Kagan is afraid to push things just yet.

It's almost too much to comprehend. All his legal and employment woes suddenly seem trivial when thrown into stark relief against the death of the woman who bore him, who raised both him and Hazel, mostly on her own and in spite of a sneering, vicious indifference from the man responsible.

The cruel irony Kagan now faces is this: Janice's tragic fate has put things into perspective, has made all his other issues seem suddenly small, wholly manageable. If taken on their own, they'd be a collection of headaches he'd be capable of wading through. But losing his mother has shaken Kagan down to his foundation. The message from Perry about Janice's death put him on his ass, left him stunned. And because of that, each of those smaller issues now feels like the drop in the bucket that finally causes the whole mess to overflow.

It could almost be funny, if it weren't so tragic.

Thank God for Gabe. More to the point, thank God for Gabe's empty apartment. Kagan's actor friend from an old restaurant job just booked a supporting role in a small studio film, the lucky son of a bitch, and he's been kind enough to let Kagan crash here for the next few weeks while he's on set in Vancouver. Gabe trusts him with the place. And he really likes the coke that Kagan's agreed to hook him up with in trade.

Kagan needs this space right now. He sensed that things were already nearing a breaking point with his sister, even before Janice's death. He could feel the resentment wafting his way anytime he'd wake up on Hazel's couch and catch her staring at him with an expression bordering on disgust. As if he hadn't supported her through a thousand breakups. Hadn't distracted her as her ego mended in the wake of countless romantic disasters.

His phone lights up from the chair, and it feels like a taunt, a provocation. A beacon of disaster. As much as Kagan dreads whatever information lies in wait for him on that screen, a piece of him is ready to invite the chaos in. Fuck it. Might as well heap it on all at once. Get it over with. He stares at the dim glow as he fishes a plastic baggie from the pocket of his suit pants and tosses it onto the coffee table in front of him.

Kagan wonders if it's the cops calling again. Or maybe it's Hazel, trying him back to apologize for her earlier tone. She was shocked to learn about Janice and took the sudden jolt out on him.

Kagan suspects that Hazel's about to run headlong into a whole patch of unprocessed guilt. Truthfully, neither of the kids was as close to Janice over the past couple of years as they once had been, but *he* at least made the effort. Kagan put in the time early on to try to get to know his new stepdad, for Janice's sake. The guy was a snooze, sure, pretty pretentious, but he seemed harmless enough. Christ, just about anyone would have been an upgrade from Charles Bailey, after all.

The siblings had gotten busier with work and were starting to carve out their own lives. Their mother seemed happily remarried, which was something of a relief. Everyone had more going on. And so there was really no one to blame, he supposes, when the distance between the kids and Janice started to grow, so imperceptibly as to have been almost unnoticeable, it occurs to him now.

A thought enters Kagan's brain and slowly seeps into the crevices: Could Janice herself have been pulling away this whole time? Subtly, subconsciously? A woman who'd been so open, so available, even over-bearing at times? Could the relief at finally being free of the emotional storm that Charles had put them all through have caused her to shy away from the kids without realizing it? Could looking into their eyes and being constantly reminded of the monster who'd charmed his way into her life, into her bed, into the fabric of the rest of her existence have somehow tainted the pure affection a mother is supposed to feel for her children?

No, he thinks, *you're overanalyzing. Reading too much into things.* He missed his mom; it was as simple as that. And he wished for a chance to tell her as much.

But in a way it's a relief not to have to face her. After the financial help Janice had given him with his Columbia tuition and with getting set up in his own apartment, it had been one tough bit of luck after another. He'd gotten canned from a few server and bartender jobs be-cause of spiteful managers or overly sensitive coworkers and was forced to crash with his younger sister while an imminent divorce loomed over him. *How cursed could one person get?*

It wasn't supposed to turn out like this. Kagan's the older sibling—the big brother—and yet it has too often been Hazel who's stepped up and handled things. Who's been his emotional caretaker. Who pro-tected him from their father's rageful lash-outs. Who's shielded Kagan from anything potentially traumatic along the way, often at great emo-tional cost to herself. And ultimately, he supposes, to the detriment of their relationship.

Kagan pushes himself up from the sofa, leans across the coffee ta-ble, and retrieves his phone from the chair before plopping back down. He taps the screen, and a text message appears from an unknown number. He opens the text and reads the reminder about the food pho-tography shoot he's got in an hour at that new spot downtown that a sommelier friend of his was cool enough to help set up. With everything on his mind, Kagan completely forgot about the opportunity, and he now feels anxious around the tight timetable but relieved to have the gig.

He wandered into this sideline years ago quite by happenstance, when things were still going his way. The restaurant job he had at the time was slow to adapt to the new reality of social media, as was Kagan himself, and management had recently made a conscious decision to play catch-up. Scrambling to get a presence on Instagram, they opted to shoot a few of their more popular dishes, without taking the time to budget and hire a professional photographer for the job.

Kagan happened to be covering a slow weekday lunch shift that particular afternoon, so the assignment fell to him. He had a brand-new phone with a good camera, and the natural light from the sunny day outside flowed through the picture windows, bathing the marble bar top in a radiant pool.

The chef brought out the dishes, and Kagan arranged the plates in geometric configurations along the surface of the bar. He figured out the best angles to catch the light and accentuate the depth of field. He used a pile of bar napkins to prop up one side of a dish, lending the food added texture in the shot. As it turned out, he had a pretty good eye.

The project was such a success that Kagan got asked to photograph food for a few smaller restaurants that were looking to expand their own social media presence. Hazel gifted him a 35mm Canon that she'd cycled through, and he picked up a tripod and small light kit and learned how to style and shoot as he went. With each job he became a little more sure of himself, and he finally reached a point of not feeling as if he were a total imposter in the field.

He's grateful for the work, especially in light of his current bind.

Without a steady paycheck coming in, he's been relying on these spo-
radic shoots—and the occasional coke sale to friends and referred
customers—to keep his head above water. And he's been managing to
pull it off, but only barely.

Kagan picks up the plastic baggie, peels it open, and taps a small
mound of powder onto the coffee table. He grabs a loose *New York*
magazine subscription renewal card and chuckles at the fact that Gabe
still reads the thing in print form before using the card to shepherd the
granules into a slender line. He leans over the table, his shoulders
hunching as he lowers his nose to the rail of coke, and inhales it in one
quick sniff.

He rereads the address of the restaurant in the text message and
begins to feel newly energized at the prospect of turning this side hustle into something big, something splashy, something attention-getting
that he can parlay into a thriving business, yeah, that's what he'll do,
update his own IG and really lean into this endeavor, yes, yes, yes, he'll
show his old manager what a mistake she made firing him, he'll show
Bethany what she gave up when she gave him the boot, he'll show his
sister that he can make it on his own, without her charity, he's got another go of it in him, and he'll fucking show them all and make Janice
proud, honor her memory by making himself a success story.

And there's the inheritance looming, it feels wrong to think about
it, he's been pushing the idea from his mind but the fact of the matter
is he's got a nice chunk of change coming after Janice's passing, much
sooner than he thought, all that family money plus the dough Charles
left behind, a little cosmic and karmic restoration of balance from the
miserable old prick, and even if he and Hazel have to cut the pie three
ways with the new husband—and he sure hopes Perry's cut will be
more of a sliver, considering it's *their* family's money—there'll be plenty
to go around, it'll help Kagan get his business venture up and running,

and hell yeah, this is gonna be it, this is gonna be huge, this is gonna be absolutely rip-roaring fucking massive.

Kagan springs up from the sofa, gathers together his kit for the shoot he's nearly running late for, and allows himself a sigh of relief. All he needed was something—anything—to go his way. And now, finally, it has.

CHAPTER 4

Hazel wakes to the screech of metal bending and glass shattering. The world below her window rocks with jackhammers punctuated by incessantly beeping construction vehicles, evidently able to drive only in reverse. Enraged by the racket, she yells "FUCK YOU" into the empty room. The violent city noises mirror her emotions throughout the mostly sleepless night.

She looks at her phone, sees nothing from Adam or Kagan, places it next to her, and then lifts it to her face thirty seconds later. Her mother is gone. She will never see her again. Never talk to her. Never fight with her. Her support system, Adam, is still MIA. She has texted and called him with the news and knows now that something awful must have happened to him to not respond. Everything is falling apart.

She lies in bed staring at the cracks in her ceiling, growing furious with each loud beep and metal-on-concrete peal, wishing painful injuries on the machine operators five floors below. Her mother has been dead for more than a day now, and the world around her continues to shriek and shatter with no regard for the enormous well of angry absence Hazel feels.

Her conversation with Kagan the day before was a blur; she ended the call abruptly and went for an hours-long walk in Fort Tryon Park to process a world without Janice. Many unsettling questions kept surfacing, intensifying her apprehension about what would unfold next. Other thoughts made her uneasy and restless. She wondered about the pain her mother might have felt upon hitting the ground, if she had any time to comprehend the fall, and why she was so close to the edge.

Hazel angrily taps a new message to Adam: MY MOTHER'S DEAD, DO YOU EVEN CARE? in caps, and tosses the device onto the floor.

Hazel inherited her extremely short fuse from her late father, Charles Bailey, whose personality type was universally inclusive resentment. No person or situation was too small to know the wrath of his discontent. And if he couldn't intimidate or terrorize whatever person into submission, he invoked the threat of his lawyer often.

His unrelenting anger and rage were fueled by nicotine, caffeine, and trans fats. Thus his massive heart attack at fifty-eight wasn't a shock. She knew her brother and mother had felt relief, too, when the paramedics finally wheeled him out of the restaurant on a gurney where they'd been celebrating Janice's birthday before the color had drained from his face and he'd slumped over in his seat.

This sudden death is so different. She's shocked that Janice is gone, and even though they were out of contact, the pain is no less debilitating. With the death of her father, her grief was tempered. With Janice, she feels rocked by regret. Her life is suddenly backward and upside down, like all her clothes and shoes have shrunk. She is confused about who to be or what to do. The contentment of her routines has evaporated, replaced by the disturbing sense that nothing will ever feel comfortable again.

Since her brother's phone call, she's been toggling between cognitive dissonance and emotional lows she hasn't felt since she was a teenager. She rolls through hours of feeling immobile and heartsick, wishing for her mother. Beyond that painful vulnerability, she experiences a slight detached appreciation for the practical opportunities stemming from her mother's fall. In a distant crook of her mind, Hazel realizes Janice's passing will resolve the problems accumulated over the past couple of years, particularly the financial struggles. Ironically, the solution to her problems had also been the source of them.

Of course, she didn't want Janice to die, but getting out from under her crippling debts could allow her to stop living the lifestyle that Janice disapproved of. Becoming the woman her mother hoped she'd be, or rather ceasing being the woman her mother didn't want her to be, felt poetic. Wherever Janice was now, Hazel believed she'd want her daughter to be happy. She would do whatever it took to make her mother proud of her.

The leading cause of their estrangement two years ago was also the primary source of tension for a large portion of Hazel's adult life. Simply, her mother was unwilling to give Hazel money when she most needed it. Janice claimed she wanted to focus on building a mother-daughter relationship that wasn't "predicated on financial support," but that was easy for her to say from her fancy ten-thousand-square-foot Upper West Side apartment. It didn't seem fair that she could unilaterally control what was meant to be the entire family's money—not to mention spend it on her random new husband while Hazel and Kagan struggled. It was truly infuriating. So Hazel resorted to cutting the only remaining currency she had to withhold: contact. It was less painful that way.

Hazel didn't feel like her anger was irrational. Her mother always had money, coming from a large multigenerational family business of department stores that had gone the way of most brick and mortars once e-commerce became king but had furnished Janice and her siblings with considerable trust funds, waiting for them on their twenty-sixth birthdays or upon their marriage to an acceptable suitor, whichever came first.

This trust bankrolled Hazel and Kagan's father's multiple businesses in insurance firms, soybeans, and a technical school in the Midwest that grew around the country in the 1980s, all endeavors that significantly increased that wealth despite the skeptics along the way. Where Charles lacked in being a father and husband, he excelled in his talent for sniffing out a worthwhile business venture. He readily wielded that success as a control instrument with his wife and two children.

Janice gave up control of her inheritance and trust to her husband because the world she'd grown up in had conditioned her to allow the man of the house all the power in every matter. Prenups weren't standard, nor was the wife controlling the finances, even if the money originated with her. Handing everything over to a man with a knack for taking everything from those around him gradually depleted her self-worth, esteem, and energy. The fact that Charles increased the family trust instead of draining it gave him justifiable free rein to treat Janice and his children like they were inconvenient and generally dispensable.

Numbers ruled him, and the size of his fortune seemed proportionate to justifiable tyranny. Charles had died with a substantial estate and a sizable life-insurance payout that went to Janice. Still, their father hadn't yet worked out the fine print on allocating his wealth to Hazel and Kagan. After he passed, Janice ceased pursuing all his pending investments, content to reap the spoils of all he had brought in to that point but let go of any connection to him otherwise. Hazel imagined that most of all, Janice was relieved that she was free from her marital straitjacket.

Hazel and Kagan's opinion that their father simply hadn't gotten around to delegating his wealth to his children was not shared by Janice. They were rudely awakened to this difference of perspective when, after Charles's death, Janice insisted that their father had wanted them to make their own money and know the satisfaction of building hard work into their personal wealth. Hazel tried to persuade Kagan to talk to a lawyer about possibly taking Janice to court and getting "their due share," but Kagan talked her out of it, concerned about Janice's fragile mental state. Hazel threatened Janice once or twice in the heat of an argument, but their mother took it in stride.

After all the Sturm und Drang around the money, Janice initially contributed generously to Hazel's and Kagan's futures. She provided college tuition, assisted on down payments for starter apartments, capitulated on occasion, and granted intermittent loans when they were allegedly going to purchase life necessities (but often were using the funds for what she considered frivolous recreational things). The financial aid had become harder to depend on as Hazel got older and then one day completely stopped. This abrupt halt in assistance had timed out with Perry's arrival into Janice's life.

Perry. Hazel hadn't considered what he must be going through since Kagan had broken the news. She'd never found Perry worthy of much thought beyond his felicitous arrival and her mother's apparent late-onset adolescence. Kagan found Perry as annoying as Hazel did but kept this to himself around Janice for the sake of their mother's feelings, something Hazel wasn't able to do. That was the nonconfrontational, peacekeeping nature of Janice coming through in Kagan. Hazel had always tended more toward her father's cynical view about people. The first time she'd gotten her heart pulverized, her father chastised Hazel. "It's your own fault for being so trusting. Even salt looks like sugar."

Hazel didn't like anything about Perry the first time she met him, or any time following. She complained to Kagan about him, but she couldn't pinpoint exactly what it was about him that bothered her. He appeared harmless. He was overly corny and pretty vanilla all around. On paper, Perry was perfect for Janice, who had served more than her share of time married to an unpredictable, abusive narcissist. Perry was friendly, accommodating, and agreeable, and, by all appearances, he adored their mother. Nevertheless, Hazel found him off-putting.

Hazel considers calling Perry and getting more information under the auspices of condolences. But the fact that Perry hasn't bothered to call her stokes hot resentment in Hazel. Janice was his wife, sure, but she was her mother for much longer than that.

Zombielike, she moves from the bed to the kitchen for water. Standing before the open fridge, she forgets why and starts scrolling through her channel, tallying views and thumbs-ups. After that, she checks the comments on her latest post—thousands of supportive words and a few critics, swiftly hidden and blocked. The post has two million views, which is not bad, but she needs to boost her numbers to monetize her profile as she envisions. The chill from the open refrigerator snaps her attention back into reality.

It hurt Hazel that her mother couldn't support her attempts to make a name for herself in an ocean of influencers. Janice didn't understand what Hazel was working toward while doing beauty tutorials and reminded Hazel often of her wasted journalism degree. Given the number of citizen reporters that permeated the new platforms springing up every other day, Janice didn't understand how impossible it was to harness that degree into a viable living. Hazel tried; she had a few under-five-hundred-word vanity profiles and pop culture lists published among the innumerable other advertorials, listicles, and puff pieces across the black hole of the internet. Every rejected story pitch to a major, serious news outlet only furthered her worst fears about her abilities.

Janice had never been politically vocal, but in the past two elections, when decisive viewpoints became a personality requirement, she came into solid opinions about what was happening in the government. Like the rest of Americans over sixty, Janice became active on Facebook in online sparring sessions with second cousins and people she'd gone to boarding school with whom she hadn't seen in four decades or more. Hazel and her mother disagreed on most things, especially her daughter's suggestion of vast conspiracies and crimes against humanity in organizations that her mother supported and relied on. It still burns Hazel that as she began to get some traction and notoriety, her mother seemed to become more critical of her life choices. It felt like Janice preferred Hazel to be unsuccessful and unhappy, even if she claimed the opposite.

Hazel's racing thoughts return to the unchangeable present. She scans her phone contacts and struggles to find Perry's phone number. Finally, she finds it under "Mom's husband" on her phone. It would be so easy to press the phone icon and get some answers, but she can't bring herself to do it. She can only imagine what he thinks of her, not that she gives a fuck.

Hazel has never had a one-on-one conversation with the man. Their interactions were limited to the handful of meals she and Kagan attended in the early courtship phase and one regretful time that she went to Janice's apartment to ask her for a loan. Perry stepped in and recommended that she try a different avenue other than hitting up her "poor mother." Janice was a lot of things, but she wasn't "poor" in any meaning of the word, and his intervention had enraged Hazel. She can't remember exactly what she said to Perry on her way out the door, as happened a few times during fits of rage, but she knows it was enough to keep her mother from speaking to her for a few weeks. Instead, it was the last time she had seen or spoken to Janice.

Hazel distractedly navigates away from Perry's info and checks her profiles. She confirms that her next MeTube video is on deck, and she is grateful she was ahead of things this week. There's no way she can focus on her online persona right now.

She taps Kagan's picture on her screen, switches to speakerphone, and lies on her couch, defeated. After a few rings, she hears his tired voice.

"Hey, K. Did I wake you?" she asks while color-correcting and airbrushing one of her photos. Someone's comment this morning about her skin looking old set her on an insecure descent.

"No, I've just been lying in bed staring out the window."

"I thought you might come here last night."

"Sorry, things went long. I was doing a photo shoot downtown and linked up with friends afterward. It got late quickly, so I crashed here."

She's a little irritated that her brother can operate like everything is normal, but she's not entirely surprised. Kagan is exceptional at compartmentalizing.

Hazel isn't entirely sure where "here" is but doesn't want to overstep. "Hey, K, I'm sorry about yesterday. I definitely could have handled things better. The Mom news completely threw me. And I'm sorry for dropping the ball on your court date."

"It was a helluva day, that's for sure," he says.

"The cops have been calling and left a couple of messages, but I can't bring myself to call them back. And to make things extra spicy, Adam has vanished."

"Does he know about Mom?"

"I've sent him many updates, to radio silence. I'm pretty worried."

Kagan groans. "Do you think he might be ghosting?"

The possibility occurred to Hazel, obviously; she isn't an idiot. But it seems so unlikely. Adam is really into her.

"That isn't his style," she replies coolly.

"People show their true selves when shit gets real."

Hazel hoped Adam and her brother would hit it off, but it's clear from Kagan's comments that he doesn't think much of him. Hazel can't worry about that now. There are too many other painful things to chew on.

"That's some shitty timing we have, huh? You got dumped, and I got divorced. I mean, I'd like to say Mom's death puts it all in perspective, but it's hard to have any of that at the moment."

"K, should we be doing something?"

"Like what?"

"I don't know. Calling people? Making arrangements? What did Mom do when Charles died?" Hazel wonders aloud.

"That was a blur. But I'm sure she did *everything*."

"Definitely."

"I'm assuming we'll get word from Perry about her service and burial. You know she had that all wrapped up tight. I've been meaning to reach out to him, just haven't had a minute to myself." Hazel picks up the same trepidation in her brother's voice that she feels.

"Okay, when do you think we'll get the money? I don't mean to be talking about the inheritance so quickly. But I could really use it," Hazel says.

"Me too. I'm not exactly solvent right now."

"I've been doing some googling, and it seems like it can take a while."

"Even more reason to hit Perry up to see what's what," Kagan says.

ELIZABETH McCULLOUGH KEENAN AND GREG WANDS

Hazel groans. "I guess so. I'd be fine never seeing that guy again."

"Well, figure we probably won't see him again once we get past all this. For the time being, we need to play nice. Hopefully, that will move things along."

"K, that's very levelheaded of you. Why don't you reach out to him?"

"Sure."

"Thanks." Hazel laughs dryly. "Also . . ."

"What?"

"We are officially orphans now."

"Well, fuck, that's depressing."

CHAPTER 5

Perry sits in a circular banquette toward the rear of the dining room at Aglio, one of his favorite Upper West Side haunts, bracing himself for the prospect of seeing Hazel and Kagan for the first time in years. He surveys the space before him. The lunch rush is in full swing, and the service, as always, is impeccable.

Perry allows himself to be momentarily swept up in the seamless ballet that is the fine-dining experience: bussers silently whisking empty appetizer plates from tables; servers swooping in gracefully to replace them with main courses; diners consulting the sommelier on which wines to pair with their meals. There's a fluid elegance to the whole undertaking that he finds calming.

It wasn't always like this. Perry slips now into the folds of memory, recalling the diner in the backwater town he grew up in—the one that served as a kind of haven during his childhood—and to all the diners in all the towns he's been to since. He holds them in particular esteem. These places know exactly what they are—no frills, no pretension, no bullshit—and provide a refreshing sense of honesty in a world often lacking it.

One of the things that first drew Perry to the idea of living in New York City was the action, the opportunity, the idea that outsize aspiration had a place to truly thrive. He felt energized by the thought, intoxicated, even a little humbled. It was exactly the type of setting he'd been waiting all his life to arrive in.

He quickly learned the flip side to this. So many of the people he met seemed to put on airs, to spend a great amount of effort and energy creating these elaborate facades. This was to be expected, he supposed, in a town where people came to reinvent themselves, to escape whatever traumatic circumstances continued to nip at their psychic heels. But Perry began to see the larger picture with increasing clarity. He was able to pick out the people who had allowed themselves to be seduced by their own embellished lore, who had lost the thread completely and fallen victim to unchecked hubris.

A city of Icaruses entangled in the thicket of ambition.

He's come to harbor a sort of amused contempt for these particular souls. It's one thing to rely on your wiles and ingenuity to try to game a system designed to bleed you dry; it's quite another to become so enamored of those supposed talents that you end up tumbling straight into a trap of your own design.

To forget who—and what—you really are.

As he sits in contemplation, a years-old memory floats Perry's way. A few weeks after they'd first met at Seasons Change, the support group for widows and widowers they both attended, he and Janice decided to take an impulsive last-minute trip to Sag Harbor as an excuse to escape the city together. They'd visited the Morton Wildlife Refuge, and the image that returns to Perry now is that of his wife standing on the beach looking his way, her gaze full of adoration, as she unconsciously fingers the gold cross pendant around her neck.

Remembering the idyllic scene, Perry finds himself charmed anew by the depth of Janice's faith. He'd never been a churchgoer himself, yet something about his wife's devotion persuaded him to attend Mass with her. The habit stuck, and he can't help but consider himself blessed as he reflects on how well the close-knit community has served him.

Perry glances up just in time to catch a young woman passing by the table, and he's walloped by a sense of recognition. Recent events could be playing into it, but this woman brings to mind an older version of *her*. The watchful eyes, the set of the mouth, the mole just above the edge of her lip. And there's something about the gait, the shift of the shoulders, that elicits an eerie feeling of sameness.

The memory's been weighing on him since the exchange with the detectives. *I had a daughter,* he'd explained. *Once upon a time.* And for a moment, it's as if he's with her again. The smart, willful, precocious adolescent he lost, all grown up.

It stirs a sense of melancholic joy.

Just as Perry settles into the feeling, he observes the siblings entering the restaurant, and the energy in the room shifts. The hostess at the podium offers the pair a smile and leads them to the table, and as the kids follow, he can already make out impatience in their expressions. They approach, an unquenchable restlessness vibrating off them.

Perry stands, hatches a grin, and extends a casual wave to each of his stepchildren. "Hazel, Kagan. Nice to see you both."

"Hello, Perry," Hazel responds. "Thank you for meeting us." Her tone is businesslike and just short of curt. She slides into the banquette next to Perry as her brother barrels in on the other side, offering a mumbled greeting.

"Of course," says Perry. "I know you must both be going through a lot, with what's happened. I'm still in shock myself."

A server approaches the table and warmly greets the trio. Perry offers to order wine for the group, and both children accede. He requests a few minutes to peruse the food menu, and the server turns on her heel and heads for the bar.

"Nice place, Perry." Kagan darts his eyes around the room. The lids are rimmed red, and his gaze seems unfocused. "This one of your regular spots?"

"We had a few. Rudolfo's, Le Croquette. But yes, your mother enjoyed it here. I thought it would be a nice place for us to remember her."

"Of course," says Hazel, her tone softer, and Perry is surprised to find his stepdaughter's hand resting gently on his forearm. Her expression has thawed, and she looks at him with something approaching compassion. "We can't imagine what you must be going through."

Perry takes a moment to answer. "It's been difficult, of course. But mostly it just doesn't feel real. I keep waiting to wake up from this."

"Hey, man." Kagan pats his stepfather clumsily on the shoulder. "I hear you. It's okay to let it out." The kid's energy is off, and Perry has to tamp down a ripple of irritation as he realizes the likely culprit.

Oh, the disrespect.

"Thank you, Kagan. I really appreciate it." Perry's perfectly capable of putting on an act too. He looks from the young man to his sister. "And how are you both processing all of this?"

Hazel opens her mouth to respond just as the server returns to their table with a bottle of 2018 Stags' Leap petite sirah. She uncorks the bottle, pours a taste into Perry's glass, and waits for him to swirl the contents and approve the wine before filling their glasses and slipping away. Perry takes the opportunity to propose a toast.

"To your mother," he says, and the children follow his lead. They clink glasses and take long sips before settling in for a moment of silence. After a stretch, Hazel picks up the thread of conversation.

"So, Perry," she says. "My brother and I are sure you must be feeling overwhelmed right now, and we just want you to know that we're here for you."

Perry finds himself momentarily thrown by the sentiment. "That's very kind, Hazel. Thank you. And the same goes for me, okay?"

"Sure," she answers. "I mean, with you having to deal with all the estate stuff, and the paperwork, I know that can be a lot. So we just wanted to offer our help with anything you might need us for. You know, communicating with the life-insurance people, or navigating the will, or whatever."

There it is. The "whatever" Hazel drops is too forcedly casual, and Perry finds himself having to stifle a laugh at the fumbling transparency of her ploy. These two layabouts are here to collect whatever inheritance is coming to them and can barely be bothered to veil their intentions or to even pretend to mourn their dead mother as they trip over themselves to get their hands on her money. This meeting is to sniff out a payday, plain and clear.

"That's so thoughtful of you," responds Perry, slathering on the sincerity. "But probably best for me to deal with the lawyer directly, as I've been the person most consistently in your mother's life these past couple of years. I'll of course keep you both updated on any developments." He offers a solemn smile for effect and watches with amusement as the masks of compassion on the faces of both children slip, revealing flashes of naked frustration. Kagan lifts his wineglass and proceeds to down half its contents in one long gulp. "Of course, with the circumstances surrounding Janice's death, the police will need to shore up their investigation before anything financial can happen."

Perry studies the kids as they eye each other, apparently surprised by this wrinkle in the plot. After a series of charged looks, Kagan finally takes the lead.

"Um, sorry, but what do you mean by the circumstances surrounding her death?"

"Have you two not spoken to the police yet?" Perry interlaces his fingers and sets his hands onto the table. "They're in the process of trying to determine whether your mother was the victim of a terrible accident or something more nefarious."

"*Nefarious?*" spits Hazel. "But who would have it in for Janice? I mean, enough to kill her? That just sounds . . ."

"I would imagine the police are looking at who had the most to gain from her death." Perry lets his stare fall heavily on the kids. "Financial expectations and all of that."

Kagan's expression morphs from bewilderment to encroaching rage as the implication of the statement settles in. "I'm sorry, Perry. Are you trying to suggest that either I or my sister had anything to do with this?!" His tone has risen to a barely contained boil. "I mean . . . just . . ."

"How dare you." Hazel manages an incensed laugh. "I don't know if this is your grief speaking, but that is absolutely beyond the pale, Perry. To think that we could have had anything to do with . . . neither of us has even *seen* our mother in—"

"And yet here you are, days after her death, inquiring about the insurance money and the will."

"We were reaching out to *you* to offer our support!" Hazel has leaned fully into indignation, the little twerp. "You have some nerve pointing the finger at us!"

"Yeah," her brother chimes in too loudly, drawing the attention of a neighboring table. "If the police are looking for motives, I'm pretty sure the spouse usually ends up at the top of that list."

Perry lets out an annoyed sigh. Since he'd gotten together with

Janice, her ingrate kids only ever came around when they needed something. If their mother were still alive to witness this callous display, it would have broken her heart all over again.

"Kagan, I'm going to do you the courtesy of chalking that comment up to the grief you must be working through. But if you'd actually bothered to stay in touch with your mother, you'd know how happy Janice and I were and what an absurd accusation you've made." He takes a sip of water. "And just for the record, I was midflight when your mother passed. Where were you, exactly?" As Kagan scrambles for a reply, Perry turns his attention to his stepdaughter. "How about you, Hazel? You've still got that apartment in Inwood, correct? Just a stroll away from where Janice was found."

"Oh, fuck you," Hazel spits as she wrings the cloth napkin in her fists, her knuckles ghostly white.

"You know," Perry continues, "as contented as your mother and I were these past couple of years, she never stopped thinking of the two of you. Never stopped worrying about you both. Never gave up hope." This felt important to say. For Janice.

"What do you mean, 'never gave up hope'?" asks Kagan.

"That you kids would finally get your acts together and become self-sufficient adults. She blamed herself for indulging you both for too long and worried that she'd sent you out of the nest ill-equipped to handle life. But Janice realized she was doing you no favors and found the strength to cut you both off and push you to make something of yourselves."

Hazel glares at her stepfather with enough heat to set the tablecloth ablaze. "My brother and I are doing just fine, thank you very much."

"I'm relieved to hear it. Truly, I am. And your mother would be so happy to know that you're both getting by on your own. Finally."

Hazel lets out a long exhale, and Perry senses the emotional reset that accompanies it. When his stepdaughter speaks again, she does so in a forcedly even tone. "Okay," she begins, "can we at least figure out the family heirlooms?"

"Family heirlooms?"

"Our parents' wedding rings, and Mom's engagement ring. Grandma's necklace. She always intended for us to end up with those." Hazel levels a defiant look at Perry. "You can't possibly have a problem with *that*?"

"Actually, I'd love to help you out there, but your mother gave those away."

"What?!" Kagan scoffs. "What the fuck are you talking about?"

"Donated them to Housing Works."

"Bullshit," whispers Hazel.

"Your mother was very generous with her possessions," explains Perry. "She donated regularly to a number of organizations she was passionate about."

"But those had sentimental value," argues Hazel. "You expect us to believe that she just got rid of them, without a second thought?"

"How can I put this gently?" says Perry, working hard to keep his tone diplomatic. "Janice had given up on the idea of you settling down." He shifts his gaze to Kagan. "And she worried about giving you anything of material value. She was afraid you might end up pawning it."

"Well, I'm just about done with this abuse." Kagan downs the rest of his wine and thrusts himself up from the table, the silverware clattering as he edges his way out of the booth. "You coming, Haze?"

"Right behind you," she says as she balls up the napkin and tosses it onto the tabletop.

Perry savors a slow sip of wine as he watches the siblings hustle out of the confines of the restaurant and into a world poised to eat them both alive.

CHAPTER 6

There is seriously something wrong with that guy," Hazel says as the pair heads down into the Seventy-Ninth Street subway station after their quick exit.

"He's a smug asshole with pretentious taste in wine," Kagan replies bitterly.

Hazel speeds up as the gap between her and her brother widens. Kagan's stride matches pace with his mood: fast and aggressive.

"His taste in wine is not the problem," Hazel responds while scrolling through her phone as they walk through the sea of people.

She fishes a MetroCard out of her back pocket and passes through the turnstile while Kagan fumbles in his jacket pocket. Hazel stands impatiently on the other side of the gateway, finally reaches her hand through, and swipes her card for her brother.

"I can't believe that fucker is stonewalling us about the life insurance and the will," Kagan sputters as they descend the subway stairs, pushing against a few hundred straphangers who've just exited an uptown train. When they reach the platform, they step aside to let the stragglers out of the car before claiming a two-seater.

"Mom would have contingencies to ensure we are taken care of, right?" Hazel asks.

"Absolutely," Kagan says confidently.

"Are you sure?" Hazel presses, feeling doubly doubtful after the Perry encounter.

"I asked her over dinner one night. I was curious about how much of her family money still existed. She was coy and told me 'plenty.' Dad left things a mess, and she didn't want that to happen when she went, and she'd intentionally put money in trusts that Dad couldn't touch, which enraged him, as you can imagine. When Mom went through her whole personal-transformation phase after Dad, she got a financial planner and took care of it all."

Hazel frowns and looks down at her phone. She focuses on her most recent post's hearts and shares. "Kind of tacky, bro." These tiny symbols of support are the only things lifting her in Adam's absence. She hates that her mood has become so affected by her followers and, apparently, her boyfriend. Hazel despises that a romantic partner has diverted her focus from her brand. She never thought she'd be one of those people.

Thinking about how her mom had changed from the meek, broken-down, disconnected self she'd been with Charles to the vibrant, full-of-faith-and-hope, strong woman she'd become before meeting Perry made her nostalgic. She'd been proud of her mother for turning things around for herself. Hazel wishes she told her that.

"I can't believe you asked her about it," Hazel says. "You are shameless. I'm kind of proud of you."

"We were having a grown-up conversation. It wasn't a secret that she was going to die one day."

Hazel feels irritated at her brother's superior attitude, but this text-book older-sibling shit isn't going to change. "When was this, anyway?"

"I think it was a Sunday dinner at her place," he replies. "If memory serves, you were on a date with the chick who worked at the botanical gardens."

Hazel knows exactly when this was. She'd been dating a woman named Amanda, whom she'd mentioned bringing to Sunday dinner, and Janice had reacted badly. She'd suggested that Hazel was going through a rebellious phase and questioned if she was just trying to make Janice uncomfortable. Hazel had furiously informed her that she had always been "pansexual" and was disappointed to realize her own mother was homophobic. Janice swore that she wasn't and was con-fused and concerned about what pansexuality meant, but Hazel made a scene about not wanting to be judged and stormed off. Things had cooled off a few weeks later, but only in the sense that they never spoke about it again. Janice treated Hazel's personal life as off-limits and stopped asking her for any updates, and Hazel's belief was that Janice preferred that she stick to men and not complicate her life any more than necessary. Janice was overly concerned about what people thought; her motto about relationships, she joked, was "Love is blind, but the neighbors aren't."

"Right, Amanda. She was cool," Hazel says dolefully, remember-ing how that short-lived romance had ended in her getting accused of "experimenting" and dumped.

Hazel looks around at the other passengers on the subway. The nice weather has brought out a collection of bare shoulders and lighter moods on the faces of these usually harried New Yorkers.

"And *the rings*!" Hazel cries out, remembering. "How could she have donated the wedding rings? That doesn't make any sense. She was too sentimental to get rid of anything that meaningful, and that engagement ring had been in the family for generations. She never would have given them away. She promised her engagement ring to me when I got married."

Hazel gets emotional realizing that Janice will never see that day.

"Who knows what Mom was thinking," Kagan says while he nibbles on a cuticle. His haunted gaze is far away.

"Hey, are you doing okay?" Hazel asks, genuinely concerned. Kagan seems more off-kilter than usual, and she hasn't seen him show any significant emotion about Janice.

"Fine," he mutters. "I'm just trying to make sense of Perry accusing us of murdering our own mother. That was not how I thought that meal was going to go."

Hazel agrees wordlessly, and the siblings sit shoulder to shoulder in shocked silence.

A garbled voice over the loudspeaker announces that the Dyckman stop is next. Kagan rises to meet her. The siblings stand opposite each other with their arms and expressions similarly crossed.

They make their way aboveground and start walking west. Hazel senses that her brother has the same destination in mind that she does when they pass the turnoff for her apartment building and keep strolling toward the park.

"Did you notice how unaffected he seemed? And how well rested?"

"You're more observant than me," Kagan replies.

"His eyes were eerily empty when speaking about the police investigation." Hazel stresses her words, hoping to incite her brother. "The only time I saw the needle move was when he realized we were asking about money!"

"Honestly, I didn't. He came off as an asshole, but I wasn't reading between the lines too much."

They walk a few blocks without talking.

"So tell me more about his *affect*," Kagan concedes.

"It was flat and rehearsed," Hazel offers, less enthused than before.

"Well, you and I aren't exactly breaking down about this in public either.

"Where are we going anyway?" Kagan asks while glancing up at the street sign.

"To the spot. Where Mom fell," Hazel says solemnly.

The pair walks in tense silence for a few minutes, the city giving way to the park's border.

"Any word from what's-his-name?" Kagan asks.

"Nothing."

"Sorry, Haze. I know you really liked him."

"It just doesn't make sense." Hazel chokes back new tears. She's so exhausted from all this involuntary crying.

As they reach an entrance to Fort Tryon Park, they both hesitate.

"Are we ready for this?" Hazel pats his arm gently. Neither sibling is particularly affectionate, but the gesture is subtle enough.

"Do you know where?" Kagan asks.

"I think so," Hazel replies, already in motion. She knows where Janice went over the edge but doesn't want to admit to Kagan that she's already been there. A few favors from her more resourceful fans with access had gotten her the coordinates from the police report.

The sounds of the city recede the farther into the park they venture. Signs pointing them to the Palisades lookout spot get closer together until they arrive at the mouth of the stone garret, peppered with obvious tourists taking posed selfies. A cloudless sky hangs clear and blue over the picturesque expanse of viridescent trees surrounding the Hudson River. They make their way to the edge of the watchtower and tentatively peer over the vertical drop into a thicket below. Like the Cloisters, where Janice worked, the lookout turret was part of a relocated medieval European castle. Hazel feels overwhelmed with nostalgia for the evenings when their mother read them *King Arthur and His Knights of the Round Table* before bed.

Hazel points at the wall a few yards from where they are standing, which borders the walking path currently cordoned off by crime-scene tape. From their view, the wall's edge is a steep drop of at least thirty or forty feet. The wall is about shin-high in some spots and waist-high in others. Hazel feels a flash of rage at two teenagers taking pictures of the crime-scene tape.

Silently, they stare at the wall. It feels like anything other than quiet reflection would be disrespectful. Hazel watches as people arrange themselves in posed stances in front of the water, blissfully unaware that someone died not far from where they are mugging so giddily. She takes in the beauty of the trees and the plants winding their way up the side of the weathered stones and again wonders what her mother's last thoughts were as she fell. Hazel sees her brother stiffen. "What's wrong?" she asks.

"We are really high up. Do you believe that Mom walked here regularly?"

Hazel can't believe that it hasn't occurred to her sooner. "K, you are so right. She never would have gone on the path, let alone gotten close enough to the edge to go over. Especially if she was alone."

"Remember the smoke alarm?" Kagan says.

"Of course." Mother's Day many years ago, when Kagan was twelve and she was ten. They'd been at their summerhouse in Amagansett, and their father was MIA for the umpteenth time while Janice was struggling to get out of bed most days.

Kagan had seen an episode of their favorite sitcom in which the dutiful kids brought their perfect mom breakfast in bed. He suggested they do the same and make the best out of their mother's self-imposed bed rest. They scavenged the pantry for pancake ingredients, and Kagan attempted to use the stove for the first time. The operation went smoothly until the bacon started to burn. An automatic shriek from the smoke detector filled the air. It could have been thirty feet out of reach of the siblings. There was no way either of the kids could retrieve and carry the giant ladder that hung in the garage that would elevate them enough, nor could they come close to reaching the blaring device with a broom handle, as their father had in the past while balancing on the countertop.

Janice emerged from her room and panicked. Her fear of heights was so severe that a trip up the ladder was out of the question. She'd hyperventilate herself into unconsciousness before she was halfway up.

Janice's acrophobia was well established, primarily by their father's endless pleasure in pushing every possible boundary around the phobia. He claimed that he was going to heal her vertigo by immersion. There had been surprise day trips to Six Flags, a tearful fight in the lobby of the Empire State Building, and several battles about vacations involving hikes and ski lifts and canyons. Kagan flew into action and pushed the breakfast table across the room, placing it beneath the detector. He positioned a kitchen chair atop the table and directed Hazel to grab the thick bound block of yellow pages. Kagan swung the very wooden spoon he'd been smacked with many times by their father until the alarm fell to the floor and broke into pieces, and Janice gratefully held them both.

Hazel stares at the ledge where their mother went over. She grabs Kagan's elbow and squeezes it harder than she means to. He inhales sharply and catches the rage in her eyes when they lock onto him.

"What?" he asks.

"We need to go to the police," she says frantically. "This definitely wasn't an accident."

CHAPTER 7

Kagan sits with his sister in an interview room inside the Thirty-Fourth Precinct station house, just south of Fort Tryon Park. Detective Gina Calabrese is seated across the table from the siblings, a notepad at the ready. She wears a navy-blue suit, hair pulled back in a tidy bun, a look of keen observation in her eyes.

"Welcome," she begins. "I'm glad you both came in. We've been trying to get you on the phone."

"I'm sorry about that," replies Hazel. "Everything's just felt really crazy, with Mom gone and all. We're going through a lot right now."

"I understand." Calabrese knits her fingers together and adopts a somber expression. "My deepest condolences for your loss."

"We appreciate it."

The detective sets her stare on Kagan, and he's hit with a disconcerting feeling. Part of it has to do with her age. Here he is, staring down the barrel of forty, and this fresh-faced young woman who's got to be more than a decade his junior is perched across the table, holding all the power in the situation. It feels out of balance and topsy-turvy and confusing as hell.

And then there are the detective's eyes. They remind him of one of those big cats, a puma or mountain lion or something, at once placid, intense, and insightful. He feels as if those eyes are drilling down into his deepest layers as he fidgets on the rickety metal chair. He's having a hell of a time trying to sit still and sets his palms onto the edge of the table in an attempt to steady his nerves. As if sensing his discomfort, Hazel lays a hand on top of her brother's.

"And how can I help you both today?" asks the detective.

"Well," says Hazel, "my brother and I have been talking, and we think you might want to look at Perry a little closer."

"Your stepfather?"

From the corner of his eye, Kagan catches a wince as Hazel stiffens up.

"Well, yes," she says.

"And what should I be looking at him for?"

"We understand you're considering the possibility of foul play," says Hazel. "And Perry's just acting, I don't know, *weird.*"

"Weird? How so?"

"Yeah, um, suspicious, I guess. And looking back at their relationship, my brother and I are coming to realize that he's always seemed a little questionable."

"Hmm." Calabrese flips open the notepad and consults its contents. "Maybe you can help clarify things for me. It was my understanding that you hadn't been in contact with Mr. Walters recently. Nor your mother, for that matter."

"Um, yeah," responds Kagan. "I guess it's been some months now, hasn't it, Haze?"

She plays along, appearing to consider the question. "Yeah, it must be by now. Huh."

"Some months." Calabrese consults her notes as she ponders the statement, then returns her attention to Kagan. "I was under the impression you'd been largely out of contact with your mother for the past couple of years."

The inquiry sets off an alarm in Kagan, and he can't help but fidget. "Detective, may I ask who you've been talking to?"

"My partner and I had a conversation with your stepfather, and he seemed to be under the impression that neither of you had been in close touch with your mom for about that amount of time."

Kagan's snort draws a quizzical look from Calabrese.

"Something you want to share?"

"I'm sorry," says Kagan. "It's just . . . 'stepfather' has an odd ring to it. We were never really that close."

"Yes," responds the detective. "Mr. Walters expressed as much when we spoke. And it sounds like that distance extended to your mother recently as well."

"Right," explains Hazel. "I guess that's true. Lots of life stuff. Just busy, you know? Families." She offers a lazy shrug. "But after Perry reached out to us with the news about Janice, we agreed to meet him for lunch. My brother and I both wanted to make sure he was holding up okay."

"Very thoughtful of you," Calabrese responds as she jots on the pad. "And how did that meeting go?"

"Not great. He said some unkind things to us and started bullying Kagan and me about money. We left early."

"Interesting. And how'd the topic of money come up?"

Hazel clears her throat. "We were offering to help Perry out in whatever way we could. I was just figuring that he'd have the insurance people and the estate lawyers to deal with, and so I told him we could help navigate those conversations, to ease his burden."

Kagan catches the uptick in tone at the end of the sentence and turns to his sister. He recognizes the smile on her face—the same one she wields when attempting to charm her way out of speeding tickets—and hopes it doesn't appear as hollow to Calabrese as he knows it to be.

The detective finishes writing and looks up from the notepad. "And you said your stepfather was acting 'suspicious'? Could you elaborate on that a bit more?"

"Hey, Haze," Kagan chimes in. "Tell her what you told me, about his affect being off and all that."

Calabrese bounces her glance between the siblings before landing expectantly on Hazel.

"Well, Detective, he seemed flat and unemotional. Like he was putting on a performance of grieving, but he could barely be bothered to even do that. He just had these, like, empty eyes. It was kind of eerie."

"I see." Calabrese shifts her attention to Kagan, and he's again subjected to the heat of her stare. "And did you pick up on this same energy your sister's mentioning?"

"I did, yeah. I've been thinking about it more since she commented on it, and I realized Perry's always had this really weird vibe, ever since we've known him. Like, *too* positive? All howdy-do. But underneath it he's really just an asshole. I mean, he practically accused us of being responsible for our mother's death, for Christ's sake!"

Kagan feels a shot of pain as his sister's foot connects with his shin under the table. She squeezes his hand too hard before addressing the detective again.

"Sorry, my brother's just . . . let me give you some context here. We were discussing the insurance policy, and I don't know if maybe Perry was just feeling really emotional at the moment, but he insinuated that the police might be considering *us* as suspects—"

"Which doesn't make any sense," interrupts Kagan. "We don't even know what our inheritance looks like!"

"What my brother means to say is that Perry seemed very cagey about sharing any info with us regarding the estate and the will, despite our good-faith efforts to assist him."

"Doesn't that seem a little suspicious to you, Detective?" Kagan feels his skin prickle as he eyes her.

"Not particularly. What you've described so far is fairly standard procedure between spouses." Calabrese sets her elbows onto the table and leans in closer. "But let me tell you what *could* seem suspicious here, Kagan. You mentioned a moment ago that you were never that close with your stepfather but also claim to have been familiar with his behavior over the course of his marriage to your mother. Am I hearing that right?"

Kagan feels as if he's slipped between the jaws of a vise and is being squeezed from both sides. "Well, you know, hindsight," he blurts.

"Hmm." The detective considers Kagan's answer before turning her attention to Hazel. "And *you're* telling me that after years of estrangement from your mother, you meet with her widowed husband to inquire about his well-being and immediately bring up your mother's finances. You also describe Mr. Walters as behaving both unemotionally *and* emotionally during said conversation. And then, when you realize your beneficiary status may be in question, you end up in my office pointing fingers at your stepfather. Forgive my skepticism, but you can both understand how this all seems a little jumbled, no?"

Kagan feels his ire suddenly boil over. "No offense, Detective, but look at you. How long can you possibly have been on the job, anyway?"

Calabrese leans back in her chair and daggers him with a look.

"Fair point there. But let me tell you a little about the job I had before I applied to the academy. Years ago, I worked the front desk at a motel out on Long Island. We had a real mix of guests there: motorists pulling off the expressway for a good night's sleep; low-level drug pushers brokering deals; and, of course, plenty of people stepping out on their spouses. I got pretty good at spotting the differences between them. And do you want to know what it came down to, every time? The eyes. That's what always gave 'em away. A person who's selling you some bullshit story will either look at you too long and too intently, or else they'll avert their gaze altogether, real cagey-like." She stares at the siblings. "And guess what? I'm getting a whole two-for-one with the pair of you."

"Our mom had a fear of heights!" sputters Kagan, and the moment the words leave his mouth he reads an incredulous look on Calabrese's face. He's immediately sunk by the realization that if he were in her place, he wouldn't know what to make of the sudden outburst either. Kagan has managed to fumble the draw on the siblings' trump card, effectively burying it at the bottom of the deck.

"Detective," says Hazel, swallowing a sigh as she does her best to crush her brother's knuckles, "are we free to go?"

CHAPTER 8

This guy is a fucking hologram!" Hazel wails as she clicks through the fifteenth page in her Google search for "Perry Walters." She usually enjoys the prospect of sleuthing online, but searching for any information about Perry has left them with more questions than answers.

"Still nothing?" Kagan sniffles. "You've been looking for like four hours. Maybe take a break?"

He's sitting a few feet from her, his restless legs syndrome in full twitch and driving her crazy.

"Perry Walters doesn't exist," Hazel says dramatically, her voice cracking. She is furious with the situation, and while uncomfortable, the anger at their stepfather is preferable to grief. "How do we know so little about a man who was married to our *mom*?"

It has been two weeks since their sit-down with the police, and emotions had been extremely high since the siblings received a letter from Janice's probate lawyer explaining how it was customary for previous beneficiaries to receive a copy of the amended will. Hazel and Kagan had been cut out completely.

They reacted to the letter in differing extremes. Kagan went on a bender and slept for two days straight, while Hazel called Perry in a storm of fury, screamed into the phone at him that this was his fault, and threatened lawsuits while Perry remained disturbingly calm. After her rage fizzled out, he pleasantly informed her that Janice had handled all her legal dealings independently of him. He didn't leave the conversation without telling Hazel that he wasn't surprised that their mother had cut them out after all the years of their taking her for granted and caring about her money to sustain their laziness, entitlement, and addictions. This stopped Hazel in her tracks.

"What are you talking about? I barely drink and never fuck with drugs."

"Your dependence on technology is just as bad as Kagan's on drugs and alcohol."

"I'm not a fucking addict, Perry. I'm an influencer."

Before disconnecting, Perry twisted the knife a few degrees further.

"I seem to remember your mother did leave you both something, though. I thought it was overly generous of her."

This sent Hazel to make multiple frantic calls to Janice's lawyer that resulted only in terse responses that their mother's estate was in limbo while her case was active. This obstacle was moot for Hazel and Kagan, who were still entitled to nothing except for a small addendum that both had missed in the probate letter:

> The deceased's estate will subsidize twenty-eight days of addiction rehabilitation for the decedent's surviving children, Hazel Anne Bailey and Kagan Charles Bailey, at an institution included in the approved list of reputable facilities.

This last vestige of their mom's concern sent them both into a tail-spin of guilt and anger.

Unsurprisingly, Perry had been unreachable since Hazel's last phone call to him. And the police continued to appease them with no real help. In the weeks following Janice's death, Hazel and her brother have cycled through every possible emotion, primarily shame and anger at their mother's footnote regarding their imposed rehab.

They hadn't spoken about it to each other for a few days after the letter came. Finally Hazel had broken the silence. "I don't even drink! What was Mom even talking about?"

Kagan had stayed tight-lipped, likely stewing over his own more obvious issue, as far as Janice was concerned. His mother had spoken to him more than a few times about her worries. Eventually Hazel had pushed him enough when she said she understood why he needed to go to rehab, but why her?

"Hazel, you're addicted to your phone. And your computer. And your smartwatch. Anything that you need to charge, really."

She'd been stunned by this absurd accusation, naturally. "Phone addiction is not even a thing, Kagan."

He'd smirked and suggested she look it up on her phone.

"Do you agree with her? Do you think I have a problem?"

In a rare moment, her brother had sat still, held her eyes, the same as his, and spoken from his heart. "I kind of do."

"That is such bullshit, Kagan. How can you say that to me? You haven't been sober since elementary school!"

"You were live tweeting my entire wedding, Haze. The whole video is you on your phone, even in some of the photos."

"K, it's not like I'm sitting in front of my computer watching porn all day. I don't need to go to rehab for it. Come on."

Later that day, when he'd run out to the store for wine, Hazel had begun reading about tech addiction online. She went through a list of signs of a dependency and stopped reading when she'd checked off ten warning signs.

Fourteen days after the letter came, they still haven't brought up rehab again or acknowledged when they were escaping into their respective hatches. Hazel is perched at the kitchen table with her computer open and her phone in hand while Kagan smokes a joint out the window.

"There are plenty of people with the name 'Perry Walters' coming up, but none of them are him. And anything that mentions him is all from the article."

They both glance at the *New York Post* spread out between them.

Hazel never buys the print edition of any paper, but the *Post* with the headline HEAD OVER HEELS: JANICE THORNHILL'S DEADLY PLUNGE was an unfortunate must-have. Kagan nabbed it from the building's vestibule, and it has been fanned out on the table, collecting crumbs and coffee stains—every time the siblings catch sight of it, the ache of Janice's death surges.

The black-and-white picture of their mother staring up at them was taken at the Women in Art Conservation luncheon at Cipriani five years ago. It is so out-of-date that Janice's hair color and style drastically differ from the last time Hazel saw her alive. At the time of her death, Janice had let her hair go completely gray and wore it in a flattering, sleek bob, which made her look sophisticated and fashionable. More jarring is that the image sits side by side with a black-and-white aerial shot of the rescue team removing a body bag from a tangle of overgrowth, likely taken around the same spot where Hazel and Kagan stood only weeks earlier.

"At least they used a good photo of Mom," Hazel says sarcastically. Janice's hair is styled in dramatic crests, her face heavily made up. She looks older than she was when she died. She would have hated that this is the photo being used, and Hazel wonders how Perry could have let them. Then she wonders if he'd provided it.

The Google alerts for "Janice Thornhill" and "Perry Walters" notified them as soon as the digital version was online, and the friends' and family's outreach followed in droves the morning the print edition hit stands. While Kagan and Hazel have no immediate family who are still alive, some of their mother's second cousins poked around, likely curious if any family money was floating about unclaimed. Kagan's and Hazel's phones are filled with unread and unchecked texts and messages from shocked characters throughout Janice's life, undoubtedly wanting information about how she ended up on the top of the Metro section for being at the bottom of a steep drop.

The shock of the article only worsened when they read the depiction of their mother's life before her "suspicious" fall, still "under investigation." The victim's "grief-stricken widower" was quoted throughout.

> He couldn't imagine that anyone would want to hurt his saintly, beloved wife, but he supposed there were always people who harbored dark motives. It was hard to sleep at night knowing that perhaps she had known her killer(s).

The piece mentioned alleged hobbies and likes of their mom's, utterly unknown to them, and sentence upon sentence of unrecognizable recollections and sickeningly saccharine platitudes that the Janice they knew would have hated. While it was true that Janice significantly transformed following Charles's death, this candy-coated version of her was a caricature created by someone who didn't seem to know her.

After their father died, Janice went from somewhat reclusive and uninterested in life, pinned down by her anxiety and insecurities, to quickly shedding that layer of herself like last season's jacket. Charles was buried on a Saturday, and by Monday, she'd gotten a therapist, followed in quick succession by a personal trainer, a stylist, and a complete makeover. Janice was joining a book club, getting season tickets to the Met, and going on group trips around the world with other single women, widows, and divorcées her age. She started going back to church regularly, which reinstilled the strong faith she'd relied upon during her childhood and gradually lost after she married Charles. This renewed spirituality and her other lifestyle changes allowed their mother to emerge a stronger, happier, and funnier version of herself. One they'd never gotten to see when she'd been in the throes of her terrible marriage.

At no point was Janice the one-dimensional portrayal Hazel holds in her hands.

After Hazel read the story out loud, she and Kagan looked at each other with the same shocked face. He could barely find words beyond, "*That* is not our mother."

They repeatedly excavated every word of the column to glean anything about what had happened and how they could prove Perry's involvement. The facts are scant, and what little there is does nothing in their favor to build their case.

"The fucking guy wasn't even in the state when it happened. But he did this. I know he did." Hazel's recurrent melancholia has persistently tried to sidetrack her, but the case against Perry is providing a new sense of purpose.

"How does someone live as long as he does without having any kind of online presence?" Kagan asks.

"You can pay to have any information about you scrubbed from the internet," Hazel replies.

"Or you aren't the person you've been claiming to be. Perry Walters probably isn't even this guy's real name. I'm going back to my older photos on the cloud. There's got to be at least a few candid photos of this asshole kicking around that we can reverse image search," Kagan says.

"From when? It isn't like we were invited on any of their vacations."

"There has to be something. Maybe from when they were first dating."

Back when they were still welcome in Mom's life, when Perry was the interloper, not Hazel and Kagan. But even then, Janice had started to put down boundaries that hadn't been there before.

"Are you finding anything?" she asks.

He shakes his head. Hazel can see the pain in his eyes, understandably, from obsessively sifting through pictures of Janice. "This would be so much easier if Mom hadn't deleted her Facebook," Hazel says, a realization hitting her hard. "You know, Perry told Mom that he hated social media and thought it was a waste of time. She deleted her account because of him. I'd totally forgotten!"

This sore point connected another set of dots for Hazel; she'd felt hurt and resentful about how much Janice judged Hazel's dependence on social media for her work, but she never actually watched her videos. Now she's wondering how much Perry influenced her mother's opinions.

Hazel postpones posting her daily video because no amount of makeup can conceal her swollen and bloodshot eyes. She also continues texting Adam, even though he hasn't responded once.

"Here's a group shot with him in profile and Mom at the Met fundraiser for the Cloisters from two years ago, but you can barely see him."

Kagan flashes his phone screen at Hazel to show her a shadowy profile of Perry off to the side in a group shot. Janice is beaming, front and center, flanked by two familiar socialites. "There's nothing at all in the images of him alone," she says, while Kagan glances at the picture but averts his eyes quickly at the sight of his mother. "The other thing that I'm realizing is that Mom hasn't been photographed at the most recent events of some of her regular organizations, not even alone. I've scoured the Guest of a Guest site for all her usual annual benefits since they've been married, and nothing."

"Huh. Mom lived for that shit. Why would she stop going?"

"I'm sure he was isolating her from her friends like he was keeping her from talking to us," Hazel contends.

"Interesting how he also managed to keep his face out of the *Post* feature. I mean, this fucking guy wove quite a fairy tale about his and Mom's marriage, but not one cheek-to-cheek anniversary picture?" Kagan shakes his head. "Where does that leave us? Private investigator?"

"With what money?" Hazel asks.

"You know, missing people were found before the internet, Haze. We have to use OG methods."

Hazel exhales frustratedly. "How do we do that if we know nothing about him?"

"Sure we do," he says slyly.

"Kagan?" She rubs her temples.

"At lunch, he told us quite a bit."

Hazel processes for a moment. "Okay, like what?"

"We know which fine food establishments he frequents, and lucky for us, that bit of business is right in my network. I have plenty of helpful contacts in high and low places."

"I may know someone who could help us too," Hazel says, excitedly thumbing into her phone.

CHAPTER 9

Kagan emerges from the subway station grasping at a shred of hope. He's at the mercy of luck and timing this afternoon, but if things go the way he prays they do, Kagan just might have stumbled onto the thing that finally gives Hazel and him a bead on the mystery man who's managed to infiltrate their lives.

Before the siblings' lunch plans with Perry at Aglio went so spectacularly off the rails, he'd let drop that he and Janice also frequented Le Croquette. The mention of the restaurant stuck out in Kagan's mind, since he'd heard through the industry grapevine that a former coworker was bartending there. He'd lost Vincent's number a few iPhones ago, but if his old pal is still on staff—and if he happens to be pulling a shift today—Kagan could be in business.

Vincent owes him a favor, and a big one at that. Years ago, when the two were working together and Kagan was first getting his food-photography sideline going, he made the misguided decision to have business cards printed up. One of the few lessons his father had bothered to impart was an insistence on the importance of a handsome, stylishly designed card. Since any sort of positive input from Charles was delivered so rarely, Kagan had internalized the advice, however archaic it had become.

He'd also recently rewatched *American Psycho*, and the iconic business-card scene from the film had made an impression on him. Kagan proceeded to have a batch of cards printed up, not realizing that in the age of social media, the accounts themselves would function as both a résumé and free advertising for his budding business.

A few nights later, postshift, the staff decided to hit a club to celebrate a coworker's birthday. As the crew sipped drinks in a banquette, Kagan showed his new business card to Vincent, who chuckled a bit as he studied—then pocketed—it. Drinks led to shots, which led to dancing, which eventually led to Vincent being approached by a pair of women who began flirting enthusiastically with him.

No one noticed the trio slip out of the club a short while later. The rest of the crew continued partying and eventually closed down the place and peeled off separately. Kagan was home and about to fall into bed when his phone rang. He picked up the call and heard a slurring and disoriented Vincent on the other end of the line.

As best as Kagan could figure out from the hazy details of the conversation, his friend had been drugged and robbed by the women and dumped somewhere out in Queens in the middle of the night with no phone or wallet. He'd stumbled into a twenty-four-hour diner and, discovering Kagan's business card in his pocket, called his pal to come save him.

Based on Vincent's description of the diner, and his mention of a few landmarks in the neighborhood, Kagan managed to figure out his location. He got dressed again and shot over to his sister's apartment, where he sneaked in and swiped the key to the Audi A3 that Hazel kept parked outside her building. With little other than the odd newspaper-delivery truck and bakery van on the road at that hour, he made it out to the diner in no time, scooped up Vincent, and got him home as the first faint light of dawn sharpened into an encroaching glare, casting the sidewalks in a brilliant glow.

By the time Kagan made it back to his sister's to drop off the Audi, Hazel had discovered the car gone and was in the process of reporting it stolen. When he walked into her apartment waving the key, she apologized profusely to the officer on the other end of the line, hung up the phone, and proceeded to scream at her brother loudly enough to wake anyone still asleep in the building. It took Kagan weeks of groveling— and several hand delivered breakfast sandwiches—for her to forgive him, and he's now hoping to leverage the incident to appeal to his old friend for a bit of help.

Kagan rounds the corner onto Columbus Avenue and sees the sign for Le Croquette halfway down the block. He's never been to the spot before, but its reputation precedes it: a hotshot young chef, an innovative French-leaning menu, and—as of last year—one highly coveted Michelin star. He's suddenly hit with the somewhat screwy feeling of being happy that his mother managed to eat so well when she was still alive.

Janice always cared about food, and not in an ostentatious way. Kagan's fondest memory of childhood revolves around a time when the family returned to the city from a weekend at the Amagansett house. She insisted on stopping at a farm stand on the way, driving Charles through the roof. He spent the rest of the drive fuming, which set everyone in the car on edge. When they returned to the apartment, his dad stormed into his office and ignored everyone for the remainder of the evening.

Janice calmly shepherded the kids into the kitchen and removed the produce from a mesh tote. She retrieved a package of bacon, a jar of mayo, and a loaf of sourdough bread from the fridge, and the kids and their mom set about preparing the best BLTs Kagan had ever tasted, made with patience, cooperation, and love. The effort had such a soothing effect that he still remembers the profound sense of calm it invoked, all these years later.

Kagan has mapped out today's visit to Le Croquette quite intentionally. The lunch rush should be wrapped up, allowing for a lull in service and some downtime for the staff. As he enters the restaurant and is greeted by the hostess, Kagan is happy to find his prediction to be accurate. A few stragglers are finishing up their meals, but the place is pretty quiet. A pair of apron-clad servers mill idly near a martini cart, waiting to clear the remnants off the last tables of their shifts. The space itself is pristine and elegantly appointed: an enormous chandelier hanging from the high, crown-molded ceiling; linen white walls displaying huge canvases of abstract oil paintings; tall potted ferns dotting the perimeter and flanking the pair of banquettes in either corner of the far end of the dining room.

Kagan spots Vincent behind the bar and feels a cool wave of relief wash over him. He thanks the hostess and beelines to his old pal's station. As he approaches, Vincent does a double take and lets the fruit knife he's been using to slice lemon wedges clatter against the cutting board.

"Kagan Bailey," his friend says, holding out his palms. "As I live and breathe."

"Vincenzo!" Kagan takes in the restaurant's interior and lets out a low whistle for his buddy's benefit. "Really working your way up in the world."

"Eh, the hustle's the hustle." Vincent shrugs. "They just make me wear a tie at this one."

"Well, you're lookin' good."

ELIZABETH McCULLOUGH KEENAN AND GREG WANDS

"You too, brother." The smile he flashes appears to Kagan to be masking an underlying sense of concern. "Hey, I was just about to go out for a smoke. You wanna join?"

"Yeah, why not."

Vincent steps out from behind the bar and tosses an arm around his old coworker. The men make for the front door and offer the hostess pleasant nods as they exit the restaurant. They settle on a stretch of wall down the block to lean against, and Vincent pulls a pack of American Spirits from his pocket and offers one to Kagan.

"Nah, I quit."

Vincent smirks as he coaxes a smoke from the pack and slips it between his lips. "Yeah, me too."

Kagan chuckles. "Ah, fuck it." He accepts a cigarette and a light, and they each settle in for a drag. "So they treating you okay at this place?"

"You know, it's a corporate gig. Manager's always looking for ways to make things more 'efficient,' which basically translates into him breathing down our necks most of the time. Nothing like the freewheeling old days." He takes a drag off the cigarette, then blows a jet of smoke from the edge of his mouth. "But I finally have insurance and a 401(k) and all that grown-up shit. I've got a wife and kid now, so the timing's good."

"Oh, no way. I hadn't heard. Congratulations, man!" Kagan plasters a smile on his face, but all he can think is, *Another poor sap, down for the count.* This seems to keep happening to him an awful lot lately.

"Thanks. Yeah, it's been a minute. Things still going strong with you and Bethany?"

"Uh, we're taking some time apart right now." Kagan's immediately hit with the impulse to kick himself for letting that clichéd—and not exactly true—bit of explanation tumble off his tongue, but he's been feeling too self-conscious and defensive about the situation to properly delve into his emotions around it.

For years, Hazel had taken some not-so-subtle shots at Bethany, insinuating that she was greedy, opportunistic, manipulative, and uncaring. "Most men marry their mother," Haze once proclaimed during a particularly savage tear, "but you went and married Dad. At least that's original." He would steadfastly shield his wife from the charges, but lately it's occurred to Kagan that his sister might have had a point all along, which really pisses him off.

"Relationships, man." Vincent drops the cigarette and stubs it out with the heel of his shoe. He turns to Kagan and sets a hand on his shoulder. "Hey, listen. I heard what happened to your mom. I'm so sorry. You holding up okay?"

The comment catches Kagan off guard, and it takes him a moment to figure out that his old friend must have spotted his name in the *Post* story and put it all together. He's had a handful of former acquaintances coming out of the woodwork these past few days, some expressing genuine concern and others in full gawker mode.

"Doing as well as can be expected," answers Kagan, shaking his head. "My sister and I are just trying to sort it all out."

"I'm sure. I mean, I never met her, but the papers made her seem like a really great lady. And it sounds like they think someone might have *pushed* her?"

"That's what the cops are trying to figure out." Kagan fishes his phone out of his pocket and keys in the passcode. "And it's actually part of the reason I came by to see you."

"Oh yeah?" says Vincent as he projects a look of curiosity.

"It's not the greatest shot, but any chance you recognize this guy?"

Kagan holds out the phone for his friend's perusal. The screen displays the photo from the Cloisters fundraiser, of a barely discernible Perry in profile. Vincent squints as he studies the image until his face brightens.

"Oh yeah, that Conrad Bain–lookin' dude."

"Who?"

"You know, the guy who played Mr. Drummond on *Diff'rent Strokes.*"

"Huh." Kagan studies the image again. "Yeah, I guess so. Never really noticed that before."

"This all makes sense now."

"How's that?"

"I think they might have used an old photo of your mother in the *Post,* so I wasn't quite sure when I saw the coverage, but I thought she looked familiar. But now that I'm seeing this guy . . . yeah, definitely. They came in for dinner together a few times when I was working. Always sat at a table, so I never dealt with them directly, but it was definitely them."

"Man," says Kagan, impressed. "Good eye."

"You know how it is, K. Names I'm no good with, but faces and drink orders? I got you all day on those." Vincent turns his attention from the picture on the phone screen to Kagan, his interest piqued. "Wait, are you thinking your stepdad had something to do with this?"

"Not sure yet. I don't want to jump to any conclusions here, but there's something shifty about the guy. Hazel and I have been trying to dig up any info on him we can find, but nothing doing so far. It's a little weird, I gotta say."

"Yeah, I hear you on that. How's your sister holding up?"

"Not bad, all in all." Kagan sighs. "The thing with Haze is she's already convinced that everything's a conspiracy, so I don't know if she's coming into this with the most objective viewpoint. But we're trying to get through it together."

"Right, right. You're each all you've got now." Vincent runs his fingers through his hair. "Listen, what can I do to help?"

"If it's not too much to ask, I was hoping you might be able to keep an eye peeled for Perry. Just give me a heads-up if he comes in, or if he seems to be up to anything suspicious. That sort of thing."

"Of course, K. You know I got you." Vincent's cheeks color slightly. "Pretty sure I still owe you one, anyway."

"Those were some times, weren't they?"

"Sure were, brother." He lets out a chuckle. "It's a wonder we're both alive and kicking."

"A miracle. Speaking of, you still party?" Kagan slips his phone back into his pocket and palms a small bag of powder. "I'd be happy to hook you up, as a thank-you."

"Naw, man." Vincent shakes his head as he holds up his hands in surrender. "Those days are well past me. I'm a family man now."

"Right, okay. Well, listen, I can't thank you enough for doing me this favor."

"Yeah, no sweat." Vincent digs his phone out of his pocket and swipes at the screen, then turns it toward Kagan. "This still your number?"

"That's me. And send a text so I've got yours. New phone."

"Cool. I'll let you know if this guy turns up at all. You said his name's Perry, right?"

"Yup. So far as we know, anyway."

"Okay. Look, I better get back inside. I'm sure my manager wants to give me notes on how to slice lemon wedges at the optimal width, or some bullshit." He locks eyes with Kagan, and his mouth tightens into a serious line. "I'm sorry again about your mom. Let me know if you need anything at all, okay?"

"Thanks, man. For sure."

Vincent pulls Kagan in for a hug, holds him for a long moment, then kisses his forehead. As they release from the embrace, Kagan detects something in his friend's expression that he has a hard time parsing. There's sympathy there, sure, and a bit of sadness, but underneath those things Kagan swears he catches traces of both pity and mild relief. This growing suspicion begins to infect the sense of optimism he felt moments before, and as he turns and walks back to the subway stop, Kagan's hopefulness is clouded by a different emotion—one more complicated and deflating.

CHAPTER 10

Welcome to another installment of TRUST ISSUES, the only ASMR, NSFW conspiracy theory channel on the internet.

I will take requests and suggestions for discussion topics in line with my content brand if you'd like to subscribe to my VIP-level Lonelyfans membership or tip extra on my page. If you'd like to sponsor me or have me wear or use your product in my videos, you can DM me for rates and more info.

Tonight's bikini is supplied by Stars and Stripes, "providing constitutionally forward pole wear for more than a decade," and the body oil I'll be applying throughout the discussion is Slick's Rub. If you watched my last video about Pornhub being a cover for population control, the bubbles I used for my bath were from the same maker.

Now sit back, get comfortable, and open your mind. As I get started on my oil massage, I'll set the scene for this week's theory:

So you've decided to dip your toe back into the dating cesspool and sign up for a handful of matchmaking apps. Some prospects will not be who they claim in their aspirational profiles; most will be shorter, balder, fatter, and *older than their pictures advertise. More than a few will probably be hustlers, schemers, catfish, or worse. We know from every third podcast you are more bait than mate.*

If you are lucky, you will be one of the two percent of people who meet a viable partner via apps. If you are unlucky, you will end up dismembered in a suitcase in the desert (see my video from May about the local law enforcement cover-up of Daphne Powers's murder).

What millions of members logging on to these swipeable meat markets don't realize is the amount of critical, vulnerable private information you are relinquishing to the United States government that can be leveraged against you. From core memories to dick pics to greatest fears, people are too willing to open themselves up to total strangers who might be their "soulmate" but are more likely to become someone's cellmate.

These prospective suitors are collecting not only emotional passwords but also actual ones. (Watch my video from December about how you can figure out anybody's password with just five questions.) Not since the Scientologists has there been such a well-organized format for manipulating blackmail material.

Hookup sites like Ember, Blissmates, and Heartstrings were created to conduct mass data collection on an unprecedented scale, all because no one reads the privacy fine print when they are desperate for love or a hookup.

/ / /

Hazel nearly slips on the body oil that has collected on the shower floor. She steadies herself on the guardrail installed for the previous tenant, who she's pretty sure died in the apartment. She gingerly steps out of the shower and dries off. Even though she's exhausted, she feels satisfied with her performance tonight. The constant dings coming from her phone suggest her fans were happy, too, and she's already received a quarter of her rent in tips.

The income from the Lonelyfans account scarcely covers her monthly expenses, and her MeTube channel has gotten big enough that she's started to see a trickle of ad revenue, but it's barely making a dent in her debt. After Janice cut her off, she continued to spend like she was still getting an allowance. The debt kept accumulating, and she forged on assuming that her mom would bail her out if things got bad. Janice always had before.

Hazel can't square up where all the money that Janice gave her over the years went. Her previous apartment in SoHo was a big chunk of it. The maintenance had gotten to be too much without a regular income, so she downgraded to her current place in Inwood with the profit from selling her downtown place and lived off the difference for a couple of years. Her closet contained luxury labels, glittery gowns, leather bags, and impossibly high-heeled shoes. Those items were merely collateral now, since she hasn't been invited to anything in a few seasons. When Hazel's money ran out, so did her so-called friends.

In the past decade, she's spent tens of thousands on credit for vacations to escape New York's stresses. Now, amid her own stress, she can't recall why she was so anxious in her twenties. She can't even pinpoint her favorite destination; every place seemed identical from the poolside chaise of a Four Seasons resort.

Hazel considers selling her car, but that idea is even less appealing now that Janice is gone. It was the last thing she purchased for Hazel before their falling out. While a car isn't as sentimental as it is practical, Hazel secretly shares her mother's sense of nostalgia. Kagan proved much better at stepping into the lifestyle of an underearner. He'd never been as showy as his sister was at the height of her spending, but she knows his ex Bethany did quite a number on his nest egg from Janice. The million-dollar wedding, the Upper East Side apartment, and the champagne lifestyle had quickly drained his resources. They never discussed it, but Hazel suspects that the dissolution of Bethany and Kagan's marriage had more to do with lack of money than love, although Hazel wonders if there was ever much of the latter.

Hazel perches her iPad on the bathroom counter and plays the rough cut of her next video. While she half watches that, she scrolls through her phone one-handed and pulls a comb through her wet hair with the other. So far, her dating app video has tons of views, including an all-capped comment, "@Tinfoilfox IS THE JOE ROGAN OF METUBE." The commenter hasn't tipped her, to her frustration. Positive feedback is nice, but only fleetingly if it doesn't help pay the bills.

Hazel feels particularly proud that she's creating new takes on cultural paranoia, sidestepping old Paul McCartney doppelgängers and Princess Diana death theories and presenting divergent content that many people seem interested in.

She's barely gotten on the second arm of her kimono when she sees a message on the Smoke Signal app. Before opening it, she knows it will be Todd, or @DickVidocq, one of his online aliases. He's the only person Hazel is in touch with who's legitimately paranoid enough to communicate on the encrypted platform. She contacted him on the secure app earlier in the day to see if he could help with the Perry investigation. He had been helpful with getting her the Janice crime-scene details and is one of her most consistent fans.

The message is one word: Call?

She presses the phone icon. Todd picks up before the second ring.

"Tremendous segment this evening, Ms. Fox. Trust Issues is getting a real following. I hope you don't forget your earliest fans when you go big-time."

Todd may be his real first name, but Hazel has no idea. She certainly doesn't know his last name, so she's been unable to do any of her own recon on the guy. What he looks like is a mystery, and she's pretty sure he uses a voice disguiser. But he's never asked her for anything in return for his favors, and she doesn't get that bad feeling in the pit of her stomach that other fans give her before she blocks them. Todd seems pretty harmless and, most importantly, is one of her top tippers.

"Todd, I could never forget you." She affects her online persona by purring, "How's life?"

"Well, the world is burning from the inside out, but I'm doing just fine."

"Isn't it, though? So glad you're good."

Hazel imagines Todd's aspirational self-image as a Sam Spade and Philip Marlowe mash-up in a perpetually smoky, black-and-white haze. The desired vibe: debonair, brilliant, and giving zero fucks. In reality, he's probably an overweight, middle-aged white guy with social anxiety in a flyover-state basement. This is Hazel's primary demographic.

His tone is flirtatious. "I was intrigued by your message. You have a proposition for me?"

"I do. I need you to track someone down for me," she replies coyly.

"Missing person?"

"The person is accounted for, but his identity is hard to pin down."

"Ah. A gentleman of the chameleonic variety." Todd's tone changes. "A boyfriend?"

"Not a boyfriend. And not a gentleman," she says darkly.

"I'm sure I can be of assistance. What do you know about him?"

"Not much. I think he scrubbed himself from Google. I have his name—Perry Walters—which I would bet is fake, and a very obscured picture of him." She puts Todd on speaker while she attaches the picture of the charity event, Perry's profile lurking in the background ominously, and shares it. "I just sent it to you."

"Got it. Give me forty-eight hours," he says confidently.

"You are my hero."

"I hope that someday, you and I will meet in real life."

Hazel disconnects without replying, feeling slightly spooked.

She puts her phone onto the counter and pulls her hair back in a tight bun. The lines on her forehead and around her eyes smooth from the tautness, and her face looks ten years younger. Hazel gazes at Adam's number but hesitates to tap the icon. Despite numerous calls, she hasn't accepted his thoughtless rejection. The weeks without him have revealed that he was a vital confidante. With Kagan absorbed in his own issues, Hazel finds herself with no one to share her feelings with.

Her iPhone buzzes in her hand with an unrecognizable 646 number. Maybe Adam has gotten a new phone?

"Hello?"

"Ms. Bailey?" an authoritative female voice asks.

"Yes," she replies guardedly.

"This is Detective Gina Calabrese. I was hoping you could come down to the Thirty-Fourth Precinct."

"What for?" she asks.

"I'd rather not say on the phone, but it's regarding your mother's case."

"When?"

"Tomorrow morning or early afternoon at the latest. We've received some time-sensitive information that I'd like you to review."

Hazel feels the adrenaline boost from a few moments ago drop heavily into her lower belly. "Do I need a lawyer?" she asks cautiously.

"You are within your rights to bring one, but this is not an interro-

gation. Your insight could help answer some questions about what happened to your mother." Calabrese's voice is warm.

Hazel's heart races, but she believes going to the station tomorrow
might be the sign she's been waiting for. She plans to file a missing person report for Adam while she's there because she's not ready to give
up hope. If he's in trouble and she's the only one searching for him, this
could be the defining moment of their relationship.

"Sure, I'll plan on being there before noon. Does that work?"

"Great. We appreciate it. And Hazel, we'd like you to come alone."

CHAPTER 11

Kagan's already seated at a table near the window of the Bean Scene, the late-morning sun warming his back, when Vincent walks in. A handful of customers populate the coffee shop, getting their caffeine fix or tapping away at their laptops, but the space is largely empty at this hour. Kagan catches his friend's eye, waves him over, and nods at the Americano he's taken the liberty of ordering.

"Ah, you remembered." Vincent plops down onto the chair, picks up the glass mug in front of him, and blows gently onto the liquid. "Good man."

"Hey, I was the new guy when we worked together. Got stuck making every coffee run for a month straight. Those orders are seared into my brain."

"I guess that's right." Vincent chuckles as he tests the temperature of the drink. "Thanks for meeting me close to work."

"Man, you're the one doing me the favor. I appreciate you reaching out. And so quickly."

"Yeah, it's no thing. I would have texted you last night, but we got rammed. Didn't make it out of there until after midnight."

"Do they have you on the schedule every day or what?"

"Sure feels like it." He rolls his head as if it's on a swivel. "But no, just the double yesterday and lunch this afternoon, then I'm off for a couple of days. Get to go hang out with my kid at the park."

"Nice. Supposed to be a warm one tomorrow." Kagan takes a sip of cold brew. "So you've got news for me?"

"Sure do." The sun's glare causes Vincent to squint slightly as he smiles at Kagan. "You know, your stepdad's a funny kind of guy."

"Oh yeah?" Kagan feels a pop of excitement as he awaits whatever developments are on the way. "And how's that exactly?"

"I'm starting my shift yesterday, before the dinner rush. It's still pretty quiet at the bar, just a couple of customers, when in walks your man. I'm playing it casual, of course, but I've got my antennae up. He orders a glass of wine, very jovial, we have a pleasant exchange, and then I go on about my business. Few minutes later, a woman walks in and sits down next to him. They start talking."

"Wait, like they were meeting, or did they just happen to strike up a conversation?"

"Oh, it was definitely planned. They hugged and everything. Knew each other for sure."

"Really?" A pang of unease needles Kagan. "What did this woman look like?"

"About your stepdad's age. Looked pretty well-off. Just had that easy air of money to her. Exceedingly polite as well. Good energy."

"Huh." Kagan attempts to mentally comb through any information he ever remembered Janice volunteering about her husband: any mention of family or people around the man's age whom he was close to. A sister or cousin, maybe? He once heard a tragic story about a daughter Perry had lost, but that's about as much as he can recall. "Did you happen to overhear any of their conversation?"

"C'mon, K." Vincent settles back into his chair as he reveals a self-assured smile. "You think you assigned an amateur to the job?"

"My apologies. Go on, Columbo."

"So this woman sits down next to your stepdad. Seems pretty smitten with him. They're talking closely, so I can't make it all out, but when I pour her a glass of wine I catch her mentioning something about *arrangements*, like they're hatching a plan."

"Shit." The discomfort oozes through Kagan's belly. "Okay." As the pair falls into a moment of quiet consideration, he notices a corner of Vincent's mouth curling into a wily grin.

"What's *that* look about?"

"I haven't told you the weirdest part yet."

"You gonna keep holding out on me?"

"Okay, so check this out." Vincent takes a sip of his Americano and settles in for the rest of the story. "When it was just your stepdad and me making small talk, he came off a certain way. And then, when the woman rolled in, his whole demeanor shifted, but subtly."

"What do you mean? Like he was flirting?"

"Well, more than that, though. It was strange." Vincent pauses. "Okay, remember at the end of *The Usual Suspects* when Keyser Söze dips out of the police station? He's walking with the clubfoot, and then it kind of melts into a normal gait, very fluidly? Sorta like that. It was as if he morphed into someone else. He sank farther into the stool he was sitting on and dropped his shoulders. Opened his chest up wide. The whole nine."

"Huh." Kagan suddenly feels as if some errant itch he hadn't quite been able to pinpoint is now being scratched. "Like a different person," he says, as much to himself as to Vincent.

"Yeah, it was wild. His voice dropped an octave, and he started speaking with almost a drawl. Real sultry, man. Layin' it on. Kinda reminded me of a young Burt Reynolds."

Nothing about this description of Perry sounds familiar, and yet Kagan can see him clearly, can perfectly picture the scenario, as if a beam of refracted light has brought an image it's fallen across into sharper focus. He laughs in spite of himself.

"I've gotta say, this does not sound at all like the version of Perry who was married to my mother."

Vincent's face screws up into a look of confused curiosity. "Okay, I'm glad you said that just now. I was afraid I might be losing it."

The comment causes Kagan to refocus on his friend. "What are you talking about?"

"Your stepdad's name *is* Perry, right?"

"I mean, so far as we know. Why?"

Vincent cocks an eyebrow. "Well, when that woman first sat down, I could have sworn she referred to him as Walt."

CHAPTER 12

How's the street noise on the weekends?"

Perry's in the midst of formulating an answer to the question from the young woman—one of half a dozen prospective buyers currently nosing around his apartment—when he spots Kagan out of the corner of his eye. *Not now, goddamn it.* The kid half glances at Perry as he flits through the main room and disappears down the hallway. Perry does his best to shake off the intrusion as he returns his attention to the woman.

"Not too bad," he explains. "We're far enough off the avenue, and the closest school is three blocks away. It stays pretty quiet, all in all."

"Three blocks," echoes a young man as he approaches the woman and slips an arm around her. "That's exciting." They exchange a smile before the man turns back to Perry. "Good school?"

"The downstairs neighbors send their children there," Perry improvises. "The kids seem to like it okay."

"Huh." The woman scopes out the living room. "Would you be

willing to sell the furniture as well? My fiancé and I are really into mid-century modern right now."

"If you're interested, we could figure something out for the furniture and the artwork."

The couple trade quizzical looks.

"My wife recently passed away," explains Perry, "and the memories we shared in this apartment are weighing heavily on me. I'm looking for a fresh start, and it would please me greatly to be able to pass on my Janice's exquisite taste to a lovely young couple such as yourselves looking to build a future together."

The couple nod sympathetically as a woman in a tailored suit and spectacles ducks out of the kitchen and joins the group. "Hey," she asks, "how's the Wi-Fi in this place?"

Perry swallows down a grumble along with his growing irritation. "Frightfully sorry, but I need to grab something from the office. Pardon me for just a moment."

He excuses himself from the group and lets the polite smile fall from his face as he turns and hustles to the office. As he approaches, Perry hears movement from behind the door. He opens it to find Kagan inside, placing a vase back in its spot on the bookshelf. The kid's sweating and as jittery as ever, and the look on his face is a mixture of anger and unease. His jaw seems to have a mind of its own. Perry shuts the door securely behind himself before squaring off on his stepson.

"And what may I ask are you doing here?" Perry hisses, working to keep his volume low.

"Just figured I'd check out some prime real estate." Kagan scowls at him. "You see, my mother recently passed away, and I'm supposed to be coming into a good bit of money right about now."

"How'd you get in here?"

"I gave the doorman your name, and he assumed I was here for the open house." Kagan takes in the room, a smirk on his face. "Imagine my surprise."

Beneath the contempt, Perry picks up on a wounded sadness in the young man and decides to change tack.

"Listen, Kagan," he begins in a gentler tone. "I'm sure this all must come as a shock. I would have consulted you and your sister about the sale, but I didn't feel like I was in very good standing with either of you at the moment."

"Hmm. Sure didn't take you long to list it, huh?"

"I'm well aware that you lost your mother, and I sympathize with you on that count. Deeply. But try to remember that I lost my wife. The love of my life. And all these reminders of her are simply too much for me to live with, day in and day out. Can you understand that?"

"'Lost my wife,'" Kagan repeats with a snort. "That's a funny way to put it."

"And whatever do you mean by that?"

"Well, I don't know, *Walt.*" Kagan's eyes narrow as he stares a hole through the man. "Care to take a guess?"

The remark catches Perry off guard, but he keeps his voice steady. "What did you just call me?"

"Walt. That's the name you're going by now, isn't it?"

Perry takes a deep breath and releases it. "Why don't you tell me what's on your mind, Kagan?"

"Gosh, where should I start? I mean, aliases, clandestine liaisons with mystery women. You're a real man of intrigue these days."

"Enough." Perry can feel his indignation climbing as the insinuations are leveled by this self-centered twerp. "Have you had me followed, Kagan? Is that what's been going on here?"

"Haven't needed to. I know some people around the neighborhood who look out for me. Who have my best interests at heart. That's all."

"I see. Well maybe there's a possibility you haven't considered."

Kagan dismisses the idea with a snicker. "And what would that be?"

"It seems to me you've been so busy thinking about yourself that it hasn't occurred to you that there are other people in this world with feelings and needs. You've been so busy thinking you're smart that it hasn't occurred to you that you might not know every goddamn thing."

The subtle crack in Kagan's veneer encourages Perry to go on.

"The woman I saw at the restaurant was a member of our congregation. She'd become quite close with Janice and is taking her death very hard. I agreed to meet with her in order to try to provide some comfort and compassion in this difficult time, as she was for me. These are the things that people in a community do for one another, Kagan."

The self-righteous look on the young man's face begins to falter. "Well, I heard there was a lot of flirting going on."

"You heard wrong. Your mother's friend was emotional and became weepy as we spoke. I comforted her. That's about as close to flirtation as anything got."

"My guy overheard you two discussing something about 'arrangements'?"

"Yes, Kagan. The woman was asking about funeral arrangements for Janice. Also, I'm planning to endow a portion of your mother's estate to the church. It's what she would have wanted. So the arrangements you mention could refer to either subject." Perry feels a sliver of satisfaction as he watches the kid try desperately to regroup.

"Okay, well . . . if that *is* true, then how do you explain the fact that the woman called you Walt?"

Perry lets out a labored sigh. "She's older and a little flaky. Somehow she's managed to get my first and last names mixed up and has fallen into the habit of calling me Walt as a result. I've corrected her a few times, but I just don't find it to be worth the trouble anymore. Especially at a time when she's in the midst of grieving and—"

"Hello." The voice and accompanying knock at the other side of the office door interrupt their conversation.

"Just a moment," Perry calls out, before returning his attention to his stepson. "So you see, it's good to think of others every now and again."

Behind Kagan's petulant sulk, a sense of doubt has crept in. He appears to be caught somewhere between the virtuous anger he came in with and the sense of contrition this new information has seeded in him. He stands there for a long moment, dumbstruck and unmoving.

"Listen," says Perry, breaking the silence, "I should really get back to my guests. But I'm glad we had the chance to iron all of this out." He sets his hands on Kagan's shoulders, which seems to snap the young man from his daze. "Are we okay?"

Kagan flinches under the touch and slips free of Perry's grip. He mutters something unintelligible, then grabs the vase from the bookshelf and tucks it under his arm. "Mom promised me this," he spits, a look of nervous uncertainty on his face, before hustling out of the office and out of the apartment.

CHAPTER 13

The midday sun warms Hazel's exposed shoulders as she rounds the corner. She glimpses the entrance to the police station, but a visceral twinge keeps her from the door. It's a little before noon, and she's not ready to face whatever awaits her. She figures a few turns around the block and a phone call might help her nerves.

Reaching Kagan has proved futile; he seems to have turned off his phone. He didn't turn up on her couch last night after meeting up with a mysterious "friend" who'd promised news about Perry, and she's vaguely worried that his afternoon meetup turned into evening drinks that turned into God knows what.

Instead, she decides to try Adam one last time and leave a message instead of hanging up. She rationalizes explaining herself, rather than Adam seeing her missed calls, might save her from appearing stalkerish or too thirsty. Her sandals are pinching from the walk over, so she finds a wall under a shady overhang across from the precinct instead of circling. Hazel leans against the cool brick and taps his name in her recent calls. Immediately, a recorded voice informs her that her dialed number is no longer in service. She tries again with the same result. She looks at her past texts and taps a quick, Is your phone number not working? A message pops up: Undeliverable.

Frustrated, Hazel ducks between two parked cars to cross over to the station. A slow-moving Ford Explorer with tinted windows takes its time passing her as she steps into the street and makes her way to the entrance.

The bland atmosphere of the police station waiting area reminds her of a DMV. After checking in, she shifts uncomfortably from one foot to the other while a surly cop minding the station's gateway calls Detective Calabrese.

"Ms. Bailey, I'm Detective Calabrese's partner, Detective Woodson; step right this way." The neutral voice beckons her through a set of half-open double doors. He nods in her direction, and she follows him in.

"Woodson! What's good, brother?" A stocky crew cut in uniform claps the detective on the back as he passes them, and Hazel feels the cop look her body up and down. She returns his leering with death daggers, and he smirks as he retreats.

Hazel follows Woodson through a cluster of metal desks littered with food wrappers, deli cups, and anachronistic file folders. A scattering of men and women, but mostly men, lean back in chairs spread in every direction, taking up as much space around them as possible, talking on cell phones or tapping away on laptops. She feels more eyes on her as they make their way to a row of glassed-in rooms on the back wall.

"Thank you for coming, Ms. Bailey," a familiar voice says behind her. Hazel swivels and spies Calabrese, closing in on them as Woodson guides Hazel into a cramped room with a table, three chairs, and nothing else.

Calabrese holds a coffee and a laptop. She's dressed in polyester black pants and a dark gray button-up. Her hair is pulled into a practical low bun, and she wears no makeup. Her outfit is as drab as their surroundings, but Calabrese carries herself with a relaxed confidence that threatens Hazel. The detective radiates natural beauty without styled hair, makeup contouring, or a curated outfit.

"Anything I can do to help," Hazel returns. "Where do you want me?"

"You can take that seat." Calabrese gestures.

"Water?" asks Woodson.

"I'm good." Hazel declines even though she is parched. She doesn't want to delay this any longer.

"Let us know if you change your mind."

"How long do you think this is going to take?"

"That depends on you. We'd like to move this along as quickly as possible." Calabrese smiles cordially.

"Great," Hazel replies, feeling anything but.

"Jumping right in. Where did Kagan attend college?" Calabrese asks.

The question immediately unsettles her. "Columbia, why?"

"Just bear with us," Woodson interjects.

"And is he right- or left-handed?" Calabrese's pen is poised.

"Left." Hazel anxiously tugs at the hem of her dress. "Why are you asking me about Kagan?"

"Do you know where your brother was on the day of your mother's death?" Calabrese asks.

Hazel hesitates. She doesn't know where Kagan was that day, but she feels deeply that whatever she says next will alter their fate. She instinctively knows the right answer will be the one to protect her brother, even if it isn't the truth.

ELIZABETH MCCULLOUGH KEENAN AND GREG WANDS

"I don't ever know my brother's whereabouts, unless he's crashing on my couch. I'm his sister, not his keeper." Her ire fills the room. "Can you just tell me whatever it is you're getting at? I need to be somewhere."

Calabrese opens her laptop and maximizes a black-and-white screenshot of trees and a pathway. "We've just gotten access to the video footage from the section of Fort Tryon Park closest to where your mother died."

Both detectives look at Hazel intently.

She desperately wants to shed a layer of her clothing in the boiling stuffiness of the room, but she is wearing only a sundress.

"What exactly is the footage of?" She wants to know if she is about to watch her mother die.

Calabrese tempers her brassbound demeanor. "We don't have a clear camera angle of the exact spot where your mother fell, but we do have a decent view of the path leading into the area. We've identified a man entering and exiting the park via this adjacent trail around the time of the incident."

Hazel wishes she weren't alone right now, cursing herself for coming without Kagan or a lawyer.

"What do you need from me?"

"We think you might be able to identify this man."

"Why me?" Her stomach somersaults.

Calabrese looks at a notepad beside her laptop, just out of view of Hazel's sight line. "Let's take a look."

Hazel watches the static image animate. The bird's-eye view of the pathway shows a few passing people, a couple, hand in hand, leaning into each other on a slight tilt. A woman pushing a stroller and talking on a cell phone, an elderly man walking a tiny dog.

A minute in, a figure emerges that saps the breath from Hazel's chest. He's wearing a familiar baseball hat, a black T-shirt, and jeans. His heavy black boots are out of season, but Hazel knows he wears them regardless of the weather. In his left hand is a folded *New York Times.*

She can feel the detectives watching her reaction.

The frame is unoccupied for a few seconds before Detective Calabrese clicks and zooms forward. Now the familiar figure is walking back the way he came, this time with a slight wobble. His Columbia University cap is backward, and his face scans his surroundings. When he disappears from the frame, Calabrese stills the screen, and the trio sits tensely for a few seconds.

Hazel is surging with shocked confusion.

"Ms. Bailey, do you recognize that man in the video?" Woodson asks seriously.

Hazel searches for what should be a straightforward response.

"Yes," she finally manages.

"And can you confirm that the man in the footage is your brother, Kagan Bailey?"

It dawns slowly and painfully. The person she recognizes is not Kagan but someone who appears to have made a great effort to look like Kagan. And inferring from the smug smiles on the detectives' faces, Hazel can tell that they have been fooled.

"That man is not my brother."

Calabrese exhales sharp frustration. "Are you sure about that?"

"But you know this man," Woodson says.

Hazel steadies her shaking hands on the table. "I do. But he isn't my brother."

Calabrese and Woodson anxiously anticipate as she processes.

"Then who, Hazel?"

"My boyfriend, Adam March."

PART
II

CHAPTER 14

Two months later

P arker, it seems like just yesterday that you were sitting across
from me for the first time, looking like a lost lamb."

"It feels longer than that," Ava replies dryly, glancing at
the clock behind Eric Prince. She musters every ounce of self-control
not to tell her boss what she really thinks of him. She is still a ward of
the US government for twenty-two more minutes, and she doesn't want
to endanger her imminent freedom.

"You look tense. Relax," he says, eyeballing her.

Ava will never fully relax around her case agent, no matter how
much time passes. His name suggests a gentle, regal type, but his demeanor is more frat than fed, and he's far from a noble. Prince would
happily judo sweep her off her feet and straight onto the ground if Ava
stepped one inch out of line. He's got the hollow-eyed, brainwashed
look of a government-issued sociopath and isn't even a computer guy,
which irritates Ava endlessly. How he landed a supervisory spot in the
cybercrimes unit is a perfect example of the ass-backward patriarchal
bureaucracy, especially at the federal level.

"I know today is your last day, but I have an employment opportunity that I think you'll be interested in."

She shakes her head vigorously. "I'm out, Prince."

"This is a plum assignment, Parker. You are the best red hat this department has ever had, and this new gig would get you out of the cave. You'd be working upstairs with me, and be able to continue to hack legally." He flashes a toothy grin.

A rotten carrot if ever she heard one.

Prince's fear of venturing into the cave was the only good thing about it. It had been Ava's workspace for the past three years. Minus the five goateed, social cue–ignoring men she's worked alongside during her time there, Ava had a full 36 square feet all to herself. Every windowless, fart-filled day was a white-knuckle countdown to freedom.

"If you stay, you can keep the apartment and car too."

"I've made other plans." Ava didn't spend the past twelve months dreaming of leaving this place only to relinquish control of her life on the final day.

"Don't you want to know what you are blindly passing up?"

"I'm good." She holds up her hand.

"You think you can do better than this? Don't fool yourself, kiddo. Using your talents outside of a government job might land you behind bars again, and not using them will land you a minimum-wage job. If I were you, I'd stick with the devil you know."

Prince pulls a legal envelope from his desk. He removes her attached picture, which he puts into his breast pocket and pats. "I'll keep you close to my heart," he says before handing her the sealed documents.

The day has gone sideways. Ava had imagined herself handing

over her credentials, the car, and the apartment keys, *not* thanking Agent Prince for the opportunity, and going on her merry fucking way.

The envelope hovers between them. He stares unblinking until she takes it. She pulls a single page from the sheath and glances over it. Same shit, different cubicle, but she can't bring herself to throw the envelope in his face and say goodbye forever.

"I'll think about it," Ava says.

"Good girl. Let me know by oh eight hundred on Monday. And don't disappoint me."

"What about these?" Ava defeatedly shakes her key ring.

"Keep 'em. You still get all the fringe benefits as long as you work for Homeland Security. And I won't say goodbye; just see you later." He smirks.

Ava rises, her body feeling far heavier than when she walked into Prince's office.

She'd felt the same heaviness when he'd informed her that the job would be the balance of her sentence on her early-release day when he picked her up at Kingsland Correctional.

That day, she learned that handcuffs came in many shapes and sizes.

/ / /

Ava feels the drag of disappointment slowing her as she walks through the parking lot. She's mad at herself for not telling Prince to fuck himself and punches her key fob angrily. She'd planned to get in and out, leave everything belonging to the government and start fresh. It would have been a clean slate, but something held her back from saying no.

Her text notification dings, and she looks at her phone. It's from Jackie, her former cellmate turned friend.

> Are you coming in tonight? There's a couple here looking for you.

She rereads Jackie's text several times, trying to decipher the two sentences. Most days, this message would read to her as a warning, and she'd stay far away. But today, she takes it as an invitation. She's tired of hiding from life.

Ava throws the car into reverse and tears out of the spot. When she hits the street, she shoots through DC toward the only place left to go today: Hell.

CHAPTER 15

Helene's Social Club & Lounge is situated among a cluster of food and drink establishments in the Adams Morgan neighborhood of Washington, DC. Helene's is a casual affair: a long, patinaed oak bar stretches along one side of the low-ceilinged and dimly lit room, the opposite wall taken up by banquette seating. The red velvet fabric that upholsters the bench is threadbare and frayed in spots, lending the place a scruffy elegance. A well-stocked jukebox tucked into the corner of the room is currently piping the sounds of Jimmy Smith's Hammond B-3 organ into the largely empty space as late-afternoon sunlight slips in through the propped-open front door.

Years before, as the story goes, half of the neon in the sign above the entrance shorted out. The back end of the name, along with half of the second "E," no longer lit up at night, shortening "HELENE'S" into the decidedly less savory "HELL." According to the older woman who's now relaying the tale to Hazel and Kagan, ownership found the scenario sufficiently amusing and decided to let things ride. Shortly thereafter, a church group caught wind of the unintentional transgression and showed up to protest, picket signs in hand. The event made the local news, and business received a healthy bump as a result. These days, the sign has become a popular background for selfies and group shots posted to Instagram. The hashtags practically write themselves.

The siblings' new friend is discussing the history of the sign with the particular relish of someone sufficiently loosened by booze. Kagan has picked up on her habit of salvaging the previous cocktail's stirrer and adding it to the incoming drink, whether out of reflex or as an accounting method he's not entirely sure. He clocks three in the vodka tonic she's currently working on. Considering the early hour, he figures the woman likely showed up today as the bartender was opening the place.

Kagan is mainlining black coffee as his sister nurses a club soda with lime. The young woman keeping bar—around Hazel's age with sleeve tattoos and a just-cordial-enough demeanor—doesn't seem to mind the fact that the siblings are abstaining from the hard stuff. Kagan is doing his best to humor the amateur historian with the stirrer fetish, but his attention is principally focused on the front door of Helene's.

He feels an anticipatory jolt of excitement as he spies a shadow stretching through the doorway, and the feeling ramps up at the sight of the woman who steps in behind it. Her pale oval face is framed by a center-parted veil of sandy-brown, razor-cut hair that falls just short of her shoulders. There's a Cindy Crawford mole above her lip. The only thing disturbing the ethereal beauty on display is a patch of scarred skin that inches up the woman's neck. Her vigilant eyes perform a quick sweep of the room as if by reflex. She steps farther into Helene's and offers the bartender a smile she doesn't quite mean. Kagan can swear he catches the bartender subtly shifting her eyes in the direction of the siblings.

"Hey, Jackie." The new arrival slides onto a stool a few seats down from the siblings and offers them a quick nod as she sets her elbows onto the bar top. "Hey, Dolly," she says, looking past Hazel and Kagan to the woman downing the dregs of her vodka tonic.

"Oh, hi, Ava. How are you, honey?"

Kagan feels the gentle kick his sister gives the leg of his barstool at the mention of the woman's name. They're in business.

"Eh, you know," Ava says in response to the inquiry. "Head above water."

Dolly chortles too enthusiastically at the remark before setting her empty glass onto the cocktail napkin and tossing a few crumpled bills beside it. She bids everyone farewell and shuffles out of the place. Jackie collects the detritus off the bar as she gives Ava an inquisitive nod.

"You don't even need to ask today."

"Went that well, huh?"

"Bureaucracy at its finest." Ava sighs.

Jackie sets a rocks glass in front of her. "I told you I could hook you up with shifts." She pours two fingers of Tullamore D.E.W. into the glass. "Just say the word."

"Appreciate it. I'll need to wriggle my way out of Prince's clutches first."

"It's your own fault, brainiac. Like I always say: set the bar low." Jackie turns to the siblings. "You two good, or you ready to get in the game here?"

"What the hell," says Kagan with a shrug. "Make my coffee Irish."

"Sure thing." She turns her attention to Hazel. "And for you?"

"White wine, please. And would you put her whiskey on our tab?"

The gesture pulls Ava's focus to the siblings. She raises her glass and waits for Jackie to pour their drinks and serve them before taking a long sip.

"That's very nice of you both. To what do I owe the kindness?"

"Asshole bosses are the worst," says Kagan. "Sorry you're dealing with that."

"You've had your own?"

"Haven't we all?"

The comment elicits a communal laugh, and everyone has a drink.

"I'm Kagan," he volunteers after a quiet moment, "and this is Hazel, my sister."

"Ava."

"Right," says Hazel. "Ava Parker, isn't it?"

Ava recoils the slightest bit. Her expression takes on a look of intrigued apprehension.

"Do I know you two?"

"Not exactly," says Hazel. "But we have someone in common."

"That right?"

"Your father was married to our mother."

Ava's eyes go wide, but she quickly recovers. "So he's still alive, then," she says, as much to herself as to the siblings.

"Yeah," answers Kagan. "But she's not."

This snaps Ava back to attention. She trades a look with Jackie before returning her focus to Hazel and Kagan.

"Listen," says Hazel. "I'm sure this is a lot to process. And just so you know we're not full of shit, here's a photo." She slides a manila envelope down the bar. "It's of the two of them, at a charity gala in New York City."

Ava opens the envelope and fishes out the picture, then consults the image quickly before dropping it to the bar top as if it's hot to the touch. "Son of a bitch." She lets out a long exhale and looks at Kagan almost bashfully. "You said your mom's dead?"

"She is."

"Under suspicious circumstances," adds Hazel.

"Man, this is sounding eerily familiar." Ava slugs down the rest of the whiskey and pinches her forehead. "Look, I'm very sorry to hear about your mom. I lost mine as well."

It takes a moment for the implication of the comment to fully sink in, but as it does, Kagan feels his gut sour and his ire climb. This son of a bitch, who'd killed their mother then gaslit them about it, made them feel like a couple of shitbags in the process, might have done this before. And who knows how many times.

"May we ask how your mom died?" inquires Hazel.

"Tragically." Ava's expression has calcified. "But the fact of the matter is that I'm estranged from my father. Have been for quite some time. So I'm not really sure what I can do to help you two out here."

As Kagan studies the young woman, he swears he can feel waves of resentment and pain radiating off of her. Beneath the detached facade, he senses the sort of wounded abandonment he himself has experienced at the hands of a parent.

"How long since you last saw him?" asks Kagan.

"More years than I can count. I needed him out of my life, or I wasn't going to make it in the world. If I'd stayed on the path I was on, I'd have taken him down and myself down with him." She says the last part almost wistfully.

"Look," says Hazel, "the last thing we want to do is dredge up the pain of your estrangement from Perry, but we could really use your help here."

Ava's eyes cut sharply to Hazel. "What did you just call him?"

"Oh, um, yeah." Hazel flashes a look of panicked embarrassment. "Perry Walters was the name he was using when he was with our mom. Kagan and I figured it might be an alias."

"Unbelievable." Rage passes across Ava's face, followed by an acid-tinged laugh. "You know where he got that from? There was a show called *Home Movies* that I used to watch when I was a kid. It was the one thing he'd do with me, when he could be bothered. There were these two characters on it named Perry and Walter." She shakes her head in disbelief. "The nerve of this fucking guy."

"What did you know him as?"

"Pick your favorite expletive."

Kagan realizes this is hardly the time for laughter, but he has to make an effort to stymie a chuckle. He's finding himself drawn to Ava Parker's alluringly wry sense of humor. "We think he's currently using the name Walt as an alias, for whatever new con he's got going at the moment." He digs into his pocket and pulls out the Connecticut driver's license he found while rummaging through Perry's office desk during the open house two months prior. Kagan had turned up the ID just before Perry barged in and quickly dropped it into the vase on the shelf that he later stormed out of the apartment with. He slides the license across the bar to Ava.

"'Wyatt Ellsworth,'" she reads with a snort. Kagan studies Ava's expression as she does her best to downplay the discovery, but he can tell something about the reveal cuts deeply. "Looks like the guy's been keeping busy," she says too breezily before returning her focus to the siblings. "And you two think he was behind your mother's death?"

"We can't prove anything," explains Hazel, "but yes. The morgue finally released her body for lack of evidence, and your dad buried her without telling us, so it doesn't look like we'll ever know for sure."

"In my experience, the guy's hard to nab. He rarely does his own dirty work."

Kagan feels the air catch in his throat as Hazel flinches next to him.

"Well," she says, "we're pretty convinced he enlisted my boyfriend to knock off our mother. So I guess that tracks."

"Your *boyfriend*?"

"We're still trying to figure out the connection," adds Kagan. "Our mom and Per . . . well, your dad . . . they met through their church. And her ex must have gone there too. We think your father manipulated him somehow into murdering her."

"Jesus." Ava shakes her head. "I wish I could say that any of this sounds surprising. But I *am* sorry about your mother. Truly."

"Would you be willing to help us catch him?" asks Hazel.

"Listen, I'm not really trying to—"

"For the sake of *both* our mothers?"

Ava blows out a slow, measured breath as she weighs the proposition. "How long are you two in town for?"

"As long as we need to be."

"Okay, give me a number I can reach you at."

Hazel procures a pen from the bartender, jots her cell number on a cocktail napkin, and slides it toward Ava. Ava stands from her barstool. She returns the photo to the envelope, pockets the number, then pulls out a few bills and slips them beneath her empty rocks glass. She turns to the siblings, eyes narrowed.

"How'd you two find me, anyway?"

"Wasn't easy," explains Hazel. "But I've got a guy who knows his way around computers."

"You bet your ass he does, if he tracked me down." She scoffs. "I'll be in touch."

As a small group of after-work patrons enters the bar, Ava Parker crosses the room, slips out through the front door, and disappears into the dwindling light of day.

CHAPTER 16

To Ava." Kagan raises his plastic cup and taps it against Hazel's.

"Today went surprisingly well." She surveys the food choices scattered between them.

"Much better than you imagined," Kagan jabs.

"I'm not the only one who was nervous."

"Your cheese appetizer, madam." Kagan dodges the comment and hands her a bag of Cheetos.

The Days Inn lacks room service, and the siblings' financial resources are scant. They'd scrimped on a celebratory restaurant meal so they could spring for adjoining single rooms. Both agreed that a brother and sister sharing a hotel room at their age—one thirty-five and the other thirty-eight—would be weird.

Yet here they are, sitting cross-legged on the same bed, splitting a stoner's feast. Hazel twists the cap of the off-brand wine from a shady liquor store with a bulletproof divider. Their current digs are a stark reminder of how far they've fallen from their economic origins, making the wound of Perry's crime all the more painful.

"She wasn't what I expected," Hazel says as she rips open the first course of their vending-machine dinner.

Her brother refills the plastic cups with the cheap merlot. They share their first real laughter since Janice's murder, creating a lighter atmosphere in the room. Hazel is reminded of the comforting moments of sneaking into Kagan's room during their parents' fights and sleeping on his floor. The soothing glow of his lava lamp, casting ever-moving shadows on the wall, is vividly imprinted in her memory.

"Yeah. Ava isn't a total shithead like her father." Kagan sucks bright orange powder off his thumb before grabbing a bag of Funyuns from the bounty. "My daily vegetable serving."

Hazel laughs.

"She was much better-looking than I expected," Kagan adds, offering her the bag.

"What were you imagining?"

"I guess Perry in a wig," he deadpans. "What about you?"

Hazel laughs again and almost spills her wine onto the cheap duvet. "I don't know, not as together as she was. For someone who's been in prison and with a father who's also a criminal, I think I was picturing more *Orange Is the New Black* than *The Good Wife*."

Ava *is* much prettier than she'd counted on. She was surprised by how much chemistry she'd felt with Ava, and how intriguing the subtle scarring that crept over her shoulder and up her neck was. Hazel caught a glimpse when Ava's T-shirt was displaced after she pulled off her coat. There was something unexpectedly intimate about Ava's fingers lingering over the scars before absently pulling the fabric back into place.

Sexual attraction was the last thing Hazel expected today.

"She does have major Julianna Margulies vibes," Kagan says while crunching loudly.

Based on Kagan's energy, Hazel is worried that he already has designs on Ava. They certainly didn't need to fight over a woman right now, especially this one.

On the ride to DC, the siblings vowed to keep the drama to a minimum. They'd been hard on each other recently. The ten weeks since their mother's murder had felt like unending gut punches; the only bright spot was the twist of Perry's very much alive daughter.

Stability crumbled for Hazel after the police revealed Adam's footage. Kagan was no longer a suspect, but they were instructed not to leave the state and made to endure numerous interrogations about Adam, who, as it turned out, was completely fictitious. The shame of falling in love with someone who didn't exist significantly intensified her post-breakup turmoil. Coping with the loss of her relationship, the death of her mother, and the realization that her ex was her mother's murderer was quite the mindfuck.

The detectives had gotten a warrant for Hazel's phone and computer for any information about Adam, but there was no determined return date. She was unplugged for a nail-biting twenty-four hours before she caved and bought a new phone and laptop with her last remaining credit. She'd thought reconnecting to her online life would lessen the despair, but it only made it worse. It was a perverse mash-up of conflicting feelings; Hazel wanted Adam caught and punished severely, but she also missed him. Even though he'd done this unimaginable thing, she still felt the heartache, no matter how hard she tried to shake those feelings. She would never admit it to Kagan or anyone, but she longed for what she and Adam had. She wasn't sure how to untangle the person she'd thought he was with the murky character outline the police had given her about him and the evidence. The detectives didn't have any more of an idea of who he was than she did. And Adam was still at large.

Kagan had been kicked out of his friend's apartment for unexplained reasons, and he'd been on her couch for weeks. During that time, the siblings received several emails and texts from Janice's friends, who were upset they'd been left out of her funeral and burial, not realizing that Hazel and Kagan had also been excluded. The siblings had gotten the burial information from the funeral home's website and gone to visit Janice's grave after the fact, standing speechless over their mom's headstone with scentless deli flowers in hand.

And a final pleading conversation with Janice's estate lawyer verified their mother had left them nothing. All of this culminated with the confirmation that Perry Walters had vanished into thin air. This appeared to be of little concern to the authorities, as he was not a person of interest based on his rock-solid alibi. But Kagan and Hazel knew he was involved; he had to be. He had too much to gain from Janice's death, and the detectives had confirmed with Janice's priest that their mother's church connected Adam and Perry. But the active investigation fizzled out after a sweeping gang bust in Washington Heights had taken the local headlines and subsequent police resources.

It had been bleak until Dick Vidocq reached out to Hazel with information that Perry's deceased daughter lived and breathed in Washington, DC. After so many dead ends, they agreed that Ava Parker was the closest they could get to Perry and, hopefully, someone who might know where he would end up next. They'd decided not to share her info with Calabrese and Woodson, who barely returned their calls and emails. Finally, with the success of making contact today, things felt like they were turning around.

"She handled our ambush well. Much better than I would have." Hazel feels massively relieved. She'd been dreading the confrontation since they decided to make the trip. "Do you think she'll help us?"

"Hard to say," Kagan says as he works a Slim Jim from its plastic tubing. "She did seem pretty miffed about his alias. That could work in our favor."

Hazel scrunches her face. "K, you realize no percentage of that 'meat' stick is meat?" She fishes a roll of TUMS out of her purse. "Here." She hands him the tube. "Preventive measures."

He helps himself. "Haze, no part of this meal is what its packaging claims to be."

"Our life theme, so it seems." Hazel switches to dessert with a peanut butter cup. She hands one to Kagan. She also observed Ava's reaction to Perry's alias, but Hazel spotted something more subtle when they showed her the fake license. The second, longer look at the photo stilled Ava's breeziness. It was less of an expression change than an energetic shift. One Hazel identified with.

"I think she was downplaying how hurt she was." *And how angry.*

"That could also work to our benefit." Kagan considers this while he washes down the chalky tablets with the last of his wine. His face shows how vile the flavor is.

"Perry has done this before; she wasn't shocked," Hazel says.

"I might have picked up on that too," says Kagan. "What do we do if she doesn't call?"

Hazel thinks for a minute and chuckles. "We kidnap her and demand our inheritance from Perry as ransom."

"Or strongly suggest that we'll point Perry in her direction if she doesn't help us."

"Vicious!" Hazel laughs. "But that could work!"

"She'll call," Kagan says in a tone of hope and doubt. "She probably needs the money."

"What is the going rate for what we're asking her to do?"

"Let's tell her a percentage of the inheritance, and we can see how things go. I imagine we can renegotiate at the end if we aren't entirely satisfied with her services."

"You sound like Dad," Hazel says, and Kagan frowns. "It's true, though. How many jobs did Dad stiff people on because he found something wrong with what they did? It was a Charles Bailey special."

"He was his own special brand of asshole, wasn't he?"

Hazel nods. "Is this insane, what we're doing?"

"You know what Dad always said: 'Go big or go broke.'"

"Well," replies Hazel, "we're halfway there."

CHAPTER 17

Ava can't go home. She needs to do some major recon on her surprise visitors tonight, and the software monitoring on her devices would alert Prince the minute she started googling. It's early enough in the evening that Ava doesn't feel bad about dropping in on Sam but late enough that she wants to give him fair warning.

She parks the car outside his building and texts, r u awake?

He replies immediately, as expected.

> Always. U ok?

> I just met "Jack's" stepchildren

> Is this a joke?

> I wish

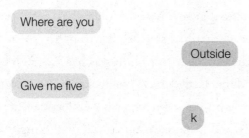

> Where are you
>
> > Outside
>
> Give me five
>
> > k

Ava taps on "Sinnerman" in her music app, closing her eyes as Nina Simone's timbre sends chills down her spine. In just six hours, her once mundane life has spiraled into chaos. Earlier this morning, she began her routine, thinking it would be the last time. Come Monday, her plan was to start her day with no goal other than seeing where her newfound freedom would take her. And it sure as hell wasn't going to involve her father. She feels a twinge in her scars at the thought of him. Years passed when she didn't even think about her burns, but a dull, aching phantom pain has begun radiating up her shoulder and neck since the siblings showed up.

She stares at her unfortunate options on the passenger seat—the envelope from Prince and the cocktail napkin with Hazel's number—and wonders how her bright future has gotten so dark.

There's a peculiar harmony to the timing. Ava was also on the verge of freedom the last time she saw her father. She felt a similar exhilarated terror when she finally walked away from him. His name was different then—Jack Latham—though she only ever called him Dad or Uncle, depending on the scam. It was easier to keep from calling him the wrong name.

After her mother, Hope, had died, he quickly became someone who didn't remotely resemble the father he'd been before. This post-Mom version was cold, distant, and nasty if she didn't do as told. Ava eventually realized that he'd always been horrible; she'd just been too young to see it, and her mother had shielded her from his true nature.

The week before she ran away from him was her sixteenth birthday. They spent it in Magic Kingdom. Though she'd long outgrown Mickey and Space Mountain, Ava's preferences were beside the point. He was between marks, and his money supply was dwindling.

It wasn't the bittersweet nostalgia of happier days that prompted their return to the amusement park; it was the attention that Ava attracted, particularly from mothers. Her father made Ava wear her childhood back brace and a sleeveless shirt showcasing the scars she normally worked hard to cover. Her pitiful appearance usually got them free admission and bumped to the front of any line. Ava assented to the humiliating charade, knowing this would be the last time she would be his pawn.

The theme park was a well-tested, high-return setting. The Happiest Place on Earth lulled its visitors into overstimulated ignorance, making it rife with marks. Parkgoers had abundant cash and were distracted and frazzled as Ava's dad worked them over with various sob stories and promises to pay them back. He banked on at least one of them being single and easily endeared to a widowed man with a disabled daughter. And more than once, he'd successfully hooked a single mother who was lonely and happy to join forces with another single, beleaguered parent for a few days of shared park time, or even longer.

Ava hated herself every minute she was part of his manipulation but wanted to keep the status quo leading up to her escape. The final days of fake crying in the park restrooms to attract a kindhearted woman or nabbing wallets and bags from distracted parents solidified her shaky nerve to walk away from him as she finalized the last arrangements of her getaway.

Ava had been fantasizing about her escape since recovering from the house fire that killed her mother and Uncle Wyatt five years earlier. With each passing year and scheme, her father's behavior became increasingly unconscionable, and Ava began to worry that he might decide that she was more valuable dead than alive. It was a deeply disconcerting evolution of realization, going from thinking her father loved her more than anything to realizing his love was an act to seeing the apathy in his eyes when she looked at him. Finally wondering if he might just abandon her outright in the middle of nowhere, or worse.

By fifteen, she'd begun actively preparing her exit, carefully taking small amounts of money from the petty crimes she was forced to commit. The amounts were so meager that her father wouldn't notice, so it took a long time to amass a chunk that could sustain her. But she patiently waited, saving enough to get her a ticket to freedom.

Every day without him, even when she was arrested and federally convicted, was free of wondering where he was and who he was scamming. She'd forgotten what it felt like to think about him and the unshakable worry and dread that immediately overtook her when she did. Her nervous system was shocked into hypervigilance at just the mention and images of him today.

Ava turns the car off and approaches Sam's building. With each step, her worry increases. She's unsure how this news will affect her stepbrother, and she considers treating the drop-in as a wellness check and nothing more. Any news about her father could send him into a dark place.

Before she can change her mind, Ava books it to the building's front door and leans on the buzzer until it clicks. She sighs when she spots the out-of-order sign on the elevator and pushes the stairwell door open. With every step, she swats thoughts about the past away. She's winded when she reaches the sixth floor on foot and sees the door to his apartment cracked open a few inches for her.

"Sam?" she calls as she steps inside and locks the three deadbolts. She removes her shoes and puts them into the closet along with her purse, out of sight.

"In here," he says from the darkness.

The ambient light from numerous monitors and an enormous flat-screen TV casts a kaleidoscope effect on the open-plan living room and kitchen walls. Sparse but practical furniture populates the space, including a dining table, four chairs, a love seat, and a coffee table. The walls are completely bare. The countertops, appliances, and cabinets starkly lack personal items and emit a faint ammonia odor. Sam's extreme minimalism imparts an eerie, perpetually unlived-in atmosphere to the apartment. Although she assumes he possesses essential tools for daily life, she has never actually seen them.

Sam sits in his throne-like gaming chair facing her. Behind him, three monitors display hundreds of lines of code—his command station.

"Hey, Sammy," she says warmly. Ava is immediately comforted by the sight of him.

"I thought you'd be celebrating your last day of indentured servitude."

"I may still work at DHS in a new post. I have until Monday to decide."

Sam's eyebrows lift. "You got a job offer?"

"Two, actually." Ava shakes her head. "Today has been weird."

"Well, I'm always glad to see you," he says, glancing at the envelope in her hand. "Although I gather you're here with a handful of troubles."

Ava gingerly hands him the photo.

He examines it and grimaces. He knows the silhouette well. "Like Bigfoot, but scarier."

Ava chuckles and positions herself on the love seat. "So that happened."

"This came from his 'stepkids'?" He looks pained.

"They were waiting for me in Hell."

"Doesn't get more appropriate than that." Sam's chair creaks as he reclines and scrutinizes the ceiling. She expects he's contending with the same surge of post-traumatic recall that she's been battling all evening.

"Are you okay?" Ava asks, concerned. "I debated bringing this to you."

"I'd be upset if you hadn't. Let's not pretend I haven't been wondering when this psycho would resurface for the past decade and a half. I was hoping it would be in the form of an obituary, though."

"Me too."

Ava finds it challenging to remember life before Sam. It feels like he has always been there, and she tries to avoid dwelling on life before him. It's surreal to consider that she wouldn't have encountered him if her mother hadn't died. The two most important people in her life couldn't exist together on the same timeline.

"What do they want?" Sam asks.

"To hire me. They think he had something to do with their mother's murder."

"Sounds like him. What are you supposed to do?"

"Track him down for them. They want their money back."

"That seems like an easy pass," Sam replies.

"I know. That was my first instinct, but I keep thinking about it."

After her mom died, Ava lived for a summer in Hilton Head with her father's reclusive sister, Constance. On her twelfth birthday, he showed up without warning. He took Ava on a two-year cross-country road trip, which was a series of stalled cons and close calls, where her father would use Ava as pity bait to romance a vulnerable woman with money and live off her lifestyle until she realized and they had to leave town. During this time, Ava's dad would dump her with these women he hardly knew and disappear for weeks, leaving her to wonder if he'd ever return. Most of the temporary "stepmoms" treated her fine, but some took their anger and disappointment over her father's erratic behavior out on her. There was never time to enroll in school, settle any roots, have a bedroom or clothes of her own, or make friends. The temporary families often came with half siblings who would ignore Ava in the best cases and, in the worst, mess with her in various ways. These were the memories she'd worked hard not to dwell on.

At fourteen, Ava's father took her to the bright yellow ranch house on Peace Road in Virginia, where sixteen-year-old Sam and his mother, Alison, lived. She instantly fell in love with the house and its occupants.

Her father, known to Alison and her son as "Jack," ordered Ava to pretend she was his niece. It felt easier to be his niece than his daughter, as if he had less claim on her. He was always nicer to her when other people were around, so she went with it.

It took her little time to gather that her father was married to Alison. When he finally admitted it, he claimed they'd met and fallen in love the summer when Ava visited her aunt Constance. Still, he'd waited to tell her because it was so soon after the fire. Ava was shocked and began to cry. Her father shamed her. "Don't you want me to be happy? How long does your mother need to be dead before I can have a life again?"

By that point, Ava was already learning to conceal her feelings. It was easier than navigating the emotional manipulation he unleashed if she let go. This coping mechanism would work against her in her adult life. She'd been accused more than once of being insensitive or cold. She was neither; she'd just mastered emotional concealment.

After about a year of attempting to live as a content blended family, Alison grew suspicious of Jack's lies. The tipping point came when she tried to enroll Ava in school during one of Jack's extended business trips and couldn't locate the necessary documents. Realizing that no faux mother had cared enough to take this initiative, Ava improvised poorly, claiming she'd been homeschooled since the accident, lost her birth certificate in the fire, and didn't have a middle name. This sparked Alison's quest to uncover the truth about Jack and Ava.

Ava and Sam were in the finished basement when their parents faced off. They listened through the vent from the living room that opened into the space below. Jack reassured Alison that he'd invested her money as a surprise and would prove everything the next day.

Sam turned to Ava and said, "Your uncle is lying, isn't he?"

She betrayed her father for fear of losing Sam. "He is. And he's not my uncle; he's my father."

Ava knew their time in Virginia would end abruptly and felt desperate to stay put for the first time in their cons. She'd grown to love Sam and Alison and their sweet little yellow house on two rolling acres with views of the Blue Ridge Mountains. She had her bedroom and a closet full of clothes that fit her, which Alison had taken her shopping for, and home-cooked meals. She didn't wake up every day with a gnawing dread already consuming her; she often felt excited. Happy.

"So? You're considering it?" Sam asks wearily.

"You have to admit the timing is kind of crazy. My last day in the cave, I have nothing to do, and they show up with news about my father?"

"I think the answer is pretty obvious."

Ava fidgets, feels herself becoming defensive. She knows Sam is right, yet she's resisting. "I'm guessing that the money will be good. I haven't exactly amassed a fortune working for DHS."

"There are other ways to make money."

Ava sighs. "I feel bad for them. The police aren't any help, and the case is already cold. Remember how that felt?"

The creases in Sam's forehead deepen. "Of course I remember," he says testily, "but that doesn't mean you should get involved. Your father has always been able to weasel his way out of things."

"Exactly, he shouldn't keep getting away with it," Ava counters, holding Sam's gaze until he turns his attention back to his monitors.

Like everything positive in Ava's young life, the house and family on Peace Road was fleeting. Alison vanished a few days after the showdown while Jack was away on another trip. She'd left for the store one morning and never returned. Jack played it like she'd gone away to cool off from a fight when the police questioned him after he rushed back from his trip.

He departed abruptly, leaving Sam alone in the house at seventeen to continue attending school while he took Ava on the road on a supposed search for Alison. Jack convinced Sam that involving the police would lead to foster care, urging him to hold off on calling them and focus on school while waiting for his mom's return. Jack promised to continue searching with Ava. Despite the house being paid off and Jack covering the bills for about six months, they never resumed the search for Alison, and they never returned.

Though Ava lived with Sam and his mother for only thirteen months, it was the happiest time she could remember since her mother had been alive. Sam became the closest thing to a sibling she'd ever had, and Ava couldn't let go of that connection. Over the years with her father, she never allowed herself to get attached or stay in touch because of her father's strict forbidding. After he took her away, Ava would call Sam from pay phones across the country whenever she could sneak away. Despite Sam reporting his mother's disappearance to the police after a month, little effort was made to find her. They wrote her off as a neglectful mother who'd likely run off with a new boyfriend. Sam managed to avoid being placed in a group home by persuading a neighbor to watch over him until his mother's return or until he turned eighteen.

Between the time they left Sam and Ava running away from her father a year later, they spoke a few times a month and planned for her getaway. Ava got on a Greyhound bus in Pigeon Forge, Tennessee, while her father wined and dined a divorcée from Kissimmee, rode to Roanoke, and walked five miles to the house on Peace Road.

"Maybe this will help get authorities interested in your mom again. If I can get him to confess or find some new evidence. He's older now; maybe he's gotten careless or remorseful," Ava says to Sam.

Sam snorts. Ava knows that she's insulting her stepbrother's intelligence by bringing his mother's disappearance into this. Her hypocrisy is glaring. Since being released from prison, Ava has encouraged Sam to move on from the past and let go of the unanswered questions, though she knows he'll never give up hope. He still trawls the internet weekly, looking for anything that might bring some understanding or mitigate the terrible guilt he's been living with all this time. He exists in a vacuum of true-crime message boards and police reports, hoping someone will take interest and thaw the deep freeze of his mother's case.

"What was the point of running away if you're just going to return to his insanity?" Sam asks seriously.

Ava was certain her father wouldn't come searching for her in Virginia; he never revisited places where he had been married. He was already grooming a new lackey, and Ava wondered if one day she'd be a target. The increased tension and simmering resentments from both sides were unignorable.

When she rolled in, exhausted and dazed, Sam welcomed her, understanding that her father's indoctrination was going to take some time to dissipate. He was patient and kind while she regained some equilibrium around being independent. After a few days of head clearing, Sam and Ava went to the detectives handling Alison's case and shared everything about Ava's father and their suspicions. However, lacking a body or concrete evidence linking "Jack" to her disappearance and with no new evidence beyond Ava's claims, there was little else that could be done. This was just the beginning of Ava's education about law-enforcement limitations. She learned quickly that she and Sam were the only people who cared about finding Alison.

Sam was used to being blown off by the underfunded local law enforcement and had been using his self-taught hacking skills to investigate his mother's case. He taught Ava, too, and the subsequent few years of rooming with Sam, learning how to hack, and living free of her father were the best of her life.

That was until she was caught, arrested, and sentenced for things Sam had no part in. Sam sold the yellow house to help pay Ava's legal bills. Ava had many plans for how she was going to repay him.

"There are a few things that I can't shake."

"Like?" he asks.

"They were able to find me; you know that wasn't easy."

"They could be working for him," Sam says.

"Their hatred for him feels genuine."

"Ava." Sam's concerned tone is obvious. "Are you actually considering helping them?"

Ava looks at her feet. "Maybe."

Sam stands, walks to the kitchen, and grabs two bottles of water from the fridge. He hands one to Ava, and she can see his hands shaking.

"Please don't do this," he says with real fear.

"I can't ignore this. I feel like I've been comatose for the last half a decade. I want to have a purpose again."

"This isn't a purpose; this is self-sabotage. What about all the work you've done to get over him?"

"Maybe I've just gotten good at convincing myself that I am."

"This will be bad, Ava."

"Sammy, this could be a chance to balance the karmic scales."

"You were a kid, and you didn't have a choice. Your father is a monster," he growls.

"Well, I'm not a kid any longer. I can handle myself. Don't forget where I spent five years." Ava rarely references her jail time, but she needs him to understand.

Sam's surprised expression settles into sadness.

"I need to use the bathroom." Ava excuses herself, requiring a moment before resuming the conversation. Splashing water on her face, she opens the medicine cabinet in search of something for her pounding headache. Among the multiple prescription medications of Sam's—antianxiety, antidepressants, pills for sleep and to stay awake, for ADHD—there's no aspirin. It's a stark representation of the aftermath of her father's damage. Or the aftermath of hers.

Ava glares at her reflection. The dull aching in her scars radiates again, along with an old worry. She vowed never to become like him, yet she found herself behind bars. The only difference between Ava and her father is that she was caught.

They never found Alison, and her case had long gone cold. She was finally declared dead by absentia seven years after her disappearance, which devastated Sam, who'd never stopped waiting, hoping she'd return. Ava could see the long-term effects every time she visited him. He barely left his apartment, didn't trust people, and was painfully OCD. Ava had wanted to hug him for years, but she'd never gotten close enough to him to do that.

When Ava rejoins Sam, his back is to her, and he's clicking away on his keyboard at warp speed. He's on a message board, probably one for unsolved murders if she had to guess. He never seems to find the answers he is looking for, and the glut of cold cases being solved publicly on TV and podcasts only fuels his obsession that the answers he needs are within reach. Ava wants Alison's remains recovered almost as much as Sam does. She believes that he won't be able to have any kind of life outside the walls of his apartment until he can bury her and make peace with what happened. Ava knows he'll never stop looking.

"How the hell *did* they find you?" Sam asks her.

Ava pauses, still unsure how to articulate what has bothered her the most about her encounter. "The brother had one of my father's fake IDs, and it is haunting me."

"Why? Your father had dozens of aliases."

"The license was my uncle Wyatt's."

Ava doesn't have to spell it out for him; Sam knows about Ava's mother and uncle. When the two weren't trying to find Alison, they were trying to prove that Ava's father had been responsible for the fire that killed her family members.

"Oh. Shit," he says softly.

"I need to know more about the siblings and their mother before I decide anything."

Sam stands and gestures for Ava to take his place in the chair. "Have at it."

She hesitates and shakes her head. "I was hoping you could do it.

I'm still on probation, and it's probably better if I don't open that door anyway."

"Yeah, of course," he says.

Ava is aware that Sam doesn't believe her when she insists she doesn't miss hacking, but he's kind enough not to pressure her.

"What do you have on them?" he asks, and sits, swiveling to face his keyboard.

Ava hands the napkin with Hazel's number to Sam. "Not much, I'm afraid."

"This is plenty," he says. "How deep do you want me to dig?"

"As deep as it goes."

/ / /

"Wakey, wakey."

Ava opens her eyes, confused.

"You were snoring," he tells her as he hands her an iPad with several tabs open. There are numerous stories about Hazel and Kagan's mother's death in New York City, a slew of MeTube videos starring Hazel, and a court transcript featuring Kagan.

"Start with these, and I'll forward along more as I find it. I'm just getting into the NYPD's database. It took me a minute; their firewall is markedly better than Virginia's," Sam says.

A video of Hazel is suspended behind him, frozen on her heavily made-up face, wide-eyed and midthought, half-dressed while writing on a whiteboard.

Ava raises her eyebrows. "Enjoying the research?"

Sam reddens. "She's wacky but also compulsively watchable."

"I'm not judging. She's definitely easy to look at."

She begins scrolling through the information, only half-aware of time passing. Caffeine drinks are cracked open as Sam shares information as he uncovers it. The familiarity of the two deep diving into the late hours is a rare comfort for Ava. It's one a.m., then three. She immerses herself in the Bailey family until they no longer feel like strangers.

When she finally looks up from the iPad, she sees the sunrise creeping over the trees.

"Thanks for helping me," she says.

"Like old times, eh?"

"Yeah, I was thinking that too."

"Don't make me regret it."

"I think part of me thought you'd be excited to try to catch him, finally," Ava says.

Sam's face constricts. "I'm not interested in giving that guy any more of my time or energy."

"Wouldn't it be better for me to chase him down than working for the man?"

"You can do anything you want," Sam says.

"Why does it feel like I'm trapped? Maybe this is the way out."

"Your father is a black hole; if you get pulled in, you'll never be free."

CHAPTER 18

As Kagan and his sister tumble into the Starbucks on the corner of Columbia and Calvert, slightly unnerved, Ava is waiting for them.

The siblings have arrived on time for their meeting, but the walk over managed to rattle Kagan. They'd left the hotel and headed toward the coffee shop, noticing the sights and storefronts as they went. The pair had barely stopped chuckling at the signage for the Grill From Ipanema when they stumbled upon a restaurant named Perry's, shutting them right up. The coincidence struck Kagan as ominous, but he knew Hazel would want to chalk it up to kismet, as was her way. He'd decided to try looking at things from that angle of positivity instead.

Ava sits in a booth near the rear of the shop, a paper cup on the table before her, eyes trained on the front door, reminding Kagan of that trope from all the old spy movies. She reveals the subtlest hint of a smile as she catches sight of the siblings. God, this woman is intriguing, and not just because—despite Perry's reports to the contrary—she's actually still alive. Kagan finds her alluring. Beguiling. Quite frankly, sexy, both in spite of and *because* of the scars peeking out from the neckline of her shirt. He hasn't been able to shake the thought of her for a second. It strikes him as a little funky to be considering romance under the circumstances, but would it really be the worst thing if he found someone amid all this tragedy?

Following yesterday's initial meeting, the young woman had kept the siblings in suspense before finally texting Hazel's phone this morning with a request to convene at this coffee shop at this appointed time. She'd given them short notice, which only added to Kagan's impression of Ava as a calculating and wily woman. As the pair approaches the table, she rises from the bench to greet them.

"Hazel, Kagan, thanks for coming."

"Thanks so much for meeting us," he answers.

"Yeah," adds Hazel. "We started to worry we might never hear from you again." His sister's tone is sardonic and bashful in equal measure, and it takes Kagan a moment to realize that it puts him most in mind of Hazel's usual attempts at flirting. So this is how it was going to be.

"But we're glad we did," Kagan blurts out.

"Right." Ava eyes him warily before glancing toward the counter. "Hey, you two want anything?"

"My brother seems a little jittery as it is. I don't think we need to add caffeine on top of that, do you?"

Kagan catches the women exchanging conspiratorial smiles and feels that familiar twisting of his insides. As kids, growing up the way they did, the siblings were always very attuned to each other's frequencies. That level of sensitivity helped them key into any discomfort the other might be feeling, usually at the hands of their father. Hazel would regularly swoop in and rescue her brother from Charles's fits of anger. But other times, when it suited her, Hazel could use her knowledge of her brother's emotional circuitry to humiliate him, out of opportunism or sheer spite.

This felt like one of those moments.

"May we?" asks Kagan, indicating the bench across the table from Ava.

"Please," she answers, and they all take a seat.

"So," begins Ava, "in all honesty, I almost didn't reach out to you guys."

"Oh?" responds Hazel, and Kagan is pleased to see a trace of the self-satisfaction drain from his sister's face. "Well, what made you change your mind?"

"I'm still on the fence, quite frankly. I don't know that you trying to track down my father is the best way forward, for anyone involved. But I did figure I owed you the courtesy of hearing you both out, considering everything you've been through recently."

"We appreciate that," says Hazel, propping her elbows on the table and settling in for the big presentation. "Let me start by telling you a bit about our mother, Janice. She was a kind, caring, selfless woman who regularly put the priorities of others over her own. She volunteered at a museum, out of a love of art and a belief in furthering people's education around it. She was unlucky in relationships, first with our father and then with yours, but she threw herself into them completely, out of a desire to be loved. Out of a need to believe in the good in others, and in the world around her. I know that sounds naive, and our mom may have been exactly that at times, but it was all driven by a pure sense of optimism and an underlying belief in humanity, as corny as that probably seems."

As Kagan watches his sister's performance, complete with a well-timed crack in her voice and a tear threatening to spill down her cheek, he finds himself nearly buying it. He barely registers the glaring omissions: Hazel's deep resentment over the sense of abandonment she felt, both emotionally and financially, and her anger toward Janice for what Hazel considered to be a weakness of will when it came to romantic relationships. The version of his sister telling this tale in this coffee shop at this moment could not seem more devoted to their dearly departed mother if she decided to dig up the coffin Janice occupied and hop in with her.

"She sounds like a pretty wonderful human being." Ava bites her top lip, and Kagan can feel the woman's sympathy and curiosity rubbing up against the sense of resoluteness she opened the exchange with. "I'm sure you miss her. And I'm sure you're hurting. And angry. I know I would be. But there's a gift staring you in the face here that I don't want you to overlook."

"And what would that be?"

"My father is gone. For good, I have to imagine. As much as you might be thirsting for vengeance, I assure you that this is exactly where you want that man to be."

"Where's that?"

"Out of your life." Ava taps the tip of her middle finger on the table to accentuate each word.

"That might be a little easier for you to say," responds Hazel. "You've had the man gone forever. My brother and I are still dealing with fresh wounds."

"I understand that. But you know what they say about letting wounds heal."

Hazel suppresses a huff. "Enlighten me."

"Don't pick at the scabs." Ava's cavalier tone scrapes at a raw place in Kagan, and he feels his fingers curl into fists.

"I'm glad you can manage to be so trite," he says, "but Hazel and I don't have that luxury."

"Trite?" Ava leans across the table, her face unnervingly close to Kagan's. "Look, I'm sorry you had to deal with my father for a few minutes of your *adult* lives. But I was attached to the guy right out of the gate, so maybe you could consider what I'm telling you with a little less attitude."

"And maybe you could be a little more sympathetic to our cause," barks Kagan as several customers turn to register the disturbance.

"Guess I'm not feeling all that charitable today." Ava's tone is tinged with a sense of disappointment that stings Kagan worse than her flash of anger did a moment ago. She glances at Hazel furtively before slipping out of the booth and squaring herself to face the siblings. "Good luck to you both. I really hope you find the peace you're looking for."

And with that, she's off.

CHAPTER 19

What the hell is wrong with you?" Hazel snaps at Kagan as Ava books it toward the exit and wades through a tour group donning "Flights, camera, action!" T-shirts. The siblings watch Ava become momentarily trapped inside the vestibule in the congestion of a slow-moving crowd, an awkward obstacle to her escape. Still, she refuses to turn in their direction.

"You scared her away!" Hazel glares at her brother.

"She isn't going to help us," he spews bitterly.

Hazel watches his eyes glaze over as he settles into total shutdown.

The group finally trickles in, and the last person holds the door for Ava, who zips through and turns left. Hazel watches her flash by the storefront and disappear out of view.

"This trip was a complete waste of time and money," Kagan mutters, defeated.

"Not yet it isn't." Hazel grabs her purse, gets up from the bench, and bolts for the door. When she emerges into the muggy, non-air-conditioned outdoors, she hangs a quick left and spots Ava a block ahead of her, stopped at the crosswalk. Hazel's stomach somersaults as she sprints to catch up, reaching her just as the light switches over.

"Ava," she utters to her back.

Ava startles and glances over her shoulder. "Hazel? What do you want?"

She matches Ava's stride across the intersection. Ava stops under a tree a few feet from the main thoroughfare and the two women stand a foot apart in the shade. Hazel is surprised by how flustered she feels; she hasn't chased her that far. Her racing heart is from more than physical exertion. Ava brushes stray hair out of her eyes and squints. She extracts a pair of aviators from her messenger bag and puts them on, enhancing her striking look.

"Thank you for stopping," Hazel says.

Ava sighs and switches her weight from one foot to the other. "Look, I'm not interested."

"I'm sorry my brother doesn't think before he speaks," Hazel replies emotionally.

Ava softens, slightly. "I get it. You guys have been through hell."

"We shouldn't have ambushed you. I can't imagine how you're feeling. You probably thought this man was out of your life for good, and then Kagan and I just showed up and destroyed that," Hazel says apologetically.

"It didn't help." Ava chuckles. "You and Kagan are catching me at a strange time in my life."

She senses an opportunity. Ava seems softer one on one. Hazel is grateful that Kagan is somewhere behind them, but she doesn't want to risk him catching up with them and intruding on the improved energy.

"Could we get a coffee somewhere else with fewer tourists?" Hazel asks. She detects hesitation in Ava's body language. "I promise I won't bring up your father."

"I really should get home. I've got some fairly major life decisions to determine before Monday."

"Please? I haven't had a normal conversation since our mom died."

Hazel watches the discernment in Ava's face turn in her favor.

"I'm not sure how normal any conversation between us would be."

"Fair. But nothing ventured?"

"There's a place around the corner that has great matcha. Are you a fan?" Ava asks.

"Love it," Hazel lies, thinking about the first and last time she drank the earthy beverage. It was with Adam. "Lead the way."

/ / /

The home of the great matcha is a lovely Japanese teahouse–inspired café. The place is empty when they arrive except for a few staff members, who whisk them into a cozy ruby-red corner banquette.

"Wow," Hazel says as she scans the stunning surroundings. "This place is gorgeous." She wants to go live on Instagram to showcase her backdrop, but she controls the urge.

"Yeah, I love this spot," Ava says, her tone warming.

Hazel peeks at her phone while Ava settles into the booth. Thousands of comments pour in from her latest video about a list of high-ranking Illuminati members reserved for a Mars flight in the event of a nuclear war. She streamed it from the bathtub of her hotel room at two a.m.

A message appears from Dick Vidocq, and Hazel feels a pang. She's been ignoring his comments and messages since he gave her all the info about Ava. She's worried that he wants to be paid after all. Hazel deletes the message and blocks him.

"Do you need to let Kagan know where we are?" Ava asks, and Hazel snaps her phone into her purse.

"Sorry," Hazel says, flustered. "Kagan can take care of himself."

"I didn't mean it like that. I don't mind if you want him to join us. I'm embarrassed for storming off."

Hazel's disappointed that Ava is considering Kagan's feelings. However, she has grown used to friends developing crushes on him through the years. More than a few friendships and hopeful relationships have fizzled out when ulterior motives became evident.

"Kagan's fine. He's probably numbing his pain in the nearest dive," she says. "I love him, obviously. But we've been together constantly since Mom died, and it's probably not healthy for us. It's good to have some time apart."

Ava remains silent, scrutinizing the menu—a gorgeous parchment-over-wood treatment embellished with Japanese characters alongside lush, inky images of each menu offering.

"Sounds like you guys are tight."

"Since our mom died, we're the only family left for each other. There are some second cousins, people we don't really know, so it's just him and me. That's part of why finding your father is so important to us. Janice would have wanted us to work together, take care of each other, and recover what she meant for us. Kagan is probably the only person on the planet whom I trust."

Hazel studies Ava's face and observes a subtle warming in her demeanor. She also sees her scarred skin peeking out from her sweater. She notices some mottled skin on Ava's hands as well but looks away to avoid making her uncomfortable.

"Do you have any siblings?"

Ava hesitates. "I have a stepbrother."

Realizing that she's broken her promise to not bring up Perry, Hazel doesn't press. "Are you close?"

"Yeah, he lives nearby," Ava replies.

Hazel nods, and the two women sit silently as soothing koto music fills the space between.

"Have you ever been to Japan?" Hazel asks.

"Not yet. I wanted to go when I graduated from college, but when I tried to get a passport, I discovered that my father had sold my identity. That and other bureaucratic hurdles have significantly delayed my leaving the country."

"He *sold* your identity?" Hazel asks, stunned.

"Apparently as soon as I got a Social Security number when I was six weeks old."

Hazel's phone buzzes every few seconds, drawing their attention to it. Hazel can't resist any longer and lifts the phone, half looking at the new messages, half looking at Ava.

"Sorry," Hazel apologizes while scrolling and tapping. "I just posted a video that is getting a lot of play."

"So, I checked out your channel, Trust Issues," Ava says, side-eyeing the device.

"You did?" Hazel feels excited that Ava's taken the time to look at her stuff, but mildly concerned. Her content isn't for everyone, and she doesn't want it to be a turnoff.

Ava nods. "I've never seen someone combine ASMR and conspiracy theories."

"I'm the first one to do it, but there are already copycats cropping up," Hazel says proudly.

"You're a good storyteller. It's impressive to be able to keep people's interest for more than thirty seconds these days, and you have a lot of followers."

"Yeah, thanks," Hazel says, feeling like a fraud for having paid for half her followers.

"Do you subscribe to your own content? Some of it is pretty far-fetched."

"Aspects of it. I'm interested in what makes people believe in conspiracies. I guess it's a social experiment for me."

Hazel can't tell how much of her bullshit Ava is buying, if any.

"What have you learned?"

"Many people are unsure of what and whom they can trust. My ideas comfort them because they confirm what they're afraid of."

"What are they afraid of?"

"Of being kept in the dark. Of being insignificant and disregarded by the people and institutions claiming to protect them."

"So you're protecting them?" Ava asks, pushing Hazel into territory that feels similar to past conversations with her mother. This makes her dually resistant and excited.

"I offer alternatives to the explanations they've been told and create a place for people who want to feel a sense of control and understanding about things they can't understand."

"Where does the ASMR fit in?"

"Everyone is stressed, burned out, and traumatized. Creating a positive sensory experience simultaneously can offset the negative vibes. I'm helping people reprogram neural pathways."

"Well, you seem to have filled a niche," Ava says.

Hazel feels proud by Ava's acknowledgment but slighted too.

"The larger my following gets, the greater the community becomes."

"Hazel, are you trying to start a cult?" Ava chuckles.

"No! I don't have enough patience to be a cult leader; I'm only an influencer. Maybe a cultish influencer?" She smiles coyly.

"And you chased me down to influence me into helping you?"

Flustered, Hazel feels her cheeks begging to burn. "I followed you because I didn't want you to think we were doing this for the wrong reasons."

"Why do you care what I think?"

Before she can respond, a traditionally dressed Japanese woman approaches their table. Hazel feels relieved by the pause.

"Do you know what you'd like?" she asks.

"I'll have matcha and kuzumochi." Ava pronounces each word beautifully.

"I'll have matcha too. Thanks," Hazel replies.

Ava eyes her phone as a call shows on her screen. She quickly puts it into her purse.

"Work," Ava says.

"What kind of work do you do?" Hazel asks.

"You guys must know all about me if you managed to track me down," she replies edgily.

"It probably seems like we have a dossier on you, but we don't."

"Well, you know where I work. And you know where I go after work. Is it safe to assume you know I was incarcerated too?" Ava snaps.

Hazel feels stung. "I know only what my source told me, which wasn't much. He tracked down a group photo of you at some trivia night thing at Helene's. I don't know how he knew you were a regular there or where you worked. And he didn't tell me anything about incarceration." This was a lie; they knew from Dick Vidocq that Ava had done time for wire fraud and conspiracy and that her "tracks had been very well covered" before and after her legal issues. Hazel was endlessly curious to know more about Ava's past, but she knew she needed to stay focused on persuading her to help them. She'd have plenty of time to get Ava's story if she was successful.

"Well, I hope he overcharged you," Ava says sharply.

"I'm sorry for invading your privacy. We were so desperate to find anyone who could help us." Tears stream down her cheeks, and she quickly swats them away. The tears aren't performative. Hazel genuinely feels upset. She's realizing that she can't persuade Ava to help them, and the bleak thought of going back to New York empty-handed is crushing.

Ava begins digging in her bag and fishes out a packet of Kleenex. "Sorry. I've worked hard to avoid my father for a long time, and I'm still adjusting to being found."

"I'm sorry to put all this pressure on you, but you're our only hope." Hazel thinks of Janice, and her tears flow.

"I haven't seen or talked to my father for almost fifteen years. I'm not sure what you think I can do for you?"

"Well, we figured you know him better than anyone. And maybe you would know where he is and could reason with him about doing the right thing."

Ava laughs while Hazel frowns.

"Sorry. You don't know any better, but even if I was in touch with him, which I'm not, there is no reasoning with that man."

Hazel remains quiet, searching for another foothold. "Honestly, I also really wanted to meet you once I discovered Perry had a daughter."

"Why's that?"

"Well, I always wanted a sister," Hazel says softly.

Ava looks out the window. "So he never mentioned me?"

"He did." Hazel looks down at her hands. "He told us you were dead."

Ava's face hardens. "In his mind, I'm sure I am."

"Ava, can I ask what happened to your mom?"

"I was just a kid, so I could never prove anything."

"Neither can we," Hazel says ruefully.

A server sidles up to their table with a tray in the crook of his arm. He places a glass mug of chartreuse liquid in front of Hazel and another on Ava's mat, followed by a rectangular plate of gelatinous squares sprinkled with crumbled graham crackers. Ava thanks the server and carefully sips her matcha. "Look, I've spent many years letting go of that anger and frustration around not knowing."

"Don't you want your father to pay?" Hazel sips the hot beverage and is surprised by its deliciousness.

"I did, for a long time."

"You gave up?" Hazel presses, looking for the tenderest spot. She clocks the slight clench in Ava's jaw and realizes she's found it.

"I didn't 'give up.' I stopped fixating on my father. I grew up. I worked on myself," she says, clearly unnerved. "You said earlier that you didn't want me to think you were going after my father for the wrong reasons. What are the right reasons?" Ava asks quietly.

"I didn't want you to think this was just about money." Hazel closes her eyes, unable to maintain Ava's intense eye contact. She searches deeply for the best answer, realizing she has no reasoning for this absurd vigilante road trip. Of course it's about the money. They need the money. And for Perry to feel as humiliated and powerless as they do.

"Then what is it about?" Ava asks thoughtfully.

"We both failed to save our mothers. I can't live with that; can you?"

Ava looks dubious, and blood rushes in Hazel's ears. She considers what Janice would do in this situation. She'd use her greatest power of persuasion and influence—guilt.

"Ava, he'll do this again. Someone has to stop him, and it should be you."

CHAPTER 20

Something strange happened when Hazel and Kagan showed up. Ava has begun hearing her father's voice so clearly that it sounds like he's crawled inside her head.

This isn't the first time in her life she's been haunted by his negative commentary. It followed her on the bus when she first escaped and lingered for a few weeks after while she settled into life with Sam again. When she was in prison, she'd hear her father's voice late into the night, chastising her for thinking she could outrun her destiny and for being stupid enough to get caught. This round ended when she was released and reconnected with Sam. Both times, his protective comfort drowned out her father's mind games.

Now her father's voice is louder, incessantly daring her to find him. His tone is condescending and doubtful of her ability to face him, drowning out Sam's warning pleas.

Ava walks south to distract herself from the unsettling chatter, replaying the past two hours. When Hazel went to the restroom, Ava powered down her phone and asked to borrow Hazel's, blaming her own older model for the poor battery. Hazel hesitated but eventually handed it over. Outside, Ava made a call before her rationality could intervene.

When the women parted ways, Hazel hugged Ava hard, pleading with her to help the siblings. While Ava hadn't committed to anything, she'd already decided. She just needed some time before she let the siblings know. She had one more call to make before she could feel resolved.

Ava stops in front of a bar and leans against a parking meter across from the entrance. She turns her phone on and pulls up Prince's number. He answers on the second ring.

"Thrill me," he says.

"I can't take the job. Something's come up."

"What's more important than this?" Prince asks.

"Family."

"Parker, you should take the rest of the weekend to think this over. This offer won't come again—"

"I'm banking on that. Have a nice life, Prince."

"Hold up one sec—"

Ava drops the iPhone onto the open spot in front of the meter just as an enormous tinted-windowed Suburban zips in. The glass and metal crunches under the wheels as she tucks between the SUV and the car behind it before darting across the street. She expects Prince will dock her last paycheck for the unreturned work phone. It's a small price for untethering herself.

Feeling lighter, Ava floats past an excited group of overly made-up underage girls sharing a vape pen behind velvet ropes. She enters a dingy apartment building when a delivery person exits. She presses the button for 2D and puts her weight on the interior metal door as the intercom crackles and buzzes her inside a low-lit hallway. She begins to ascend a stairwell littered with dirt and paint chips from the crumbling walls.

Ava sprints up two flights of stairs to the second door and knocks lightly. A cat-eyed woman with a shaved head and facial piercings motions for her to enter. Ava follows her down a dark hallway into the apartment's kitchen.

Ava can hear movement in another room but keeps quiet while the woman counts the cash she's just handed her. Cat Eyes stashes the wad in her bra, reaches under the table, and places a large plastic bag on top of the table. She pushes it across to Ava.

"Check everything now. No returns once you leave."

Ava pulls a laptop, phone, and wallet from the bag. She takes a cursory look at each item but feels confident that she is holding what she came for.

"Looks good," she says, dropping the items into her bag as she swiftly moves to the door. She has breached multiple points of her probation in one sitting.

Upon returning to the street, Ava hails a cab to her government-owned apartment, where she swiftly tosses the contents of her closet and desk into a duffel bag. The place never felt like home. Her go bag, prepared since her first week there, awaits in the hallway closet. Ava adds a framed picture of her mother, clothes, and other essentials. She walks out, pulling the door shut behind her.

Ava slides into her company car one last time and drives the same route she's been traveling to DHS headquarters on St. Elizabeth's Campus. Instead of pulling onto the parking deck, she enters the reserved parking section and glides into Prince's designated spot. She retrieves the oversize legal envelope from the passenger seat, containing her work laptop, apartment keys, and ID lanyard. After pressing and clicking the lock button and adding the car keys, she walks the envelope to the night drop slot, watching the last letters of her block handwriting disappear through the opening.

Strolling in the dark until she's sufficiently distant from the campus, she takes a seat on a bus-stop bench. There, she fires up her new phone, inserts a SIM card, and gets to work. Setting up her new credentials, activating credit cards, and reserving her bed, she's absorbed in her tasks when a car pulls up beside her. Her chest tightens, but after confirming the license plate, she relaxes and slips into the back seat.

The driver listens to a baseball game and doesn't talk, which Ava is grateful for. She sits back while the streets of DC whiz by, each neighborhood falling away as she moves further away from yesterday's predictability into tomorrow's unknowns. As the car slows down and her destination appears, she tips the driver on the app and wordlessly exits the vehicle, her heavy duffel slung over her tired shoulders.

As she slides her new ID and Amex across the counter, a bushy-browed clerk absently types on his keyboard. She refrains from repeatedly glancing over her shoulder every time the electronic sliding doors swoosh open behind her. She's defaulted to hypervigilance, the cost of her father's return and her questionable decisions today.

The Days Inn clerk smiles while handing her a door key card. Overwhelmed by the rush of blood in her ears, she barely registers details about the continental breakfast. Following his finger to the elevators, she floats to the doors, stepping aside for a woman with a little girl. Both smile at Ava, and the mother thanks her as they pass.

As the door closes, tingling sensations run through Ava's extremities. She feels electrified though somewhat ashamed as the elevator rises to the fourth floor. This is a familiar contradiction of feelings from her lawbreaking days.

Approaching the room, Ava internalizes that she's just a few feet away from altering everything. The option to walk away and salvage her life is still within reach. Hasn't she been striving for that ever since her release? She followed the rules and avoided so much as a parking ticket, rebelling against everything he'd taught her—a daily penance. But now she's on the verge of undoing it all.

Knocking on the door, Ava acknowledges that this is the only way to truly move on instead of pretending. She has to fight his way in order to find hers.

The door swings open, and Hazel and Kagan wear triumphant expressions, holding plastic cups filled to the brim.

"You came," Hazel squeals.

Kagan beams with stained teeth and dilated eyes.

Ava steps inside the room and accepts a tight hug from Hazel.

"What now?" Kagan asks.

"We have a lot of work to do to ensure he never does this again."

"How are we going to do that?" Kagan asks.

"We're going to get him where it hurts the most," Ava tells them.

The siblings' eyes widen.

"We are?" Kagan smiles.

"We're going to find him, and then I'm going to steal your money back."

CHAPTER 21

As he steps out of the hotel lobby and into the early-morning glare, a sudden gust whaps Kagan straight in the face, cracking through the remnants of his mental haze. The sluggishness he woke up with from the red-wine hangover was quickly tempered by his sense of excitement at the adventure that lay before them today, and particularly by the addition of Ava to the mix. This bit of fresh air is putting the final touches on his return to the land of the living.

Kagan still can't quite believe that Ava's decided to join Hazel and him on this mission. He'd have sworn after his outburst at the Starbucks that she'd sour on the whole deal and shake herself loose of the siblings. But then last night she showed up at their door, laden with an overstuffed duffel, looking like a weary, windbeaten traveler.

He'd be more than happy to serve as the port she takes refuge in.

Kagan's assignment this morning is twofold: track down caffeine for the trio and gather some recon on the way. They've planned to push off from the Days Inn and hit the road shortly, hopefully armed with a lead or two to follow up on. As he heads in the direction of the coffee shop, Kagan slips his phone from his pocket and dials a familiar number. She picks up on the third ring.

"Kagan." Detective Calabrese's voice sounds tentative, resigned. "Haven't heard from you in a bit."

"Well, I thought it was about time I checked back in."

"Uh-huh." Kagan hears what he assumes to be Calabrese's hand covering the speaker, followed by a jumble of muffled sounds, before her unobstructed voice returns to the line. "And what can I do for you today?"

"Just wondered if you might have managed to get a bead on my dear stepfather? Or maybe the guy he put up to killing my mother? You know, if you haven't been too busy."

The detective sighs before adopting a more formal tone laced with a just-discernible trace of sarcasm. "As you know, that case is ongoing, which means I'm not at liberty to discuss it. And none of the leads we've pursued have turned up anything on Mr. Walters or Mr. March."

"Well, of course not. How can you ever hope to find a couple of men who don't exist?"

"I'm sorry?"

"That makes two of us."

"I'm not sure wha—"

"What I mean to say is, Perry Walters and Adam March were fakes, remember? Aliases used to scam my mother out of her money before they disposed of her. So we're not going to have any luck finding them that way, are we?"

"I'm well aware of the aliases, Kagan. And I don't like the sounds of this 'we' you're referring to."

"And *I* don't like the thought of you giving up on this investigation, Detective."

The line is quiet for a moment before Calabrese returns, her tone slightly softened. "Listen, I'm really sorry about Janice, but you have to understand that there's nothing I can do right now, okay? Not with the evidence we have. It's completely out of my hands."

As Kagan stands at the curb readying to cross the street, an oncoming Nissan swerves briefly into the opposite lane, eliciting a honk from a startled delivery-truck driver.

"Wait, Kagan, is that . . . Where are you?"

The question causes him to feel suddenly exposed, reprimanded.

"I'm, uh, just out making a coffee run."

"Yeah, but where? I'm watching a torrential downpour outside my window right now. You're not in New York." The last sentence comes across as an accusation.

Stay cool, stay calm. You haven't done anything wrong. "Hazel and I are down in DC for a few days."

"Huh." That inquisitive edge is back in Calabrese's voice. "Visiting friends, or just sightseeing?"

"We came here to get out of the city, clear our heads. My sister and I are still in mourning, you know."

"Of course. I just don't want to imagine that you're off on some vigilante business, Kagan. That wouldn't sit well with me."

"You have nothing to worry about, Detective." He crosses the index and middle fingers of his idle hand. "I promise."

"Well, I'm glad to hear that. Because if these men are actually the kind of people you say they are, I'd hate to think of you putting yourselves in danger by looking for them. Can you understand where I'm coming from?"

"Of course. And I appreciate your concern." Kagan remembers the tack Hazel reported taking with Ava in their one-on-one conversation and decides to lean into the same strategy with Calabrese. "But my sister and I aren't interested in revenge anymore."

"Is that right?"

"It is. We've been going to therapy individually and attending a support group together. It's really helped us to get a clearer perspective on things."

Kagan feels a zing of both excitement and terror as the bullshit spills from his mouth. He's committed the act of blatantly lying to an officer of the law, with no way out but to continue to build on the deception. The adrenaline zips through his body, and the nausea he woke up with comes back for an encore performance. Kagan envisions himself momentarily as the hero of one of those adventure movies, hands and feet bound together as the nefarious villain slowly lowers him into a vat of acid, the vapors licking at the heels of his feet, left to rely solely on his wits and cunning to get him out of this bind.

"I'm happy to hear that you're finding some clarity around all of this."

"Thank you, Detective Calabrese. I really appreciate you saying that."

"Of course. Now, Kagan, I have to ask: If you're past tracking these guys down for revenge, why are you calling me? You sounded pretty raw when I first picked up the phone."

"In all fairness, you *were* considering me a suspect in my own mother's murder at one point." He lets go of a chuckle to take some sting out of the statement and to assure the detective that they're on the same page now.

"Okay, I'll own that. So . . ."

Kagan's feeling dialed in, experiencing flow state, the answers materializing before him as if from the air itself.

"Through this support group I mentioned, we've learned about a national network of people who have been the targets of these types of cons and who are now working as advocates to spread awareness around how they operate, in order to help spare others the same fate. A big part of putting a stop to this kind of behavior is sharing information, whether about the signs to watch out for or, in some cases, the people actually perpetrating the scams." *Man, he's really cooking now.* "I'm checking in with you in the hopes of finding out anything we might be able to pass along about the men who victimized our mother. If we're able to share the identities of the perpetrators, maybe we can help prevent them from doing this to someone else's mother. Or sister. Or daughter. These con men get more and more emboldened as they go, and the only way to stop them is to catch them. And that happens only if people like us can access and share information. As bad as Hazel and I have been feeling, we would feel even worse if we didn't do everything we could to help other people who might fall victim to the same fate."

"I see." There's a stretch of silence, and Kagan can practically hear Calabrese deliberating on the other end of the line. When she speaks again, it's at a volume slightly above a whisper. "Listen, I shouldn't be saying anything, but between you and me, this case is still nagging at me."

Her tone elicits an encouraging zing in Kagan. "Please, do share."

"Well, I never got to speak to March, or whatever his name is. But there was something your stepfather shared when I first interviewed him."

"Okay."

"The night your mother died, he mentioned having come back from visiting a sister in South Carolina. He produced the ticket stubs for a pair of flights in and out of Savannah/Hilton Head International, along with cab receipts. We contacted the sister at the time, and she confirmed that he'd been down to see her. So if you're trying to get the word out on this guy, maybe consider that as an area he could be looking to target future victims."

Kagan is suddenly enlivened by the visceral thrill of discovery. He's got a precious nugget of information to bring back to the group, and he's particularly amped to show Ava what he's capable of. "Thank you, Detective. This really means a lot. To my sister and me both. And to all the other people this information might help."

"Nothing to thank me for." Her tone is decidedly flat. "We never had this conversation."

"Of course not."

"Hey, listen." He hears an intake of breath. "Is your sister doing all right?"

"I think she is, yes. Hazel's finally found some purpose in all this tragedy."

"I'm happy to hear that, Kagan. Take care of yourselves out there, okay?"

"Don't worry about us, Detective." He tamps down the feeling of glee threatening to burst through. "We're just here for the cause."

CHAPTER 22

Alone in the motel room, Hazel struggles to keep her eyes open. After a late-night session divulging every detail they could recall, including the mysterious woman Perry was seen with at Kagan's friend's restaurant, Ava was convinced that Perry had already moved on to a new target. The woman was likely someone he'd started priming while Janice was still alive. But they didn't have much more than the sighting to share, with no other leads on Perry or Adam.

Ava instructed Hazel to scour her phone and social media for any clue of Adam's connection to Perry, no matter how seemingly insignificant. It was a long shot, but perhaps Adam had mistakenly left a breadcrumb to his or Perry's potential whereabouts.

Kagan was tasked to press Calabrese for any intel to narrow Perry's whereabouts. While they worked on their respective tasks, Ava went on a mysterious errand.

Hazel found comfort in having someone else steer the ship, yet she couldn't shake her shame after dissecting her and Adam's relationship in painful detail the previous night. Rehashing the intense three months with a relative stranger left her primarily feeling humiliated— she didn't want Ava to perceive her as an easy mark.

Ava showed no judgment. She was practical and kind. Hazel was emotional, recounting her and Adam's origins. When Adam had first approached her in Whole Foods somewhere between the fresh herbs and the shallots, he looked harmless and unmemorable. He'd asked her if she knew how much baby bok choy equaled an adult bok choy, and she'd laugh-shrugged and walked away. After she checked out, Adam held the door for her and said, "Hey, you" like they were old friends and walked her home before asking for her number. The whole encounter felt easy and uncomplicated.

Before their first date, Hazel had conducted her usual internet deep dive. She couldn't fathom how people still fell for dating-site scams like fake profiles and pictures that were easily spotted. Adam wasn't on dating apps but had all the necessary social and professional accounts, with minimal online content reflecting his reserved nature. No red flags.

Ava pointed out that Adam had likely been casing her from the beginning, and Hazel felt sick. This persisted as she miserably sifted through hundreds of texts between them, hoping for clues. Their texts span the confessional spectrum, covering dreams and fears and everything in between, but nothing significant or helpful about who Adam is.

Now Hazel views her texts not as tokens of a blossoming relationship but as password clues and personal information—insider details that could serve well to steal Janice's identity. Hazel freely gave away the keys to her mother's life.

Hazel turns to her upcoming segment, watching it for the fourth time. Her teaser about crisis actors has garnered over three hundred thousand shares—a number she's not entirely satisfied with, but she remains confident the new video will surpass that. Hoping to capture viral attention, she critically reviews the two-minute video and, satisfied enough, decides to release it.

A knock at the door interrupts her concentration. Hazel is disappointed to find Kagan on the other side. She hoped for more time alone with Ava. Historically, Kagan tended to hog attention, forcing Hazel to fight for the spotlight.

Hazel sees that he is empty-handed and is immediately annoyed. "Did you forget the coffee?"

"Shit. I was excited after the call and forgot. It's windy as fuck out there."

Hazel releases an irritated sigh. "What did Calabrese say?"

"We should wait for Ava before I download." Kagan grins.

"You can 'download' again when Ava gets here."

He glances at his phone. "She'll be here any minute."

"She texted you?"

"Yeah. Is that okay with you?" he asks smugly.

"Did you get anything useful?"

"Well, Calabrese is a better detective than we gave her credit for," he says. "She may not have made any progress on Mom's case, but she sniffed out that I wasn't in Manhattan."

CHAPTER 23

Kagan, did you reach the detective?" Ava enters the room, harried from the outside world. The siblings are on their feet immediately, herding her into their space like puppies. She's self-conscious about the attention they're giving her, yet it's a nice change from her usual non-welcomes in the cave.

"Guys, take a seat. Relax." Ava distances herself and cracks open a water bottle.

"Perry claimed to have been visiting a sister in South Carolina as his alibi," Kagan shares proudly. "Could 'sister' actually be code for something?"

Ava's skin crawls. The house in Hilton Head floods back to her, with all its Gothic horror qualities. Ava spent the muggy days avoiding her aunt as much as possible and her nights trying to sleep amid the eerie sounds of the antebellum house settling and her aunt moving through its corridors, unsettled.

"My father did have a sister—Constance—who lived in Hilton

Head. I can't believe she's still alive. She seemed so old and had mental problems."

The scent of witch hazel, which her aunt bathed in, and the aroma of peppermint flood Ava's senses. These smells still trigger anxiety within her.

"Are you okay?" Hazel asks, finally looking up from her iPhone.

"I'm fine," she says distractedly. "Aunt Constance could be helpful."

"So what's our game plan?" Kagan hangs by the window, separating the blinds to peer outside every few minutes.

"Kagan, calm down. You're making me nervous," Hazel whines.

"We'll head to South Carolina," Ava says.

"Do you think he's there?" Hazel asks.

"Doubtful. He doesn't like to revisit places too often in a short period. But Aunt Constance might have information. Perry used her house when he needed a permanent mailing address. It's worth a shot."

Ava never wants to see her aunt again, and she doubts the old woman will be helpful, but she remembers something else near Constance that could be useful. She keeps this to herself.

"What if your aunt recognizes you and tips Perry off?" Hazel asks.

Ava has already played out that scenario. "She was going blind when I stayed with her a long time ago, and her mind wasn't very clear either. We'll handle it in a way that won't raise suspicion."

"I've always wanted to take a road trip south," Kagan says brightly. "Maybe we can do one of those catamaran booze cruises."

Ava found solace with the kids who worked on the charter and fishing boats, a bright spot in an otherwise gloomy season. That season, she learned to sail, and the ocean saved her from drowning in her grief. She wonders how many of those kind souls remained on the island and imagines more than a few. They were dock families, people who lived and worked locally for generations.

"This isn't a vacation," Ava says plainly, returning to the room. "We get in and out as quickly and discreetly as possible."

"When do we leave?" Hazel asks.

"Well, every day we don't find Perry is another that he's spending your inheritance."

CHAPTER 24

Hilton Head, here we come!" Kagan announces into the breeze before retracting his head through the rear window of the Audi, feeling invigorated by the prospect of the mission they're embarking on. Hazel's just merged onto I-395, and Ava's in shotgun, typing an address into the Google Maps app on her phone.

"So," he asks, "how old were you the last time you saw Aunt Constance?"

"Eleven." Ava taps the screen before slipping the phone into a cup holder between the seats and turning to Kagan. She appears to be working something out in her head. "Man, that's almost twenty years already. Wow. Anyway, the summer after my mom died, Perry dumped me at the Hilton Head house to live with Constance."

"How well did you know your aunt then?" asks Hazel.

"Not at all. First time meeting the woman."

"Huh," Kagan jumps back in. "That must have been something."

"Yeah. Her whole story was pretty tragic, as I came to understand it. Constance had married young. She'd gotten herself hooked up with the scion of a disgustingly wealthy sugar-farming family. Harmon Danforth was the guy's name, if I remember correctly. He died a few years into their marriage in a drunken hunting accident. She inherited the mansion and mostly just puttered around it all day, not doing much other than attending to the flower beds out front."

"Did you two get along okay?" asks Hazel.

"There wasn't much interaction. She was pretty clocked out, I guess from the sudden death of the husband. But I'd just lost my mom and my uncle and really needed someone to help me work through all of that, and meanwhile here's this grieving woman just kind of floating in her own malaise. So, not great."

"That's rough." Kagan's surprised to find that the memory of navigating a self-centered adult still scrapes at a raw place within him.

"Yeah, it was a weird time. I remember the house and everything in it feeling like it was fossilized in amber. They had this ramshackle tennis court in the backyard, and in the corner next to the door that led outside was one of those old wooden rackets with the catgut strings, just leaning there. It was covered in a thick layer of dust, like it hadn't been touched in years."

"Ew."

"The whole place was like that. The keys of the piano, the books on the shelves, the framed photos on the side table in the living room. Everything except the bottles on the bar cart." Ava frowns. "The only thing that kept the house from going full *Grey Gardens* was the fresh flowers Constance would cut and put out on the dining table once a week. It was her funny little ritual."

"Sounds grim." A nightmare scenario was more like it. Kagan can practically taste the gloom. He moves to place a comforting hand on Ava's shoulder, but thinks better of it. You never knew these days. "I'm sorry you had to go through that."

"Thanks." Ava turns in her seat, and the half smile she offers Kagan sends a charge through him. "It was okay, in the end. I entertained myself well enough, thanks in large part to the old bowrider of Harmon's that my aunt kept tied to the dock out back."

"So when did Perry come back to get you?" asks Hazel as she slips into the left lane and guns it past a FreshDirect truck.

"The end of the summer. I got a whole season at Camp Constance."

"Jesus," exclaims Kagan. "Brutal."

"Oh, but the fun was only beginning. Unbeknownst to me at the time, my father had already found his next mark."

"I'm so sorry, hon," says Hazel, keeping her attention on the highway as she locates Ava's hand and squeezes it gently. A sting of jealousy sends a flush of heat through Kagan. He now wishes he'd been bold enough a moment ago to follow through, to offer Ava comfort and establish physical contact. Having to watch his sister usurp him feels conspiratorial, vindictive. But Kagan has only himself to blame. He's squandered the opportunity, and now it's nothing more than a could-have-been.

"So where did you two go from there?" he asks, anxious to remain in the conversation.

"We hit the road," says Ava, slapping on a brittle, hollow smile. "It was time for the adventure to begin. Drove a few hours north to Myrtle Beach and set up shop for the weekend, trying to get some action with the Labor Day crowds."

"Did you understand what was happening at the time?" asks Hazel. "Like, did you get that he was scheming, or not really?"

"You know, I guess I did and I didn't. Something definitely seemed off about what we were doing, but I was also desperate for parental love and acknowledgment, so that was probably enough to keep me from thinking too hard about it. And my father always managed to make it seem fun."

"Like it was a game or something?" Kagan asks.

"Exactly. I remember he came up with this thing we called the Cone Challenge, where he'd give me five minutes to try to get some random stranger to buy me an ice cream from this stand on the boardwalk. But he wouldn't tell me how to do it, so I'd have to come up with a compelling story, like I'd dropped my last one in the sand, or I'd lost my allowance money. That kind of thing. Just manipulating these poor people into feeling sorry for me."

"That's pretty fucked up."

"Right?" As he studies Ava's face, Kagan recognizes a mix of pain and nostalgia in her expression. "One day, he taught me 'front and follow.' I had such a fun time while we were doing it and realized only later on that it was a way to lure potential marks. He got some years out of me with that one."

"Wait," asks Hazel, "what's front and follow?"

"It's a surveillance technique you can utilize when you're working in a team. One person gets ahead of a target and tries to keep tabs on them while the second person follows at a distance. The person in front uses reflective surfaces like windows or car mirrors to keep an eye on the target without tipping them off. Or, if you're in a beach town, the lenses in a pair of sunglasses at a kiosk. I came up with that one on my own. Ol' daddy-o was *very* proud." The sarcasm and bitterness drip from her tongue. "Then, at some point, the two people switch positions so as not to tip off the target. And if the one tucked up front loses the mark, then the back picks up the slack. I swear, it's supercool when you're a twelve-year-old."

"I'm sure." Kagan's gotten swept up in the story of Ava's spy-like childhood—playing out in his head like a movie that would have riveted his younger self—and has to remember that they're discussing the same man who had his mother killed. Somberly he asks, "And how would you use that to lure people?"

"First, we'd spot a good candidate. Usually a single woman, often with a kid about my age. Perry taught me to check for a lack of a ring. Also, someone who looked kind, nurturing. Trusting. And well-off. If I could get them a little ways away from a big crowd, I'd pretend to be lost and scared. I'd hit 'em with something about my mom having recently died, and it was just me and my dad, and he was the only person I had left in the world, and he must be worried sick about me, and . . . you get the idea."

"And they went for it?"

"Every time," answers Ava, shaking her head in residual disbelief. "I was a regular Tatum O'Neal. Of course, it wasn't all that hard. When we first started, I *had* actually lost my mom pretty recently, and some part of me had to know that Perry was not a safe person to be around. So, yeah, I sold the fear and desperation pretty well. Eventually, after I was good and worked up, Dad would come along and save the day."

"Did he ever get together with any of these women?" asks Hazel.

"Well, he was already working on the one, but I think he always kept an eye peeled for a bigger fish. And part of it was his ego. Just doing it because he could. Staying sharp."

"And what happened to that mark he'd found?"

"Turns out they'd already married, while my mom was still alive." The shake of her head suggests that Ava retains a glimmer of disbelief around the situation. "We all lived together for a while. Happy little family." She swallows uncomfortably and bites her top lip. "Until the woman disappeared."

A pall falls over the interior of the Audi, and everyone is quiet for a long, charged moment. Kagan notices that his sister has quickly picked up speed, as she tends to when she gets upset behind the wheel. Finally, Hazel breaks the silence. "How does he keep getting away with this?!"

"My father always had a knack for persuading other people to carry out his dirty work. It's how he's managed to keep his hands so clean."

As the sullen mood looms, Kagan notices Ava checking the side mirror, not for the first time. He assumes it to be a vestige of her old life, prompted by the reminiscence about Perry. "Hey," he begins, in an effort to steer the conversation into cheerier territory, "I'm impressed you remember your aunt's address. I can barely tell you what I had for lunch yesterday."

"Well, I don't exactly. But there was this café, the Salty Dog, that I used to pass on my bike when I'd ride into town. Luckily, it's still around."

"And you can find the house from there?" asks Hazel.

"I'm pretty sure, yeah. But we'll see." Kagan catches a glimpse of Ava's face in the mirror, staring absently into the distance, a haunted look having crept into her expression. "Memory can be a slippery thing."

CHAPTER 25

The Keith Carradine soundalike on the radio croons that it's midnight in Fayetteville. Hazel suspects they're on the outskirts because of the weak radio signal; every song is more static than music. Driving for over five hours, they've skirted the edges everywhere since hitting the road. As the night deepens, their road trip takes on the atmosphere of a horror movie, especially with spotty cell service for the past fifty miles, depriving them of Bluetooth-enabled playlists. Instead, there's been a lot of bickering over which FM station is the least annoying, and everyone has reached their threshold.

"We should have stopped for food at that Waffle House miles back. There's nothing out here," Kagan complains. "Where are we anyway?"

"About halfway," Ava replies edgily.

"Kagan, stop kicking my seat. What are you, five years old?" Hazel gripes.

"Gas station!" Kagan yells in Hazel's ear.

Hazel feels opposing emotions as she pulls into the station. The ride has been stressful and irritating, with Kagan's antsy verbosity. Simultaneously, Ava riding shotgun, guiding her in the dark, has been exhilarating.

"Are we sure this place is open?" The pumps are empty, and Hazel easily glides the car up to one. She looks at the yellow-lit storefront. Giant moths orbit the dirty light and flutter in and out of the sliced illumination. Beyond the grimy windows, no one appears at the register or moving around inside. Hazel taps the horn lightly, and there is some movement after a minute.

"I'm going to use the bathroom. Any snack requests while I'm in there?" Ava asks.

"Anything but Funyuns," Hazel groans. She's feeling hungover from the all-sulfite diet and craving some New York cuisine. Ava exits the car. As soon as her door is closed, Kagan simpers.

"What?"

"There was a booking error with the rooms for tonight."

Hazel feels immediately annoyed.

"What kind of error?" She knows she shouldn't have let him take over the lodging for their trip, but he'd insisted.

"I accidentally booked only two rooms, a single and a double."

She checks the store to clock Ava's whereabouts and sees the back of her head through the window. "Just book another room. It isn't that hard."

"Doubtful. The Wi-Fi is too spotty to book online, and nobody is answering the phone," Kagan replies.

"Huh." She narrows her eyes at him. "What's your angle?"

"I want to share the double with Ava," he says.

Hazel scoffs loudly. This is so typical.

"Can you tell her you need to be alone to film something? I think it's important that she and I have the space to get to know each other. Riding in the back seat isn't exactly helping," he whines.

"Can we not do this, Kagan? Just leave it alone."

"You aren't going to even think about it?"

"Why would I agree?" Hazel stink-eyes her brother. While she hasn't told him she has feelings for Ava, she feels burned by the blatant disregard that she might. But telling him the truth will only make her look hypocritical. "Why would *she*?"

"Haze, throw me a bone! I know you're picking up on the vibe between us."

"I'm picking up on your weak game."

The only things she's seen between Ava and Kagan is an imbalance; his thirstiness, and her politely ignoring it. Kagan calling dibs on Ava is infuriating.

"If she's interested in you—and I'm not getting that 'vibe'—you absolutely cannot hook up with her."

"Why?"

Hazel applies pressure to the space between her eyes with two fingers. "Because she works for us, Kagan."

"Yeah, but not like in an official HR scenario. And we haven't paid her yet."

"That doesn't make it better." She can't tell if drugs and grief have wrecked her brother's good sense on this topic or if he never had it.

"Oh. I get it." Kagan gasps jokingly. "You *like* her."

Hazel is glad it's dark in the car and her brother can't see her blanching. "It doesn't matter either way; this isn't college. You can't call dibs on every woman you find attractive."

"Well, how are we going to settle this? Should we flip a coin?" Kagan asks.

"Should we tell Ava about your idea for a coin toss and ask her whom she'd prefer to share a room with?" Hazel snarks.

Kagan smirks. "You're worried that she likes me more than you."

"Get over yourself."

The passenger door swings open, and Ava slides in. "There was nothing in there you'd want to eat; trust me. And the pumps are dry. There's a guy inside who knows a lot about unrelated subjects, though I'm not sure if he actually works here. He mentioned a Sunoco half a mile down the way."

Neither sibling speaks.

"What did I miss?" Ava asks, glancing between them.

Hazel hides her frustration with Kagan, who fidgets in the back seat. She prays he won't ask Ava whom she prefers, though she can't put it past him.

Kagan clears his throat. "I was just telling Hazel that the motel I found for tonight had only two rooms available. I know it isn't ideal, but I was thinking that you and I—"

"It's not a problem," Ava says, patting Hazel's leg. "You don't snore, do you?"

Hazel watches her brother's mouth slacken in the mirror as she turns the car onto the road and smiles triumphantly.

"Hazel sounds like a buzz saw when she sleeps, but I on the other hand—"

"Sorry, Kagan," Ava cuts him off. "No boys allowed."

/ / /

A drowsy husband and his annoyed wife, in pajamas, check the trio into the motel. The office is as barren as the parking lot. The pegboard behind the couple displays multiple available room keys. Hazel turns to Ava.

"Do you want to get your own room?"

"Nah, we should save resources," Ava says, her eyes gleaming as she meets Hazel's.

Given her past incarceration, Hazel realizes that Ava is likely accustomed to sharing her space with others. Despite that, Ava doesn't convey the hardened demeanor of someone who has been in prison that Hazel might have expected.

Kagan appears miserable as they stand in awkward silence until the wife hands them two sets of keys, each attached to a large block of wood.

Hazel raises her eyebrows.

"There's a fifty-dollar fine for lost keys," the wife tells them sternly, and all three nod.

"Is there food nearby?" Kagan asks. Hazel can see through her brother's pouting and doesn't feel sorry for him. Now that he's shown his willingness to manipulate things to get closer to Ava, Hazel must be on guard. The husband gives him a once-over but doesn't speak.

"There's a diner about twenty miles east," the wife grunts. "I'm not sure if they're still open, though. We don't get many tourists."

The pair turns out the lights while Hazel, Ava, and Kagan remain standing there.

"That was creepy," Ava says when they step outside and locate their rooms on either end of the place. "Where did you find this joint, Kagan? The dark web?"

Hazel hands Kagan the key with a grin, and he deflates even further.

"Should we try the diner?" Kagan attempts.

"I'm too exhausted to eat," Ava replies.

"If you guys can't sleep, let me know," he says gloomily.

A second wind overtakes Hazel as she and Ava walk shoulder to shoulder down the dim hallway. Cheap sconces sporadically light their way, with every third one flickering or dark. Threadbare spots dot the carpet, and the walls cry out for a fresh coat of paint. The distinct odor of mildew grows stronger the deeper into the motel they go.

"I know we're on a budget, but Kagan picked a shithole. I can't believe they're still using actual keys. And did you see the rotary phone in the office?"

Ava is already putting the key into their room's doorknob. "I love it. It is a total time warp." She smiles and pushes the door inward, and it makes a whooshing sound as it connects with the carpet.

Hazel steps through the doorway blindly while scrolling through her phone.

"You should surrender your phone and laptop to me, and we can pretend we're back in simpler times."

"Were things actually simpler?" Hazel asks as she walks farther into the room.

"Sometimes I think devices have made things more complicated," Ava replies.

Hazel looks up. "I'm surprised you think that. Aren't you a computer genius?"

"So you do know more about me than you've let on," Ava remarks lightly as she stashes her bag next to the bed. Hazel feels relieved that the defensiveness from their first solo conversation is absent but wishes she had approached the talk with a bit more finesse. "I guess I do. But I'd love to hear it all from you."

"Pull up a chair. What do you want to know?"

Ava unzips her bag and extracts a couple of mini bottles of Patrón, placing them onto the table. She reaches into her purse for a bar of extra-dark chocolate with sea salt. "Dinner?"

"That's my favorite flavor combination," Hazel marvels, her grumbling stomach reminding her of the lapsed time since their last meal.

Ava smiles. "Mine too."

"We have a lot in common," Hazel says excitedly as she sits in one of the two guest chairs. Being out of the car and free from Kagan and alone with Ava in the middle-of-nowhere setting gives her a cozy feeling she wants to freeze in time. Even if they are in a dump.

While Ava excuses herself to the bathroom, Hazel scans the room, taking in the queen bed, paisley polyester duvets and pillow shams, a small flat-screen TV smaller than her laptop screen, and the water-stained ceiling. The stark contrast with the five-star hotel rooms of the past reminds her of the urgency of her need for her inheritance. Even Ava's good company can only partly compensate for the depressing reality of this place.

"Should I get ice?" Ava asks, holding a plastic bucket from the bathroom.

"I don't need it," Hazel replies.

As Ava opens the first bottle, Hazel unwraps the chocolate bar and breaks it in half. She places the squares on tissues and slides Ava's share across the table. Hazel watches as Ava empties the first bottle into a plastic cup and then divides the liquid into a second cup by half.

"So what would you like to know about me?" Ava asks.

"How about everything?" Hazel laughs. "I feel like your life has been a real journey."

"Compared with some, but I've met plenty of people who've had crazier ones than mine."

Hazel sips the liquid and appreciates the warm sensation as it goes down her esophagus and then reverses course to her ears. "So you're a hacker?"

"Not anymore," Ava says.

"How does someone learn how to do that? I mean, I consider myself pretty damn good with computers, but not anywhere near being able to do anything that could get me arrested."

"I had a good teacher and a knack for it. It gave me a feeling of purpose for a period of time. I was pretty insecure when I was a teenager and preferred staying close to home. I needed something to focus on and, I suppose, an escape after I split from my dad. Things were tough when I was under his care, and I use that term ironically."

"I'm sorry that your dad made you a child accomplice. It's twisted," Hazel says.

"I don't think about it. At least I hadn't been until you and your brother showed up."

Like she'd conveyed to Kagan when they first met Ava, Hazel doesn't truly believe this. You don't just get over something like that, and she understands from her own experiences with Charles how hard it is to let go of core traumas.

"Our father was pretty horrible too."

"Your mom had a type, it sounds like. Do you speak to your dad?"

"He's dead. He was nothing like yours, but he was my mother's OG abuser. After he died, she did a major glow-up and had a pretty impressive second act. She was really happy. Until she met Perry."

"He has a knack for ruining things. That is why I cut him off."

"Do you ever think about how different your life might have been if you had stayed with him?" Hazel asks while kicking off her shoes and stretching her toes.

"I make it a personal policy not to dwell. 'If you keep looking back, you're bound to stumble.'"

"Huh. I haven't heard that before." Hazel laughs.

"It was something my mom used to say."

"I feel like all I do is look backward," Hazel laments.

"You're still in the thick of things. So really, you're just experiencing the present and wishing it was behind you. Give yourself some time to process it."

Her words move Hazel. "I keep thinking about Adam. I know I shouldn't, but it's all so confusing. How can you love someone so toxic? I mean, he killed my mother, and I'm still missing him. I can't believe I'm admitting that."

"It makes sense to me."

"I haven't talked about this with anyone," Hazel tells Ava.

"Not even your close friends? Kagan?"

Hazel shakes her head. "I don't have any close friends, never have. I don't entirely trust women. Maybe that comes from dating some terrible ones." Hazel pauses to gauge Ava's reaction, but she is unmoved. "And Kagan and I don't talk about our relationships."

"I don't have a lot of friends either. It feels safer that way. And to tell you the truth, I don't trust most people. I'm hoping we can trust each other, though."

Hazel feels instantly lifted by this. "I hope for that too."

"What's the thing you keep obsessing about with Adam?" Ava asks.

"How much I wanted my mom to meet him. She was critical about my relationship choices and never really accepted that I dated men and women. Part of it was her religion, but there was also a piece of her that was so scared of what other people thought. I fought her on this so hard, but I never gave her a chance to get to know anyone that I was with. Adam was different, and I knew she'd like him because he made me happy. That's what she used to say: 'I don't care whom you're with as long as you are happy.'"

"That's what a parent is supposed to want," Ava says. "She sounds like she was a good mom."

Hazel sniffs back tears, and Ava hands her a rigid cocktail napkin from the sad minibar.

"Are you okay?"

"I just thought of something horrible." As she cries, Hazel experiences a surge of calm comfort when Ava puts a caring hand on her back.

"What?" Ava asks gently.

"I got my wish; my mother *did* meet Adam."

CHAPTER 26

While Hazel is in the bathroom, Ava sees three missed calls from Sam. She texts him back, assuring him that she is safe. She feels guilty for the terrible scenarios he probably cycled through since she left DC with the two strangers connected to her father. She receives a thumbs-up in response as the bathroom door opens.

"Janice would die if she saw this motel," Hazel remarks as she returns to the table.

"I take it your mom appreciated nice things?"

"She didn't know anything else. She was born wealthy, but she wasn't an asshole. Some rich people can be insufferable. Janice wasn't a snob. She just appreciated luxury."

"She must have if my father chose her."

Ava observes Hazel processing this.

"So he targeted her, right? That's what people like him do? He picked her, worked on her, and had a plan in place? It makes my stomach hurt thinking about how clueless my mother was."

Ava nods. "That's how he works. Nothing is random. However, part of his game is to make everything seem synchronistic and magical. Especially in the beginning. It's hard to spot red flags when you're wearing rose-colored glasses."

"That makes me feel marginally better about falling for a killer," Hazel says.

"Don't beat yourself up. Adam targeted you just the same as Perry did your mother. You were both marks in the same plan."

Pensively, Hazel bites a small section of the chocolate bar, her mind wandering. "I suppose it was the last thing Mom and I did together." She chuckles while trading the bar for her phone, reaching past Ava to grab it. Unlocking the device, her focus shifts to the screen, a routine Ava has observed frequently during the trip. However, she's struck by how absentmindedly Hazel does it, even in the midst of a conversation.

"Is everything okay?" Ava asks, mildly annoyed that she's now conversing with the top of Hazel's head.

"Everything's fine; why?" Hazel replies without looking up.

"I figured something must be really important to have to check your phone in the middle of our conversation."

"Sorry." Hazel's cheeks flush.

"It's okay."

"Something's been bothering me," Hazel says, reengaging. "Wouldn't Perry have been able to get our money without throwing my love life into the mix?"

Ava sighs; she feels for Hazel. She understands what it is like to keep running through being taken and endlessly trying to make sense of how and why, like having a terrible meme stuck in your head on loop. It could drive a person crazy.

"Perry realized you and Kagan could be obstacles between him and Janice's money. It might have been your interference in their relationship, threatening his take, or simply needing you distracted for the final part of his plan. Adam's job was to get as much info as possible from you for my father."

Hazel absorbs this. "And then push my mother over the edge. So this is all on me."

"Don't do that to yourself," Ava says.

"This is going straight to my head." Hazel shakes her cup. "Whatever you do, don't let me post anything tonight." She pushes her phone away for effect.

"I wouldn't dream of it." Ava takes Hazel's phone and puts it into her bag.

"Thank you for saving me from myself," Hazel says brightening through a mouthful of chocolate. Her grin showcases her face from a completely different angle—an improvement from her usual melancholy downward cast. She looks so different from the made-up face in her videos. Sitting across from her now, in the room's low light, au naturel, she is attractive in that quiet way that grows on you the longer you know someone.

"I think this is the first time I've seen you smile," Ava says.

Hazel holds Ava's gaze. "I guess I haven't had much to smile about."

"I'm sure the past two months have been brutal."

"More like my whole life."

"Were you close?"

"Very," Hazel says sadly. "How about you and your mom?"

"My mom and I got in a big fight right before she died." Ava blames her unexpected candor on the tequila.

"You did?"

"Yeah. I still replay the fight, and sometimes I wonder if my mother might still be alive if the fight had never happened."

"So you do think about the past," Hazel says gently.

"I guess I do when I'm feeling maudlin," Ava concedes.

"You'd said he made your mom's death look like an accident? What happened?"

"When I was eleven, our house burned down, and my mom and my uncle didn't make it out, but I did. I barely remember it. I was unconscious for most of the aftermath, but I've read the police and insurance reports a hundred times." Ava takes a thoughtful breath.

"How did you get out?"

"When the heat from the fire woke me up, I tried to open my windows, but they'd been nailed closed. They hadn't been that way a week earlier."

Hazel gawks, on tenterhooks for more. This was the typical shocked response from the few people Ava had told; they always wanted more details.

"Fire and thick smoke had filled my room, and I was burned pretty badly trying to get through the door. I broke a window using my desk chair and climbed onto the roof. I got dizzy and fell from the second story. I woke up two days later in the hospital."

"Oh my God. It's amazing that you survived."

"With third-degree burns and a broken back." Ava touches her neck.

"What a nightmare. Your poor mom." Hazel shudders.

"And my uncle Wyatt. He was the closest person to us besides my dad."

"Your father started the fire?"

"He had an alibi. He was out of town on a business trip, so he had someone else do it."

"Did your mom have a lot of money?"

"Not like yours, but he had insurance policies on us and the house.

I think he wanted to get rid of her because she was going to leave him, and she'd threatened to report him to the police."

"His own daughter . . . I can't believe he would do that."

"You're looking at it from the perspective of someone with empathy."

Hazel looks gobsmacked. "Nobody suspected him?"

"He had a solid alibi, being two states away and interacting with numerous people who confirmed his whereabouts. To the authorities, it appeared as a terrible tragedy and stroke of bad luck—his wife and brother-in-law were tragically killed, and his daughter narrowly survived. I spent a month in the ICU. When I was discharged from the hospital, he took me to my aunt's place."

"When did you realize that he tried to kill you?"

"I started to suspect after he dumped me at my aunt's."

"Jesus, your life should be a podcast," Hazel says as she folds her legs into a crisscross formation and leans back on the headboard.

"When I first arrived, I was totally in a state of confusion. My mom and uncle were gone, and I was on painkillers, which had me pretty loopy for a few weeks. So I'd be on her couch for hours, watching old sitcoms from the sixties, listening to her ramble about the past. When she wasn't monologuing about her dead husband, she was obsessing about how my dad had treated her when they were coming up. He would use her as bait in little scams and let her take the fall when they got caught. She was hit by a car when they were little, and she was convinced that my father pushed her because he tried to shake the driver down for money."

"So Perry's been a psycho from the beginning."

"It seems that way."

"So your mom and uncle die, you almost die, your dad dumps you with some insane woman you've never met, and then you realize he was behind it all?"

"In a nutshell."

"No wonder . . ." Hazel trails off.

"No wonder I ended up in prison?" Ava laughs.

Hazel casts her eyes down. "Sorry. I just meant that it's no wonder you haven't had a typical life. So he came back for you? Why, if he wanted you gone?"

"He realized that having a disabled daughter would be an asset. The woman he married while he was with my mom had a son, and I think my father wanted me around to distract both of them while he was setting up his next target."

"How did you live with him after you suspected?"

"It took me a long time to see my father for who he is. Even when he used me in his hustles, I didn't think about his involvement in the fire. He was the only parent I had left." Ava struggles to keep the bitterness out of her voice, which irks her. She's past this now. Her father doesn't have any control over her anymore. She's worked so hard to move on, which makes these new feelings about ancient memories deeply unsettling.

"So your mom was trying to leave. And he found out."

"Nobody leaves my father."

"You did. He must have hated that." Hazel sways with heavy eyes.

"Are you feeling okay?" Ava asks.

"The room is spinning."

"You should probably lie down." She helps Hazel to the bed and tucks her in. Hazel's eyes flutter up at her, and longing lingers before she closes her eyes.

"Get in with me," Hazel mumbles.

Ava sees by the digital clock that it's after two a.m. Her brain is sprinting, and her body feels like it could do the same.

"I'm going to grab some ice," she whispers, although Hazel is already snoring lightly. Ava grabs the plastic bucket, kills the lights, and pulls the door closed.

As she walks down the hallway, she smells cleaner and cigarette smoke. The ice machine hums loudly. She ditches the bucket in the space between the ice and vending machines and changes course. She didn't make the trip for ice anyway.

Her vulnerability has sent her into needy desire. She knows she should stop, but she keeps moving, aware that whatever happens from here on out won't be good for the long term. But she's seeking short-term gratification, which has clouded any remaining good judgment.

She lightly knocks when she reaches the threshold to the door, hoping the sleeping body on the other side isn't too far gone to let her in. Finally, she hears rustling inside.

The door opens, and Ava smiles with her empty-handed shrug.

"Sorry. I lost my key," she lies.

"There's a hefty fine for that," Kagan replies, smiling hungrily. He doesn't hesitate before grabbing her by the waist and yanking her into the darkness.

CHAPTER 27

Kagan's still riding the high of the previous night's surprise visitor—along with the jolt from the mug of tar-thick coffee on the table before him—as the waitress shows up to their booth wielding an armful of plates stacked with various breakfast foods. He's well aware that "server" is the currently accepted nomenclature, but he's pretty sure Doris would laugh him out of the diner for referring to her as such. She sets the plates in front of the trio and drops a smattering of "honeys," "dears," and "dolls" before booking it back to the counter to take an impatient couple's order.

"Hey, Kagan," says a bleary-eyed Hazel in a cartoonishly childlike voice from across the table, "want me to make a blueberry smiley face on your panpapes?"

"Aw, Haze," he shoots back, not missing a beat. "I remember my first hangover too."

His sister smirks at him while offering a middle finger for further clarification.

"Wow," Ava chimes in as she cuts a bite of spinach omelet. "It's like dining with the aristocracy." She turns to Hazel and winks as she steals a chunk of potato and a smear of hollandaise off the platter of eggs Benedict. Kagan finishes soaking his pancakes in syrup, sets the dispenser on the table, and leans forward.

"Again, let me apologize for my sister's complete lack of manners. First, locking you out of your hotel room, and now this vulgar display."

"Oh, fuck off, Kagan." Hazel shifts her attention to Ava. "I really am sorry about last night. You should have just pounded on the door until I woke up."

"I knocked a few times, but it was late, and the owners already seemed pretty bent out of shape that we'd gotten them out of bed for check-in. I didn't think a commotion would help the cause any." She shrugs. "Plus, you looked so cute when I left that I felt bad waking you up."

As he watches his sister blush, Kagan's hit with a tinge of jealousy. "You know," he offers, "you could have come and knocked on my door. I'd have put you up for the night, no problem."

"Ew," Hazel blurts, then winces from the effort. "Don't be such a creep."

"What?" He raises his hands in surrender. "I would have been a gentleman about it. Give me a little credit."

Both women shoot him disapproving looks, but there's a mischievousness behind Ava's that exhilarates him. This secret they now share bonds them in a way that his sister can only dream about, and Kagan lets himself bask in a moment of quiet satisfaction.

"I sure appreciate the thought," responds Ava in a voice thick with condescension, "but the hallway floor seemed like a much better option." He catches a glimpse of a grin as she sips her juice.

"Sorry my brother's such a weirdo." Hazel sets a hand on Ava's shoulder, then petulantly stares Kagan down. "And I'm *not* sorry you missed out on all the fun."

"Hey, like you decided in the car, no boys allowed." A piece of him is straining at the seams to throw his conquest in his sister's face, but a sense of calm has descended over Kagan. The satisfaction of the secret liaison with Ava is outweighing his baser inclinations. He almost feels sorry for Hazel, with this pathetic attempt to box him out.

If she only knew the truth.

Years ago, Kagan discovered a way to rebalance the scales in those instances when his sister had become a little too smug, a little too pleased with herself, a little too insufferable. It was hardly his fault. After all, what was the point of possessing an abundance of charm and a surplus of charisma if he wasn't going to make prudent use of it? And so he had. First, with Hazel's high school lab partner. And then, with her college suite mate. And her *other* college suite mate.

And finally, just hours ago, with Ava.

Kagan stabs a blueberry, then a second one, before plunging the tines of the fork into the stack of pancakes and cutting off a section. He drags the arrangement lazily through a pool of syrup as his mind wanders back to the events of the night before.

He hadn't expected Ava to show up at his door at that hour, though in retrospect it didn't surprise him all that much. He figured she'd played things as cool as she could manage, made him work for it a little. But he couldn't blame her for being as eager as he was. The tension had been brewing all day in the car, and that kind of chemistry could prove combustible if left unaddressed for too long.

He couldn't remember them exchanging so much as a syllable. He'd let her in, and she'd promptly sought out his mouth with hers as she pushed him back onto the bed and began stripping off the last of his clothes. There'd been no need for words.

The sex was hot and hungry. And he'd been able to perform, thank God. Since the split from Bethany, Kagan had suffered the indignity of an equipment malfunction on a few occasions. He blamed the number his ex-wife had done on his head, and possibly the lack of stability in his life. But it wasn't an issue with Ava. They'd connected on a level that rendered all of that moot. Just two people with a raw need for each other.

It wasn't until they'd woken from their postcoital sleep that she finally spoke. The dawn light was creeping in around the window blinds, and she'd peeled her eyes open and turned to him with a satisfied smile. He started to say something, but Ava put a finger to his lips. "Let's not ruin this with a lot of talking," she said before slipping out of bed and back into her clothes. She made for the door, only stopping to add, "As far as Hazel's concerned, I slept in the hallway in front of her room last night," before letting herself out.

A wordless tryst. Steamy as hell.

"So how much longer of a drive do you figure we're looking at today?" The sound of his sister's voice plunks Kagan back into the conversation, and he shakes off the last of the reminiscence and takes a sip of coffee.

"I figure we should be able to do it in four and change, with a couple of bathroom breaks built in."

"So we'll be there by this afternoon?"

"Don't see why not." Ava mashes an errant strand of spinach with the back of her fork and brings it to her mouth.

"And what's our plan once we get there?"

"That'll depend."

"On what?" There's the trace of a whine in Hazel's question, and it elicits a frown from Ava.

"Variables." She sighs. "I haven't seen Constance in forever. We'll need to gauge what sort of shape she's in to suss out how helpful she's likely to be with locating Perry. And then, depending on how that goes, either we know where we're headed or we have to cobble together a different plan."

"Sorry," blurts Hazel, seeming to pick up on Ava's annoyance. "That tequila really did me in." His sister tries to keep her tone casual, but there's a whiff of desperation that quietly delights Kagan. He lets her sit with the discomfort for a moment before finally taking pity and stepping in for a rescue.

"So," he asks Ava, "what's the strategy when we do catch up with Perry?"

"I'll refer you to my earlier statement. I haven't had anything to do with the guy in well over a decade. He may have a whole new bag of surprises I don't even know about." Ava takes a sip of juice as she contemplates the play. "We'll need to figure out a way to run some recon without him getting wise to us, and then proceed accordingly."

"Maybe we can use that estrangement to our advantage," offers Hazel.

"How's that?"

"I mean, there's a good chance he might not even recognize you now, after all this time apart, right?"

"Yeah, that had occurred to me." Ava's voice sounds suddenly thinner, as if the thought itself has taken some of the wind out of her. "I'd like to imagine I cut a more confident figure these days."

"You know what? Screw that guy." As Hazel rubs Ava's back, she shoots her brother a self-satisfied look. "We're going to take the son of a bitch down."

Ava straightens up in her seat. "Yes, we are. And if he's working on another con when we find him, which I have to imagine he is, I'd love to figure out a way to use it against him." The canny gleam is returning to her eye. "Catch him in a trap of his own making."

It occurs to Kagan, looking at Hazel's hand on Ava's back, that he should attend to the emotional component of this budding romance. He's suffered through his own share of parental abuse and imagines the sort of feelings that must be churning through Ava right now. Kagan still blisters at the mere thought of Charles, of the way the man would dismiss his son only to soften when his daughter came into the room. What a cold, manipulative prick. Kagan reaches across the table and sets a hand atop Ava's. As he does, he feels the temperature of Hazel's stare.

"Hey," says Kagan, "I'm sure this is a lot for you to take on right now. I want you to know we're in this together, okay?"

Hazel slips her arm around Ava's shoulder and pulls her close. "Yeah, we've got your back. For real."

"Thank you, guys. That means a lot." The words belie an uncomfortable look on Ava's face that Kagan attributes to Hazel's thirsty grasp.

He gently squeezes her hand and offers up a warm smile. "You gonna be okay seeing Perry again?"

"Hey," responds Ava with a glum chortle and a squeeze of her own. "*Something* has to kill you."

CHAPTER 28

Hazel is sulking in the back seat, but no one has noticed. They've been on the road for a few hours, and she can't shake the feeling that Kagan has earned the upper hand with Ava. She swears there were subtle lingering looks between them during breakfast. And if that wasn't enough, Hazel felt a tentative foot nudging her ankle while sitting in the diner. Momentarily, she thought it was Ava, and her stomach somersaulted excitedly, but the footsie-seeking gesture was her brother. She choked on her coffee and watched Kagan's ears turn crimson when she kicked his foot away.

Hazel is furious at herself for passing out last night. She and Ava were genuinely connecting, and she'd blown it. She had gotten herself to a level of openness that she didn't think she was capable of after Adam's betrayal. Ava's childhood story was awful, but it was a good sign that she was sharing it with her. Hazel now had something over Kagan—more intel about Ava—that she could use to put him in his place if need be.

Kagan connects his phone to Bluetooth to get relief from the Bible Belt radio loop.

"Can you please not subject us to one of your 'smooth jam' play-lists?" Hazel asks while Kagan excitedly scrolls through Spotify. She anticipates that his digital selections are not much different from the compilations he used to create for Hazel's friends, attempting to impress them. She'd encountered more than one of his burned CDs in friends' and roommates' collections and promptly chucked them into the nearest trash can.

"What does the driver feel like listening to?" Kagan asks sweetly.

"I'm not picky. Something chill?" Ava replies, and smiles at Hazel in the rearview.

Hazel retreats into the comments section of her last posted video. She feels like she missed the memo and is irritated with Ava as much as her brother. Everything they say to each other feels like an inside joke that she's on the outside of.

Pouting, she surveys the online damage. If she doesn't feed her followers regularly, they bite. One commenter is being particularly nasty, saying her content is slipping and she's no longer interesting to watch. The trolls are always louder than her fans. Now she's dejected in real life and online and blocked for her next idea. Her thoughts have been so preoccupied. Finding Perry and their money is front of mind, but the drama of their road trip has made things messier than she expected. If she were a true-crime vlogger, her life would all be content gold, but the conspiracy afoot seems to be the burgeoning romance between Ava and Kagan.

The first soulful strains of "By Your Side" fill the car. Hazel loves Sade as much as the next warm-blooded person, but in the latish morning light of their mercenary road trip, the sexiness of the song feels as appropriate as sibling footsie. Her hangover has lifted enough for her to be in a moving vehicle, but not to assuage her irritability.

"I challenge anyone to listen to the first thirty seconds of this jam and *not* groove. Impossible." Kagan bobs his head in time with Sade's grainy contralto.

"Wasn't this your song with Mackenzie Stroudman?" Hazel asks.

"Under the advice of my attorney, I invoke my Fifth Amendment rights." Kagan skips to a Yo La Tengo song.

"Bad breakup?" Ava asks.

"Not one worth rehashing," Kagan says, his earlier playfulness noticeably weaker.

"We have twenty miles before we get to Aunt Constance's. I'm always game for a good heartbreak story."

Kagan sighs. "The girl was pretty unhinged, to begin with—"

Both women frown at Kagan.

"Ava, have you ever noticed how crazy *every* ex is?" Hazel interrupts.

"I may have been out of mainstream dating for a few years, but the insanity is an epidemic," Ava agrees.

Hazel can see Kagan's nostrils flaring but knows that he won't unleash on her in front of Ava as long as he's playing his charm game.

"Why don't you tell your version of my story, Haze? I'd love to hear your creative interpretation."

"Everything I know was from Mackenzie's lengthy Facebook recap post."

"This was when you guys were in college?" Ava asks.

"Mackenzie was a freshman at Fordham, and Kagan was a senior at Columbia. Mackenzie's family owned all the Happy Burger franchises in the US, and her grandfather bought major sports teams for fun; which ones were they?" Hazel pushes.

"Does it matter?" he mutters.

"She was a major catch. And she was enamored with my brother, which I still don't get."

"Until things went horribly wrong, I'm guessing?" Ava chuckles.

"Mackenzie chose to surprise Kagan after a weekend trip when he was visiting our sick mother. He told her he wouldn't be reachable until Sunday morning and would call her to come over. Mackenzie had duplicated his apartment key and let herself in, assuming he would appreciate returning home to a warm surprise-welcome after tending to his mom."

"She made a copy of your key without you knowing?" Ava asks.

"Kind of crazy, right?" Kagan looks to Ava for validation, and she raises her eyebrows.

"A little. It was nice that you were looking after your mom, though."

Hazel jumps in. "Except that our mother was not sick; if she were, Kagan most definitely would not have sacrificed an entire college weekend to care for her."

"We should listen to a podcast," Kagan suggests.

"No way, I'm invested now," Ava says, her hands steady on the steering wheel.

Kagan subtly shrinks in his seat.

"So Mackenzie cleans the place, probably snoops a bit, arranges a whole lunch spread, and then gets all cozy waiting for him to return home, ready to comfort him—"

"Jeez, for someone who wasn't even there, you remember a lot of details," Kagan interrupts.

"Mackenzie's post was extensive."

"The age of oversharing," Ava says.

"By noon, she hadn't heard from him and texted him a few times. He doesn't know that she's texting from inside his apartment. He tells her that Mom is feeling better and he'll call her later. At some point, Mackenzie gets into his bed completely naked. She wakes up to the sound of his key in the door, waits for him to stumble in for his happy surprise and gratefully jump into bed with her. . . ."

"Uh-oh," Ava says.

"Kagan saunters in, dressed to the nines, trailed by his other girl-friend and her parents, who were dropping Kagan off at home after he spent the weekend at their Kennebunkport compound."

Ava covers her open mouth with her hand. "Oof!"

Kagan is staring straight ahead at the road. "Mackenzie had an immature understanding of our relationship."

"His apartment was a studio, so when the girlfriend and her parents stepped into the place, they immediately saw Mackenzie in Kagan's bed. Her Facebook post about the whole messy situation was a thesis on Kagan. And that was back when everyone was on Facebook. Multiple girls commented about their experiences dating him. This was pre-canceling, but it didn't help his reputation. At least seven people who didn't even realize it was about my brother forwarded it to me, and a dozen more who did realize. . . ."

"Haze, you're leaving out a few critical details, though."

Hazel feels her face begin to burn.

"Like what?" Ava asks.

"Mackenzie was Hazel's freshman roommate, and she had a major crush on her."

"No, I did not," Hazel defends.

"Okay, are you more comfortable with 'fixation'? Because she sure wasn't," he cracks. "Mackenzie came onto me during a weekend visit at our house, and I was into it. After we got together, Hazel made it a whole drama, and Mackenzie even switched dorms in the second semester because she felt like Hazel was creeping on her all the time."

"That isn't true. She moved because she felt weird about having you over to our room while I was there, for obvious reasons," Hazel counters.

"That's what she told *you*," Kagan says, and turns to Ava. "She's conveniently leaving out the part of Mackenzie's Facebook post where she called Hazel 'Single White Female' after putting me on blast. So we both got heat for that viral mess."

"That's terrible," Ava says.

"It made things uncomfortable for the rest of the semester," Kagan says.

"No, I meant it's terrible that you dated someone that Hazel cared about."

Hazel's heart soars while Kagan's shoulders slump.

"We were young."

"Right, and we are so mature and past that stuff now. Right, K?" Hazel asks haughtily.

"You don't want to start dragging out the worst thing our exes ever did to us, do you?" Kagan cracks.

Hazel feels slapped and stares out the window.

"Low blow, Kagan," Ava says, turning to Hazel and smiling at her sympathetically.

"Why don't we change the subject?" Hazel offers.

"Here's a question: How is it that Perry has never been caught? He's been scamming people for a long time, yet he hasn't done any time. But *you* have? How did that happen?" Kagan asks.

"Kagan, that is really rude!" Hazel snaps.

Ava's cool demeanor remains, though Hazel can see her thinking.

"My father has always been very adept at staying a few steps ahead of the authorities. He prides himself on being smarter than local law enforcement and never offending twice in the same area. He's got a photographic memory, so he never slips up with his aliases. And he's always had someone who will do the really dirty stuff, ensuring an indisputable alibi. I did try to get him caught when I ran away from him. You can see how well that turned out."

"But how many wives of one man can go missing before it catches up with him?" Kagan asks.

"Enough that there is an entire cottage industry of murder content," Hazel says.

"He's ripping off isolated women over a certain age, who don't have a lot of family who care about them, and who aren't going to make a big deal when they go missing."

"He must be slipping because he seriously miscalculated with our mom. We will make this guy's life a living hell," Kagan says.

The car's navigation interrupts the tension by announcing their arrival. The Salty Dog Café is in front of them, its patio bustling with the lunch crowd.

"We're close. I can navigate from memory here," Ava says. She inhales sharply as she turns the car left onto a long road flanked by magnolia trees. A house emerges from the dense overgrowth.

"This is some *Gone with the Wind* shit," Hazel says.

Ava pulls over a few yards from the enormous, dilapidated antebellum house with a second-floor wraparound that appears to barely support the weight of the squirrels running to and fro on the shoddy roof shingles.

"What a creepy shithole," Kagan says through a whistle.

"Exactly as I remember it."

CHAPTER 29

As Ava exits the car, she catches the sweet scent of Carolina jessamine lining the long drive; in the next breath, the putrid stench of pluff mud from the nearby marsh overpowers her. The combination is a sensory reminder of this place's extremes.

A peculiar sense of déjà vu overwhelms Ava upon stepping onto the porch. Having dreamed of this house and her aunt so frequently, she cautiously tests the porch's wood to ensure its reality. She imagines how odd this must appear to Hazel and Kagan in the car.

Every wave of insect acoustics transports her back in time. The oppressive humidity and heat of the low country make sweat pool at the base of her spine and above her top lip. Her brain tells her to turn, run, and never look back. She swore she'd never return under any circumstances. Yet, here she stands, her legs solidly in front of the door.

Ava recalls watching the house shrink through the rear window of her father's car. At that time, the prevailing emotion was relief. It was when she still believed her father loved her despite her growing suspicions. His return had momentarily reset the emotional balance, prompting her to bury any negative thoughts. His arrival to pick her up at the end of the summer felt like an answered prayer, and escaping from her aunt was the only thing on her mind.

Aunt Constance was a character straight out of the dusty old books she always had in her lap. She worshipped Tennessee Williams, Charles Dickens, and Shirley Jackson and their Gothic stories about madness, abandonment, and melancholy. Ava knew these works well because, at her best, Aunt Constance would dramatically retell them from memory while her niece recovered from her injuries on a threadbare fainting couch in the parlor. At her worst, Constance would forget who Ava was, calling her by the wrong name and accusing her of plotting against Constance. She'd laugh or cry uncontrollably, wandering the house in ratty nightgowns with her wild maroon hair calling out for people and pets long gone. Sometimes, she would have brief moments of clarity in which she recognized Ava and took care of her, but most often, she was trapped in her own distorted reality of dueling paranoia and childlike innocence.

The unpredictability of Constance terrified Ava.

The white paint on the weather-beaten planks is nearly all chipped away. The front door hasn't fared much better. Ava shudders as she pulls back the enormous pure-brass knocker and releases it. The heavy ring through the mouth of a menacing lion is hot to the touch. She couldn't reach it when she was last here without standing on tippy-toes. Now she's eye to eye with the wild face and is struck by how innocuous it is. Her chest aches from the anxiety.

The windows along the front of the house are grimy with pollen and dirt, and the curtains are closed. She knocks again. Have they traveled all this way to find the house empty, her aunt long dead or institutionalized? This sinking realization is at odds with the rising emotion of relief. Isn't it time to call this thing off anyway?

Ava remembers something, checks her watch, and heads down the porch steps. She walks through the overgrown, parched grass toward the side of the house, her gaze fixed on the car. A temporary cloud-covered sun allows good visibility into the parked vehicle; Hazel and Kagan talk animatedly, and Ava gathers that they're arguing. Ava has observed a pattern with the siblings. She doesn't know if the power struggle for alpha status between them is exclusive to her presence, but they've been ceaselessly competing for the spotlight and stepping on each other's toes trying to get there. Ava worries that her impulsivity last night in going to Kagan's room will present problems, but if she'd learned nothing else from her father, people are easier to control when enthralled. The sex was useful because she needed to escape her feelings, and he did too. Grinding their emotions away made for good friction. But he might have gotten the wrong end of things by thinking her pop-in was more than it was. She allowed herself a night in his bed because she knew there was no chance of falling for Kagan. However, something he'd told Ava afterward had troubled her all morning. Despite her attempt to shut down any conversation, he spoiled the moment by speaking.

They've stopped bickering and are watching her from the car. She gives them a little wave, and Kagan gives her finger guns. She nods and smiles, fighting the urge to roll her eyes. Hazel's head is down. She is undoubtedly soothing herself with her avatar.

Ava hears the sound of a boat horn and wonders if she knows the owner. By the time she'd healed enough to get up and walk around, her burns were improving. In a moment of clarity, Aunt Constance sent her into town to see a doctor, who cleared her to remove the back brace and encouraged her to be more active. He insisted Ava see him every week to check her progress. This standing appointment led to

Ava getting out of the house, a reprieve from Constance and an opportunity to explore the island.

The doctor's son occasionally hung around the office and invited her to the marina one day, which became a weekly routine after her appointments. When the locals found out whom she was staying with, they embraced her, giving her odd jobs like delivering lunch to dockworkers, assisting tourists on day trips, teaching her about boats and sailing, and inviting her for family dinners. Years later, she realized these kindhearted people had felt bad for her. She never told anyone that she was leaving or stayed in touch, but she also never forgot their grace.

Ava creeps around the side of the house, past the battered tennis courts and through the thicket, and is shocked at how unkempt the property is. Aside from her gardening, few things made the older woman smile, and now, in place of her prized oleander and hydrangeas is a gnarled sea of Spanish moss and dog fennel.

When Ava wasn't able to avoid her aunt, she tried to make the best of it. It was a fascinating spectacle watching her move around the property, relying solely on her other senses to dig in the dirt and tend to her plants. As much as Ava feared her mood swings, watching her work away in the soil was enthralling. Aunt Constance would hold things close to her nose to identify them, singing to herself as the sun beat down on her giant straw hat. But she moved with such ease most of the time. Ava wondered if the woman was truly sightless or had created the disability out of self-protection. She'd seen so many terrible things; Ava understood if she'd rather be blind.

Sometimes, Constance would make Ava kneel beside her and prattle on for hours in the heat about each of the plants they were tending to or the ones around the property. Some of the trees and flowering bushes were ten times older than Ava was, and Constance loved to muse about the things the ancestral trees had witnessed. It surprised Ava how much she remembered those impromptu horticulture lectures. When outdoors, Ava would have to wear high-necked shirts and one of Constance's large hats to protect her burns. The muggy heat made her sweat, and the perspiration irritated delicate skin, still healing and concealed under bandages. Even with her dementia, Constance was sensitive to Ava's injuries. She would harvest her giant aloe plant in the kitchen and squeeze the jelly into her niece's palm, encouraging her to apply it to her neck and hands.

Before bed, her aunt would have her roll fresh peppermint between her hands to release the spicy oil and apply it on her wrists and philtrum, explaining that the menthol would trick her body into feeling cooler. And it worked; her daily searing sensations would decrease noticeably. This ritual prompted Ava's nickname, "Peppermint Patty," which she didn't love but pretended to like to keep her aunt happy.

The flower beds have disappeared, and Ava has to navigate through denser areas where overgrowth has created a tangled web of moss, leaves, and thorns. As she reaches the back of the house, she spots Aunt Constance's silhouette beneath the enormous oak tree, where she always sits this time of day. Constance's aging is evident from her wilting posture. Her once deep burgundy hair now appears clownishly red, dyed to cover white hair instead of her natural dark brown. Ava approaches slowly, taking a wide berth and coming from the side to avoid startling her aunt.

"I wondered when you'd show up." Constance's throatiness hasn't changed.

Ava immediately feels sick and doesn't move. "You did?"

She nods. "I've been waiting for a very long time."

With her back to Ava, Constance faces three small gravestones a few feet before her. She is wearing her hallmark oversize dark glasses, to conceal her milky irises.

She doesn't know how Constance knew she was coming but recalculates her approach.

"I'm sorry I kept you waiting," Ava says, looking over her shoulder, half expecting her father to emerge from the house.

"Well, since it took you so long, I already took care of it myself. Mother will be very pleased with my good work," Constance boasts.

Ava feels the oxygen returning to her brain and extremities. With all the memories of her aunt, she still hadn't accounted for her warped sense of time. She hasn't been waiting for Ava. Whoever Constance thinks she is is likely long dead and buried.

Ava calls on her eleven-year-old self, who used to be able to navigate Constance's confusion. Aunt Constance spoke like a Lewis Carroll character, even at her most lucid, and Ava had to learn to speak her surreal language, often having to solve riddles for the most basic information. She'd gotten so used to it by the end of their summer together that it had taken some adjusting when she was back with her plainspoken father.

"I'm sure your mother will be very impressed," she says.

Constance turns her head and grins at Ava.

"Do you know if Jack is here?" Ava asks, realizing how tricky her father's many aliases and her aunt's scrambled name recall could be.

Ava can see her aunt's posture change slightly.

Constance smooths the fabric of her skirt. "Jack, be nimble, Jack be quick."

"How about Perry? Is he here?"

Her aunt cocks her head to the side and starts to sing quietly,

I had four brothers over the sea,
Perry Merry Dictum Dominee;
And they each sent a present unto me.
The first sent me cherries without any stones. . . .
The second sent a chicken without any bones. . . .
The third sent a blanket that had no thread. . . .
The fourth sent a book that could not be read. . . .

When she finishes, Constance becomes still again. It was foolish for Ava to come here. She wouldn't break her brother's confidence even if she knew where he was. Maybe she didn't come here to find her father. She came to confront one of the monsters from her past.

Unmoving, Constance looks like a waxwork sitting on the cracked bench as a gentle, hot breeze ruffles the dried weeds on the gravesites. A new headstone has appeared since Ava was last here. The small stone shows the name Archie and a paw imprint. As a child, Ava always wondered if Constance's dead husband was interred in one of these graves.

"I'm sorry for bothering you; I've made a mistake," Ava says, losing her nerve.

Constance stands more spryly than expected. She moves her cane from its spot on the bench to the ground. Age appears to be compressing her; she is about a foot shorter than Ava remembers and thinner.

Ava is humbled by the frail appearance of the woman and how utterly harmless she seems now. "Nothing that has ever happened will happen in the future," Constance says cryptically.

"I think you're the only one who can help me."

Constance smiles. Ava can see a glimmer of something.

"I've been hoping you'd come," she replies.

She remembers how Aunt Constance regressed when her brother

showed up to take Ava back. Her behavior was at odds with her age; she idolized and feared him. It was the perfect mix of what Ava's father wanted in people. Ava knew she needed to tap into the fear to get what she needed.

"I have a package for your brother."

Her aunt stiffens. Ava contemplates the possibility that Constance might have been more aware than she let on, leveraging her apparent confusion to divert her brother's attention.

"Do you know where he is?" Ava asks sweetly.

"Where have you been? I've wondered."

"Don't you want to be a good girl and help?" Ava asks in a child-friendly tone.

"I want to be helpful," she says innocently.

"He'll be so happy with you if you are."

Constance looks at the sky. "He took the flowers to the pink tower for happily ever after."

Ava realizes she hasn't factored in how far gone her aunt would be. At this rate she won't be able to track her father down. Maybe it was foolish to think she could. She looks around the emaciated garden. This trip wasn't all for naught. The fear of Aunt Constance has dissipated after seeing her in real life.

"Thank you for everything," she says. "You've helped me."

Constance sits back down on the bench under the tree and starts singing again. Ava turns to leave until she hears the lyrics.

My name is Peppermint Patty, and I lost my daddy
And this is how my story goes
He ran away to the pink tower
To marry a beautiful flower
And now I'm chasing a ghost

An unsettling smile lingers on Constance's face.

Ava walks quickly to the car, haunted by something chasing her. She allows herself a glance over her shoulder, but only her aunt and the house are behind her.

Ava slides into the car. "I know where he is, and he's not alone."

PART
III

CHAPTER 30

Walt Pierson stands beneath the massive chandelier inside the Dunes Ballroom at the Beach Club at the Boca Raton, the blue of the carpet humming beneath his feet as the blessedly cool air circulates through the room, his linen shirt not clinging uncomfortably to his skin for the first time today. His fiancée, Iris, looks to Walt, slightly befuddled, white curls of hair brushing the shoulders of the floral-print chiffon dress that casually drapes her slim figure. Esteban, the couple's wedding coordinator, tugs at the cuff of his blazer as he consults notes in a binder. He smiles at the pair.

"This really is a dream come true." Iris plants a kiss on Walt's cheek and lets out a jubilant squeal as she takes in the room. Walt works hard to keep his lunch from coming up. "Esteban, we're so looking forward to Saturday."

"And I'm excited to help make your big day as special as can be!"

"We're so delighted to have you! Though I have to admit, I do feel a bit guilty about such an indulgence."

The wedding coordinator crinkles his brow. "How do you mean?"

"I'm not sure if my fiancé's told you," says Iris, "but we're having a small, very informal ceremony. Just the two of us and an officiant." Walt delighted in how quickly she agreed to the idea. He'd convinced Iris that the sense of intimacy would make it all the more special.

"Oh, don't you worry one little bit about that." Esteban pats her hand reassuringly. "I'm here to make sure the flowers look fabulous, the music goes off without a hitch, and there's a cocktail waiting for you at the end, to toast your love."

"Bless you, young man."

"And tell me, how did the two of you first meet?"

"Bird-watching in Central Park." Iris slips her arm through Walt's and pulls him close. "It was springtime in New York City. My favorite season there. I was relatively new to birding, having only taken it up earlier that year on the recommendation of a friend. I'd gravitated to an area in the park where there seemed to be a lot of activity." Iris sure loved to include the play-by-play like it was a goddamn movie scene. As if this guy gave a shit about any of it and wasn't just going through the professional motions. "One particular morning, I saw this tall drink of water sitting on my usual bench with a pair of binoculars, watching the action.

"He invited me to join him and pointed out a mourning warbler he'd spotted. The bird was partially camouflaged in the tree, and Walt was so patient, helping me locate it through my binoculars. Then he gave me some background about the species, and how rare they were, and how special it was to see one. There was this wonderful whimsy in Walt's voice as he spoke and a gleam in his eye. Not to sound crazy, but I almost felt like he was talking about this chance meeting between us. Like it was fated. There was a hint of magic to the whole thing."

"So romantic!"

"We got to talking, and he was very attentive and inquisitive. I felt engaged in a way I hadn't in so long . He mentioned that he'd taken up birding after losing his wife several months prior. It was very disarming, the way he shared. So vulnerable. We really bonded over that." She gazes lovingly at Walt. "I don't know that either of us was looking for anything, exactly, but love finds a way."

"It certainly does," agrees Esteban. "And what marriage will this be for you both?"

"Second for my Walty." Iris blushes. "And lucky number three for myself. I like to think of those first two as trial runs, though I shouldn't complain. They left me very comfortable."

This was one hell of an understatement. As Walt had gleaned through his conversations with Iris, she was sitting on a veritable fortune. The woman hailed from the sort of background where money was neither intimidating nor the main motivator in any potential relationship. And due in part to this comfortableness around wealth, Iris managed to land herself a couple of well-to-do husbands.

The first was the sole heir to a vast pet food fortune. A charming playboy, ready to settle down. A few years into the marriage, after Iris had failed to produce any offspring, the brute unceremoniously announced his intention to end things, but not before offering up a handsome settlement. Husband number two was the CFO of one of the big banks. Also charming, if occasionally volatile. Somewhere past the five-year mark, the guy had grown to enjoy his after-office extracurriculars more than his home life. He, too, sent Iris out the door armed with a generous sum.

The money was a nice concession, but Iris had married for what she considered at the time to be love. A true romantic, now swimming in an ocean of dough. Just the kind of woman Walt Pierson could see things through to the end with.

"How fortunate for you." Esteban claps his hands together. "And now you've finally found your person. What was it that brought you two lovebirds down to sunny Florida?"

"Well, Walt and I each adored New York while we were there. Lots of great years and fond memories. And a few painful ones as well." She squeezes his arm. "So we were both ready for a fresh start. A slower pace, some time to unwind and really *be* with each other. And Walt's discovered a lovely place for us to live, just as soon as we're back from our honeymoon."

"Wonderful. And where will you be spending it?"

"I'm surprising my bride-to-be," Walt chimes in.

"How enchanting!"

"And Esteban," says Iris, "I have to tell you, this week is something of a homecoming for me. I used to vacation at this very hotel with my parents when I was a little girl."

"You don't say."

"It's true. In fact . . ." The blush returns to Iris's cheeks.

"What is it?" he asks, tilting his head inquisitively.

"This is going to sound so silly, but at the time I dreamed of walking down the aisle right here, at the Boca Raton. Of course, I was convinced it would be arm in arm with James Dean. But I'm glad I held out."

"Oh, my goodness! How sweet." The kid can hardly contain himself.

"Isn't it?! My knight in shining armor finally showed up, just in time to whisk me away."

"Just in time, indeed." Esteban holds a grin in place as he slips the binder from beneath his arm, flips it open, and consults his notes. "And you mentioned it'll be the two of you, correct? No family attending the ceremony?"

"Mine are all passed." A melancholic cloud settles over the conversation as Iris speaks. "Walt's, too, I'm afraid."

Walt summons the waterworks and clears his throat. Iris slips her arm from his and fully embraces her fiancé.

"Are you okay?" asks Esteban.

"I'm sorry." Walt lets a tear escape before wiping it away and pulling himself together. "It's just . . ." He sniffles. "I only wish my daughter could be here, to meet the wonderful woman I've found and to share our special day. Together. As a real family."

"Oh, honey." Iris attends to Walt before turning to the coordinator. "Walt's daughter, Ava, passed away tragically in a horrific fire many years ago. It's still so hard for him, each and every day."

"I'm so sorry." Esteban brings a hand to his chest. "I'm sure wherever she is, she's smiling down on you."

"Thank you, young man." Walt musters a smile. "I have to believe you're right about that." He wonders momentarily what's become of that precocious young girl he'd helped wise up to the ways of the world. They'd made a good team once upon a time, before his own flesh and blood had up and abandoned him. And she may as well have been dead after pulling a stunt like that.

"Well, listen," says Esteban, the buoyancy returned to his tone, "we're going to make this day magical for the two of you. It'll be the wedding of your dreams, I promise."

"Ah," says Walt, "we can hardly wait." It was all so close to happening for him. And this time it would be for good.

CHAPTER 31

The pink tower of the Boca Raton hotel, with its Mediterranean Revival and Spanish Colonial architecture, is visible through the lobby's large windows, giving the space an airy, open-air feel. Its iconic structure also appears in gold embossing on the cocktail napkin magnified under Hazel's glass of cucumber water.

Megan, the woman behind the check-in desk, is being held hostage by the audacious woman who pushed in front of Hazel. She is going through a litany of demands while her identical twins run figure eights around Hazel and scream at the top of their lungs. Hazel tries to keep herself as still as possible, though she is agitated. She's a sitting duck; every minute standing here is one closer to getting spotted by Perry.

One of the pigtailed girls stares at Hazel strangely every time she makes a loop. Finally, she stops chasing her sister, halts in front of Hazel, and sticks her little hands on her hips.

"Why are you so ugly?" she asks in a spitty lisp.

"Excuse me?" Hazel replies.

"Your face looks so weird." The other little girl has stopped, too, and the two of them are staring up at Hazel and laughing through the gaps in their teeth.

"Yeah," her sister chimes in, "you have a dog face!" The girls scream with laughter.

Hazel drops the smile. "If you don't have anything nice to say, you shouldn't—"

"Don't talk to my children," their line-cutting mother hisses, finally paying attention to them. She huddles her demon spawn on either side of her and turns back to torturing the desk clerk.

"I am tired of asking for extra towels and not getting them fast enough, our room service has been subpar and tepid, and the water pressure in our rooms is abysmal. Say my name back to me so you remember me."

"Marilyn McGunthrie, suite sixteen oh five," the woman behind the desk repeats through a clenched smile.

Hazel sees Ava standing a few feet away. She wears a similarly outraged expression. Hazel waves her over, but Kagan walks up and leans in to whisper something. They walk over to a giant palm and step out of sight. She assumes this is in case Perry walks through the lobby, ruining the only thing they have in their favor right now: the element of surprise.

Hazel withdraws a compact from her bag and sees dark rivulets of mascara and eyeliner streaking her cheeks. Her lipstick has bled past her natural lip line, and she understands why the girls were negging her. The humidity is melting her makeup, and she looks like the Joker. Hazel blots away as much as she can and puts on sunglasses.

Marilyn McGunthrie finally finishes haranguing the woman at the desk and shepherds the bad seeds away. Hazel smiles at Megan, her gold-plated nametag shining from the many ornate light fixtures suspended above. Hazel hopes Marilyn's horrendous behavior has primed Megan's appreciation for Hazel's markedly better attitude. Maybe she'll even get an upgrade for being nicer.

"Good afternoon, checking in?" she says with a trace of friendliness left in her voice.

"Yes, checking in for Patricia Devlin."

"I see three rooms under that name."

There were no side negotiations about the sleeping arrangements. Everyone is getting their own bed. The hotel is enormous, with over a thousand rooms, and they reserved the least expensive ones to lessen their chances of being in the same section as Perry. Even then, the nightly rate was more than she and Kagan had in the bank combined. They are officially running out of money. Apparently, revenge is a luxury experience. They'd had to come clean to Ava that they were running out of funds after their stop at her aunt's, and she'd taken it surprisingly well, reassuring them that they'd be fine.

"I'll need a license and a credit card for incidentals," Megan says with forced brightness. Hazel steadies her hand as she passes over the fake credentials and Amex from Ava and looks away from Megan as she scans the license and runs the card. After Aunt Constance's house, they'd stopped at a diner across from a long-term self-storage facility. Ava instructed Kagan and Hazel to sit tight over their all-day breakfasts while she took the car and stopped at the storage place without much explanation. She was gone over an hour before Hazel started to worry.

"She could ditch us here, and we'd be stranded in some bumblefuck backwater town."

"Ava's not like that, Hazel. We've already been through too much for her to do that."

The "we" had felt woundingly exclusive.

When Ava returned to the diner, she handed Hazel a Coach wallet containing three credit cards and a driver's license for Patricia Devlin, a woman ten years older than Hazel but with the same hair and eye color.

She handed Kagan a billfold with a driver's license and credit cards for Matt Devlin. He had at least fifty pounds on Kagan but was another generic, decent-looking white guy.

"We look nothing like these people," Hazel pointed out.

"They'll look at the name to match the cards. Just don't hand them to any cops."

Kagan immediately wanted to know if the cards worked. Hazel asked if they were stolen.

"Use them only at the hotel. And the less you know, the better."

This exchange excited Hazel. Their time with Ava increasingly resembled a heist movie, a welcome shift from the horror drama it had been up to this point. While Hazel had engaged in some petty crimes as a teenager, like shoplifting small items from drugstores and skipping out on the bill with friends, this adventure felt thrillingly next level.

Ava instructed Hazel to check in when they arrived at the hotel. Hazel assumed it had something to do with Kagan's erratic energy. He had disappeared around the back of the diner for about twenty minutes "for a smoke" while Ava was on her secret storage stop, and Hazel suspected Kagan had found a hookup based on his changed mood when he returned. She wasn't clear on where her brother was getting cash for party favors, but asking him was futile, and she was tired of fighting with him.

The lobby is bustling with guests in brightly colored beachwear with frosty drinks in hand.

"Can you ensure two rooms are adjoining and the third is on a different floor?"

Those were Ava's instructions, and Hazel hopes the adjacent rooms are for the two of them, to get back some of the quality bonding time she and Ava missed. "And is there an upgrade available?"

Megan types away while Hazel tries not to look around the lobby too much. The threat of Perry appearing at any moment has all their nerves up, but Hazel feels like the sacrificial lamb out here while Kagan and Ava are cozily out of view.

"Here you go, Mrs. Devlin. Three of our single garden-view king bedrooms."

She is annoyed they haven't been upgraded to oceanside and tired of second-class travel.

Megan nods at the suitcases next to Hazel. "Did you need a bellhop for your luggage?"

"Yes, please."

After a bellman wheels their luggage away, Hazel walks toward the palm, which now stands alone. After an increasingly irritating twenty minutes, she drifts outside into the blaring sun and surveys the luxury cars coming through the valet station, an army of luggage racks and families streaming into the airy entranceway. In another version, this could be the beginning of a great trip. But the warm, clear Floridian afternoon is spoiled by Hazel's hot frustration with each passing minute that her brother and Ava are missing.

A quick wolf whistle turns a few heads around her. Hazel spins toward the lobby and spots them. Ava looks stunning in a sleeveless patterned dress, her scarred neck and shoulders exposed in the bright sun. By her side, she holds a peach wide-brimmed beach hat. Kagan has a large ivory shopping bag with the Boca Raton Beach Club emblem and gold-and-white braided handles.

"You guys went shopping?" Hazel asks, stung by the exclusion.

Ava puts a warm hand on her elbow before gently pulling the ponytail holder from Hazel's hair and sliding it off. When her hair cascades down, Ava places the sun hat onto Hazel's head and smiles. Hazel's stomach flips with the sweetness of the gesture.

"Ah, that looks great," she tells Hazel. Ava takes the bag from Kagan and hands it to her. "We got you some things from the hotel boutique to blend in. I noticed that all the clothes you packed were black."

Hazel peeks into the tissue paper–wrapped contents and sees brightly colored patterned silk and gauze. Her irritation subsides significantly.

"There are some sarongs and a couple of dresses for dinners, a swimsuit, and some sandals. I guessed your size," Ava says. "We can pick up some more as we need it."

"Thanks," she says as she looks through the swag, surprised by the gifts. "I didn't think we'd do much swimming or dining out."

"We're undercover. We have to blend," Kagan says.

"Not to be ungrateful, but we can't afford this stuff."

"We didn't buy these; Marilyn McGunthrie in suite sixteen oh five did."

Hazel gawks. "Are you serious?"

Kagan nods, pleased with himself. Hazel is too. *Fuck you, Marilyn.*

"Let's talk more in one of our rooms." Ava pushes them inside the entrance.

The trio walks toward the elevator bank and hangs back as a group of college kids jams into an available car. Hazel flinches when the doors open again, quickly letting a straggler friend dart by her and squeeze in.

"Don't look so conspicuous, Haze," Kagan says.

Hazel clocks the goofy smile on his face, jaw grinding.

"Why don't you worry about yourself?"

Another car opens, and Hazel is relieved to see it's empty. Ava looks at all the key-card sleeves and presses the twelfth-floor button. "Great, they had adjoining rooms."

Hazel's heart skips.

"This will make it so much simpler for the two of you to come and go from the same door," Ava finishes.

"Excuse me?" Hazel feels behind again until she sees Kagan's matching bewildered look.

"It must appear like you guys are staying in the same room. It's a critical part of the plan."

When the doors open, and they find 1212 and 1213, Ava swipes the corresponding key card, and with a click, they're in.

Ava immediately opens her laptop. She has an intense look of determination as her fingers sail across the keyboard. Hazel watches her silently from the other side of the room while Kagan paces before the window. Ava is impervious to his motion, but Hazel throws a pillow at him.

"Quit it."

He glares at her but takes a seat and communes with his phone.

After ten minutes of tense silence, Ava pushes her computer away and acknowledges the siblings.

"So here's the plan," she starts. "My father is here under the name Walt Pierson; his mark is Iris Garrett. They checked in yesterday afternoon, and they're here for five days. They are doing a wedding package and having a small ceremony in three days."

Kagan and Hazel look at each other, impressed.

"How did you do that?" Hazel asks, wide-eyed.

"I hacked the hotel's database and looked through the guest roster for the honeymoon suites and VIP rooms. Knowing my father, he'll go for the most expensive suite in the place or the next-best one available.

Sure enough, there was a booking for a Walt Pierson in the four-bedroom cloister suite."

"So what do we do now?" asks Kagan. "I'm ready to nail this fucking guy to the wall."

"Me too," Hazel agrees.

Ava looks between them, her face serious. "I know this has been a team effort up to this point, and that's been fine. But you guys hired me, so you need to step back and let me call the shots from here on out. Can you do that?"

"Yeah, sure," Kagan replies.

Hazel nods. "Okay, but can you tell us the plan? What is our part?"

"Look, the truth is, I could just hack their bank accounts right now and get your money back and then some. I don't even need you guys here," Ava says gently.

Hazel feels insulted, and judging by Kagan's slumped shoulders, he does too.

"Okay," Hazel responds.

"But it occurred to me that taking him down a few notches would be a lot more gratifying."

"Fuck yeah," Kagan yells.

"I figured you'd feel that way. So the plan is to destabilize 'Walt' at the most critical part of his operation. Right now, he's resting on his laurels, feeling like he's in the last few days of locking this one down and getting access to everything this woman owns. Let's force him to juggle his past life with his present."

Hazel vibrates excitedly. "Yes! How are we going to do that?"

"Patricia and Matt Devlin will become Iris Garrett's new best friends."

"No offense, Ava, but that seems kind of boring. Maybe I should sweet-talk this old gal and steal Walt's broad from under him? Older ladies have always had a thing for me."

Hazel rolls her eyes.

"Kagan, honey." Ava pats his arm, and he beams. Hazel burns from the inside with jealousy. "Patricia and Matt are here celebrating their fifth wedding anniversary, which happens to be the same day Walt and Iris are getting married, right here in the hotel. The coincidence is too perfect. So, Hazel, charm your way into her good graces."

"Do we have to be a married couple? Really? I know this is Florida, but I mean, yuck." Hazel gags.

Ava shoots her an impatient look. "You guys don't have to make out. Just convince people that you're married."

"So bicker in public and eat in silence—we can do that," Kagan quips.

"I think this will be an excellent relationship-building exercise for you both."

"Okay, tell me what to do," Hazel says with a forced brightness.

Ava pulls the laptop closer, clicks a few times, and refers to the screen. "Iris is booked at the spa for a royal ritual bath at ten a.m." Ava types quickly. "You're also booked for a royal ritual bath at ten a.m. Then a facial, a vaginal steam, and a massage, same as her. You will meet cute in the dressing room and have a relaxing day of pampering together."

"And what will I be doing, in lieu of a vaginal steam?" Kagan cracks up.

"You will be on call if either of us needs backup," Ava says. "Stay sharp. Stick to water."

"You just booked all that from your laptop?" Hazels asks.

Ava nods. "I can do a lot more than that."

The TV comes on, and the pay-per-view menu scrolls without anyone touching the remote. The lights dim, and the AC kicks on.

"What would you guys like to watch this evening?"

"You can control our TV from your computer?" Hazel laughs.

"I can control everybody's TV from my computer. And the lights, the AC, room service orders, the bills . . . ," she says.

"Really?"

"I'll wipe everything off Patricia and Matt Devlin's tab when we check out. But don't draw attention to yourselves."

Hazel can see her brother fantasizing about the open bars waiting for him.

"And what will you be doing?" Kagan asks.

"I'm going to spend the afternoon with dear old Dad."

CHAPTER 32

M att?"

The sound of a woman's voice bleeding across the pool deck plucks Kagan from his daydream. He's been basking on a lounger sipping a piña colada as he enjoys some decidedly impure thoughts about Ava. Kagan was temporarily stung by her disadvantageous maneuvering of the room arrangements, but now realizes it was sound strategy. The three of them need to operate as a team over these next several days if they're going to bring down Walt Pierson, and any fracture in their group dynamic might jeopardize the plan—and their money.

"Matt? Honey?"

In retrospect, Kagan's feeling a little silly about the whole thing. He was practically bragging to his sister about the sexual tension brewing between himself and Ava, not considering the damage it could do to their mission if Haze slips into feeling like a third wheel. She'd been sulkier than usual on their road trip, likely a reaction to the heat that's continued to build in the wake of the stealth liaison three nights ago.

So of course Ava had erred on the side of diplomacy, in the interest of restoring balance. Always thinking, that one.

"Matt!"

Kagan jolts upright as he realizes the voice belongs to his sister, and that she's addressing him. The fog of lust put the alias he's supposed to be operating under out of his mind. He stands as Hazel approaches with the older woman in tow. She radiates a carefree spirit and wears a caftan in a pattern that so deftly walks the tightrope between elegant and garish as to suggest an obscenely steep price tag.

"You're not going deaf on me already, are you?" Hazel brushes his cheek with a kiss.

"Sorry, babe." *God, this is going to be tough.* "I guess you should have booked me an appointment for an ear candling while you were at it. How was your spa day?"

"Let me introduce you to the best part. Matt, meet my new friend, Iris Garrett." Haze seemed to be handling this phase of the operation quite effortlessly. "Iris and her fiancé are also from New York."

"You don't say." Kagan takes Iris's hand in his and gently kisses it. "Nice to meet a fellow northerner. What a small world."

"Well, technically, I'm a Montana gal. Grew up on a cattle ranch near Billings before I made my escape to the big city."

"How rustic!" Kagan lifts a finger to flag down the cabana boy. "I was just about to refresh my glass. And what are *you* drinking, Iris Garrett from Billings, Montana?"

"Why, chivalry lives! I'd adore a margarita."

"Honey." Hazel clears her throat. "Are you pacing yourself? You know how you get, lying out in the sun all day."

"Oh, Patricia, let the young man have a little fun." Iris languidly swats the air between them, then breaks into an impish grin, endearing herself to Kagan. "Gosh knows we've had ours."

"Sounds like a well-deserved day of pampering." Kagan prays he can avoid learning the finer details of vaginal steaming at any point in this conversation. The kid working poolside approaches and takes their drink order before booking it back to the bar.

"The massage was simply divine!" crows Iris.

"How marvelous! Ladies, shall we take a load off? I'd love to hear some more about our new friend."

The trio makes themselves comfortable on the loungers. Iris fans her face with a hand as she blows out a labored breath. Hazel subtly mirrors the older woman.

"Matt, honey. You won't believe this, but just guess when Iris and her fiancé are getting married."

Kagan's hit with a shot of panic. He's not sure if guessing correctly will seem intuitive or suspicious. "Uh, this weekend?"

"Well, yes. But more specifically, on our anniversary."

"Oh, wow. What a coincidence."

"I can hardly wait." Iris trembles with excitement. "I'm so smitten with my Walt, and the whole weekend is just coming together so perfectly. We're only having a modest ceremony, but it's going to be so intimate and romantic."

"Your fella sounds like a regular Romeo." Kagan grits his teeth. "How did you two meet?"

"One fateful day, both of us bird-watching in Central Park. We got to talking, and the hours simply flew by. I knew he was the one for me, right then and there."

"You had a lot in common, eh?"

"Walt was just so attentive and interested, asking questions and wanting to really learn everything about me."

"I bet," mumbles Kagan. He catches a glare from his sister.

"I'm sorry?"

"Oh, I just meant that he sounds like a real catch."

Iris turns to Hazel. "Not always the case with the menfolk, am I right?" Hazel snickers in agreement, and Iris directs her attention back to Kagan. "Present company excluded, of course. But it was just so nice to have someone who seemed truly invested in knowing who I was. And so comfortable in who *he* is. I've been married twice before, and between us, both husbands ended up not being at all who I'd thought they were."

The comment catches Kagan off guard, and he falls into a coughing fit. "So sorry," he hacks. "Just a bit parched. Where's the cabana boy with those drinks?"

"Matt, dear, are you okay?" Iris displays a show of concern that touches Kagan. It suddenly feels like forever since he's been the recipient of this sort of warmth.

"Fine, I'm fine." He waves her off and clears his throat as Hazel shoots him a look so acidic it could strip paint. "Just making a spectacle of myself. Anyway, where were we? Oh, yes, your fiancé. Walt, you said his name was?"

"That's right."

"And has Walt ever been married?"

"Just once. He lost his wife several months before we met, in fact. He was still grieving at the time, but I'd like to think I helped him get through some of the rough patch."

"I see." Kagan feels his stomach churning and has to temper his tone. "And when exactly did you two meet?"

"This past spring. His wife had passed the fall prior, and he'd endured a very lonely winter, by the sounds of it." Iris frowns as Kagan works out the timetable and quietly seethes. "My poor guy."

"So a whirlwind romance for the two of you, then." Kagan catches the edge to the comment as it escapes his mouth and immediately regrets it. His sister looks as if she's on the verge of an aneurysm, though Iris herself seems unbothered.

"I suppose it is, but at my age, sometimes you just have to take a chance on love. Throw caution to the wind and all those silly clichés. Walt's really encouraged me to lean into my spontaneous side, and it's opened me up to a whole new perspective. I'm so thankful."

The young man approaches the group with a tray of drinks. He sets a sauvignon blanc on the table beside Hazel, then the margarita next to Iris, and another piña colada by Kagan.

"Thank you, Rafael." Iris offers the kid a genuine smile, and Kagan's left baffled as to how she knows his name, sans tag. As he retreats to attend to the next customers, she sets a hand on Hazel's shoulder. "Well, that's quite enough about me. Patricia, tell me a bit about how you and Matt . . . Now, wait a minute. I just realized, Pat and Matt. Isn't that just adorable."

"Yeah," says Hazel, "we try to avoid shortening mine, honestly. Makes us sound like brother and sister or something."

A little close to home with that one, Haze, Kagan thinks, but Iris snorts as if it's the funniest thought under the Florida sun before raising her glass. "A toast to love, both old and new. Happy anniversary, you two."

"And congratulations to you and Walt."

They clink glasses and quietly enjoy sips of their drinks. Kagan's eye is wrangled by a leggy brunette in a metallic-silver bikini positioned across the deck in full recline, skin glistening, pouty lips peeking out from beneath the brim of the sun hat she's—

"So tell me how you young lovebirds met."

Fuck. After they'd split from Ava and settled into their rooms, the siblings had followed her instructions and done their due diligence in researching Iris. They'd forgotten, however, to hammer out an origin story for their own supposed relationship.

"Um, well, Iris, that's a funny one. And, honestly, I think Patricia tells it much better."

Kagan watches as his sister does her best to tamp down the sudden feeling of panic that's apparently churning inside both of them. "Oh, honey, don't be so modest," she says. "You're such a gifted narrator. You should really take it."

"You flatter me, sweetheart." Kagan tosses a grin Iris's way as he mentally spins through the info they'd gleaned from the Google search: *Iris Garrett, socialite, philanthropist, on the board of the Met museum, also Scholastic, big proponent of the arts in education.* . . . "So, Iris, Patricia and I met as volunteers for this after-school program we'd both signed up for, out in Brooklyn." Years ago, he'd been hooking up with some chick at one of his old jobs. She'd been a volunteer with one of these organizations and would constantly yammer on about it. He now gropes around for any details he can drop into this story. "Uh, there was a big creative-writing component, which is actually what drew me in. And the space had a superhero theme and, like, a secret door to the classroom. The kids went bonkers for it."

"Oh, how wonderful!" Iris holds the cool glass to her chest. "Volunteering is so dear to my heart, Matt."

"Ours too, for sure. A life of service is a life well lived." *Jesus, where the hell did he pull that one from?*

"I couldn't agree more." Ice cubes clink as Iris rolls the glass against her skin. "You know, when I was a young girl, I was something of a wallflower. Extremely shy. One Christmas, my favorite aunt got me an art set, and I just fell in love with drawing and painting. It was such a welcome escape from the awkwardness I felt around my peers, and it grew into a lifelong passion. How marvelous that you were both able to give a similar gift to those kids through your selflessness. Good on you."

"Oh, thank you," says Kagan before continuing the embellishment. "So—confession time—I'm pretty bad at math. Part of our volunteer days were spent assisting the kids with their homework, and I was pretty useless with anything past basic arithmetic. I was helping this kid out one day and got totally stumped, so I hit up Patricia here for a lifeline."

"And I was so impressed that he actually asked for help. You know how boys can be." Hazel and Iris trade a look. "So after the session that day, I waited around and gave him a chance to run into me on the way out the door."

Iris is aglow with the account of blossoming romance. She hangs on every word.

"Which is exactly what I did, quite literally. I was so nervous to talk to Patricia that I actually stepped short as I was approaching and stumbled right into her. Nearly knocked her to the ground. So embarrassing."

"Of course all the kids were laughing at him, but I have to say, Matt rebounded very smoothly."

"What did you do?" Iris asks, spellbound.

"Well, after we recovered from the near fall, I asked her if she always made men weak in the knees. She responded that she did so only in front of large audiences, and then I asked if we could try somewhere quieter for my next humiliation. She agreed, and I took her for a drink at a place down the street."

"He was so charming, and before I knew it, the sun had gone down and we were still gabbing away. We found a little café in the neighborhood for a late-night bite. He put me in a cab after and asked me to text when I made it home."

"She called instead, and we stayed on the phone for another hour. I took her out again a few nights later, and then the night after that, and a few months down the road we were shacked up together."

"Wow, that is just the most romantic thing I've ever heard." Iris clutches her chest and lets out a contented sigh. "You give me hope, you two." She glances at her watch, and a look of mild alarm sets in. She places her nearly empty drink onto the table and eases herself out of the recliner. "I'm frightfully sorry to do this, but I have to run. Walt's going to be back soon, and we've got early dinner plans. But we simply must get together again. What room are you staying in?"

Kagan blurts out "twelve twelve" at the same moment his sister announces "twelve thirteen." He quickly apologizes, tapping the side of his glass by way of explanation, and defers to Hazel.

"Twelve thirteen," concludes Iris. "Wonderful. I'll call up to the room tomorrow. In the meantime, thank you both for an exquisite afternoon." As she blows them kisses and shuffles off toward the entrance to the hotel, the siblings let go of relieved exhales.

"Man, Haze. I think we pulled it off."

"Yeah." She kills the last of her wine and sets the glass down. "Nice work, K."

Kagan's struck by a warming sense of nostalgia. The tale they just cobbled together on the fly reminds him of their childhood. With Charles's volatility keeping every member of the family on uneven terrain, the kids had gotten pretty good at riffing their way out of trouble, with one sibling regularly backing the other's play. There was something reassuring in the knowledge that those muscles hadn't entirely atrophied.

As the elation of the moment fades, a nauseated sensation sets in. Kagan feels the sourness climb his gullet.

"K, what's wrong?"

"You heard what Iris said before, about the timeline? I know I'm no math wiz, but even I can figure out that Mom was still very much alive when those two met."

Hazel's face drops. "The grieving widower act. It's like the son of a bitch already had half a mind to take her out. Like he saw the opportunity coming and seized it."

"Uh-huh." Kagan straightens up and turns to face his sister. He sets elbows on knees and leans toward Hazel, a renewed sense of vigor kicking in. "But if we play it right, he's not gonna see any of *this* coming."

CHAPTER 33

Ava spots him two steps out of the elevator, and her ears begin to ring. She's been casing the area all day, knowing he'd have to emerge eventually. His gait is the same, even with slight stiffness. She can't tell if he has placed a small pebble in his shoe for the character of "Walt," an old method acting trick, or if her father has finally succumbed to aging. She hopes the latter; he always believed you could buy youth like everything else if you had the money. Watching him from afar, she thinks he hasn't made enough.

Ava is startled by how strongly the ancient feelings resurface. The weight of the anger, resentment, and hatred slows her reflexes only momentarily until he glides past her without a glance. Her skin burns at his lack of response. It's not that she expected he would recognize her after all this time, but it's dawning on her now that part of her hoped he would. It feels cruel that she's having such a strong physical reaction to his presence when he hasn't even registered hers.

Ava brings herself out of the heat, a surprising rush of courage lengthening her body and rooting her feet. She moves to follow him, prepared for the moment of recognition that may throw this whole ruse into ruin. Maybe this is the point of her being here: to confront him, hear whatever horrible thing he'll undoubtedly say to her, stand her ground, and finally put this to rest. Emboldened, she removes her sunglasses and hat just as he stops a few feet before her. Ava steels herself, slides up next to him at the concierge, and catches his eye when he turns to her.

"Excuse me, sir? Do you know what time it is?"

Perry lifts his wrist, and she sees the Rolex, the gold catching the sunlight shining through the open entryway. "Certainly. It's half past three."

"Thank you," Ava says.

He glances at her face, and his eyes betray no flicker of recognition, no tremor of fear that she's returned. His eyes are empty.

"Absolutely," he replies, his attention shifting to the attractive concierge who's just finished assisting someone else.

Stunned, Ava slips away, overhearing him asking for directions. It's precisely where Ava predicted, and she's already instructed the valet to bring the car around, slipping him fifty bucks to ensure it's ready.

While Walt engages in small talk, Ava discreetly exits, nodding to the valet as she slides into the Audi. Pulling out of the turnaround, she activates her hazard lights, moving her head out of view from passing cars as she waits. A few minutes later, she observes Walt getting into his car. Ava accelerates to get ahead of him and onto the highway.

Watching Walt's conspicuous red Alfa Romeo in the rearview mirror, she maintains a perfectly legal sixty-five miles per hour along Route 1, with his car a few vehicles behind hers. Pleased with herself, she sees him pull into the Driftwood Diner parking lot moments after her, confirming her ability to anticipate his next moves. This small detail reinforces what she already knows: her father hasn't altered his routine in the years they've been apart. He remains a creature of habit, providing her an advantage over anyone else trying to pin him down.

Pulling around behind the diner while he secures his spot in front, Ava anticipates his desire to keep an eye on the car. It took her less than a minute to find the nearest diner on Google, and she knew by its cookie-cutter design that Walt would choose it over the hipper, higher-rated options in the other direction from the hotel in downtown Boca. The only predictable thing about her father was his penchant for finding local greasy spoons, no matter where or who he was.

Ava always hated these dime-a-dozen diners and had been inside more of them in the past few days with the siblings than she'd been in over the past two decades. She'd spent more of her young life sitting in uncomfortable, hard plastic booths, flipping through seat-side juke-boxes or hypnotized by dessert carousels than in school. But they were the one place where her father's demeanor was neutral, sometimes even kind. It was also his workspace, whether planning for a new mark or, as was the case now, putting the final touches on the grift. Once the siblings reported back about the state of Walt and Iris's relationship, Ava would have a clearer picture of what she was dealing with. Regardless, the days leading up to the wedding were crucial in Walt's timeline with his bride-to-be. He would likely be subtly manipulating the unfortunate lady, leaving her alone for extended periods, creating a sense of neediness in her. Perhaps he would even provoke some fights, maintaining the highs and lows and fostering a make-up, break-up dynamic, ensuring she wouldn't focus on her bank account. Ava couldn't help but feel sorry for this new woman, wondering whether it was worse to be neglected by her father before her wedding or to be befriended by Patricia and Matt Devlin.

Ava had been truthful with Hazel and Kagan—taking money from him would be easy. He would be preoccupied with maintaining appearances and engaging in behind-the-scenes maneuvers. She didn't necessarily need the siblings' presence for this task, but they needed to feel included. Ava wanted to help them gain power and agency over their healing process.

Ava was reluctant to admit it, but she was energized by the mission. It was a welcome change from her routine at the cave, dealing with government firewalls and enduring condescension from Eric Prince. Nevertheless, the antics of Hazel and Kagan could be grating as much as they were entertaining. Ava had received texts from both of them the previous night, each asking to visit her room for a talk. She ignored both, not wanting to complicate matters further.

As Walt crosses the parking lot into the diner, Ava pulls down the driver's side visor, anticipating he will choose a window booth. The overcast afternoon allows her a decent view of Walt's profile through the car window. Ava experiences a twinge of shame as she realizes she's deriving some childhood excitement from watching her father work. She learned the art of cons through observation and tutorials on his more talkative days. Ava received an unconventional education despite missing out on a traditional school experience.

She presses Sam's name on her phone, and he answers promptly.

"Waiting by the phone for my call?"

"I thought you were my Seamless guy." He chuckles. "But I'm glad to hear your voice. How's your Scooby-Doo Mystery Tour going?"

"It hasn't been boring," Ava replies.

"You don't sound like yourself," Sam says.

"I don't feel like myself."

"Is that a good thing?"

"I'm looking at him right now," Ava says seriously.

"Well, shit. No wonder. How do you feel?"

"Like I'm twelve years old again."

"I gather you aren't feeling the lightness of childhood innocence and wonder."

Ava laughs. "Sam, what am I doing here?"

"That was my question." He's momentarily quiet, and Ava watches her father's silhouette through the smudged glass.

"I think you are trying to answer the unanswerable."

"Deep, Sam."

"Why do you think you're there?" he asks gently.

"I thought it was because I needed a purpose. Now I'm not sure."

Sam exhales, and Ava senses the concern in the breath. "Want to come home? Before anything goes south?"

"Too late for that; I'm in Florida," Ava says. "And I need a favor."

He doesn't hesitate. "Anything."

"Thank you. I'll call again soon. Love you."

Sam doesn't reciprocate before disconnecting, as Ava knew he wouldn't.

While waiting for her father to finish, Ava delves into her findings from Iris's financials. Over the past year, there has been a series of in-bank cash deposits into the primary checking account, staying under the ten-thousand-dollar threshold that requires reporting to the IRS.

Ava knows that the recurring deposits are from Walt slowly siphoning money from Janice's accounts into Iris's. He would've told Iris that he needed to park the money in her accounts to shelter it from money-hungry relatives or some variation of that. This approach would have stabilized any worry that Walt was after her money if Iris saw how solvent he was and that he was willing to dump large amounts of money under her name. The bonus would be endearing Iris's sympathy around the fact that Walt had to cope with such a terrible experience settling his late wife's estate. And if too many questions ensued, Walt could play the "too painful to talk about it" card, which would quickly shut down suspicious curiosity.

This banking pattern confirmed that Walt was running his standard money-transfer scam and would be reasonably easy to undermine. But there also had to be a more extensive system in place. Based on Iris's assets and investments, Iris was a white whale compared with Janice and the women before her. Knowing this, Ava figured that he had to be working on something much more substantial. She had her suspicions, and once she clicked on a few images of Iris's checks saved in her transaction records, they were confirmed. Ava feels high, knowing how easy it will be to take everything from him. She can no longer deny the electrifying experience of hacking again. As soon as she'd cracked into that black-market PC and jumped headfirst down the rabbit hole, that part of herself sprang open as though it had just been there waiting patiently.

Walt exits the diner and gets into his car.

Ava waits until he pulls out of the parking lot and keeps going in the direction away from the resort. She follows from a few cars behind and prays that he isn't watching his rearview too closely. He signals for the highway exit with barely enough notice for Ava to cut across two lanes of traffic. Walt's car turns into a bank and pulls into the drive-through in the lane farthest from the teller's window. Ava edges her vehicle into a spot a few yards away. He retrieves the plastic tube from the shaft, places a handful of paper checks into the vacuum chamber, closes it, and sends it back through the pneumatic chute. Ava is unsurprised that her father's chosen a bank that still uses this low-tech relic.

This used to be one of Ava's favorite parts of their routine; she would sit up extra tall in the back seat and make eye contact with the bank teller, telegraphing how badly she needed that lollipop sent back through the tunnel. More than once, her father had taken the single lolly for himself. "My money, my lollipop," he would say as he popped the Dum-Dum into his mouth and smiled at her disappointment.

Walt receives the returned tube and fetches what appears to be a decent clutch of cash based on the thickness of the envelope. Ava clocks the surveillance cameras on either side of the lane as he pulls away. She lets him go, pulls into a space, and heads into the bank once she's confident he's not doubling back.

There isn't much activity: a sweet elderly couple in line hold hands while a single teller helps a man in a construction vest. Ava surveys the space and clocks a perky guy in a suit a size too small for him beelining for her.

"Can I help you?" He smooths his longish hair behind his ears and smiles solicitously.

"Yes, I just moved here and wanted to open an account."

"Super. I can help you with that." He whisks her to his cubicle sandwiched between two fake ficus trees.

"I'll just need a few pieces of ID and some basic information to get this started," he says while logging into his desktop. Ava watches his fingers dance across the keyboard and memorizes the login and password by the shape of his keystrokes.

"Sure thing," she replies sweetly, and unlocks her phone. "What is your Wi-Fi login?"

He taps a card on his desk with the bank Wi-Fi login and info, and she keys it in and gets into the bank's network.

CHAPTER 34

"Pick a hand."

Walt stands before his bride-to-be, both arms tucked behind his back. He's just returned to their hotel suite and caught Iris in the midst of getting ready for dinner. Her face brightens at whatever surprise he's got in store, like an enraptured kid attending their first magic show.

"That one!" She points excitedly toward his left hand. He slips the items into his right before pulling the empty hand from behind his back and displaying a bare palm. Her face drops for a split second, then she smiles as Walt produces a single pink rose and a grape-flavored lollipop with his other hand. "Oh, honey," she coos. "My favorites."

"Who knows his special gal?" He steps toward Iris, who wraps her arms around his neck and pulls him in for a slow kiss.

"That would be my big bear." She brushes his cheek with her free hand, then breathes in the rose's fragrance and smiles brightly. "How considerate, Walt. Thank you."

"Mere trifles compared with the enormity of my love for you." He catches a whiff of his underarms and frowns. "Let me go ahead and freshen up before dinner."

These past couple of days have made Walt realize how comfortable he'd become with New York weather. Manhattan got plenty hot in the summer, sure, but it was nothing compared with the all-day sauna that was Florida in July. He'd lapped up lots of air-conditioning over the course of the afternoon, and yet still feels he's ready to be wrung out into a bucket.

"How was your day, sweetheart?" There's a cloying quality to Iris's tone that's lately begun to set Walt's molars on edge. He finds himself wishing that the woman would embrace a basic sense of self-respect. Make him work for it a little.

"Oh, just fine." Walt slips into the bathroom. He removes his shirt and hangs it on the back of the door, then blots his armpits with one of the spare cotton hand towels and discards it on the floor beneath the sink. "Was shoring up a few odds and ends before the big day." He pumps a couple of spritzes from the bottle of Tom Ford Ombré Leather that Iris got for him and lets the mist settle on his skin. "Did you enjoy your spa day and afternoon by the pool? Any cabana boys I should be worried about?"

"Oh, you rascal." Iris slips her head through the door to stick her tongue out at Walt. "You know you're the only one for me."

"I also know you're the hottest thing going down here." Walt musters as much of a flirtatious tone as he can stomach. "I have to be able to handle a little competition from these virile young fellows, I suppose."

"Yeah, yeah." She steps into the bathroom and hands him a freshly pressed linen shirt on a hanger. "I *did* make the acquaintance of a lovely young couple today. And guess what? They're here from New York City too."

The mention of his former town looses a split-second vestige of panic in Walt, but he tamps it down. In a place that large, what are the chances he'd crossed paths with whomever Iris is going on about? After all, for a couple of months he'd deftly juggled two well-heeled socialites living on opposite sides of the park. A little risky, sure, but immensely gratifying when he'd managed to pull it off.

"You don't say. What a coincidence."

"Isn't it, though? Matt and Patricia Devlin. Just the sweetest, most charming couple. They're here celebrating five years of marriage. And their actual anniversary falls on our wedding day!"

"How about those odds?" Walt fumbles with the top button of the shirt until Iris steps closer and deftly pops it through. She kisses the tip of his nose, then looks bashfully at the floor.

"I was thinking," she begins, "how nice it would be to invite them to dinner tomorrow night." She returns her eyes to Walt's, and he reads in them a nervous hopefulness. "What would you say to that idea?"

"Oh, my little social coordinator." He smiles through a cresting wave of annoyance and kisses the top of her head. "It's very sweet of you to want to include them, but I'm sure the Devlins have better things to do than dine with a couple of old-timers."

"Speak for yourself." She swats him playfully. "Weren't you just saying how I was the hottest thing on two legs?"

"And that's why I want you all to myself." He nuzzles her neck. "I'm sure these new friends of yours wouldn't want to impose, just like we don't want to get in the way of them celebrating their anniversary, am I right?"

Iris appears miffed by the comment. "I'd like to think I'm a reasonably good judge of character, Walt. And we had a truly lovely afternoon together."

Here we go, with the nitpicking. This recent habit of hers was really beginning to wear thin. "Honey, I didn't mean to suggest otherwise.

But wasn't a big part of the reason we decided to come down here to get away from the bustle of city living? To kick back and just concentrate on each other, and on our new life together?"

"Well, yes, I suppose you're right. But Walt, you're out during the day, flitting here and there, and I could just use some company. Is that so unreasonable?"

"Iris." He unsheathes a look of disappointment and watches as it hits its target. A brief flash of panic on his fiancée's face confirms that Walt's still steering the conversation. "All this flitting around, as you put it, is to have everything lined up ahead of the wedding. Trying to make this day the most romantic it can possibly be for us. It's not as if I'm just running all over town getting up to no good."

"Of course not." Iris looks sufficiently cowed. "But we'll be married in a few short days, and then we'll have the rest of our lives to spend together. I guess I was just hoping that we could share some of our time tomorrow with a nice young couple." She pitches him a hopeful smile. "And I really think you'd like them."

Walt is working to maintain an even temper by reminding himself that all of this will be over soon when a new thought floats into his head: What if these Devlins are a fresh opportunity? Maybe he can engineer a little side score on his way out the door, rack up a few extra style points as a way to augment an already illustrious run. This couple must be reasonably flush to be able to afford the Boca. And during Perry Walters's tenure in New York City, he'd come across more than one cocksure young fellow who'd possessed a dubious understanding of finance, though it was the exact field that many of them worked in.

"Always thinking the best of people," Walt says with a sigh. "Okay, dear. You've talked me into it. Let's go ahead and have your new friends join us for dinner tomorrow evening."

This meal might hold a bit of promise after all.

"Oh, Walt!" She lays a kiss on his cheek and pulls him in for a squeeze. "You won't be sorry, I promise. We'll have just the best time with Matt and Patricia."

"The things I do for you, my love." As Walt shakes his head, he allows the suggestion of a smile to bloom.

"Don't you worry." Iris lets a hand slip down Walt's back and plants it on his butt. "I've got a few things in mind to do to you."

"Why, Iris Garrett." Walt makes no attempt to mask his surprise. "You might just be the death of me."

CHAPTER 35

B eing married to my brother is as stressful as it sounds."

Hazel hugs Ava as she steps into the hotel room. She is delighted when Ava returns the warm embrace. The marathon spa treatments, sun, and poolside drinks have left Hazel feeling looser than she realized.

"How did today go?" Ava asks. She sits in a guest chair by the window, the sunset her backdrop.

Kagan gives Ava an approving once-over while he sings along with Bruno Mars from the de facto bar he's made on the credenza. Hazel regrets not asking the hotel staff to empty the minibar when she checked in.

"We killed it," he says as he stirs a cocktail with a swizzle stick.

"I'll admit we did a pretty great job ad-libbing our origin story," Hazel concedes. The day has left her with opposing emotions. She's happy their plan went smoothly; everything Ava asked them to do has been accomplished. But she's hollowed out from the afternoon's disturbing revelations.

Kagan hands Ava a tumbler full of chartreuse liquid. A sprig of mint floats on the drink's surface. Ava raises her eyebrows as she accepts the beverage.

"What is it?" she asks.

"A mash-up of a mojito and a gimlet."

"A mimlet?" Hazel cracks with a laugh. Her shoulders burn when she moves them, and she regrets forgoing sunblock today.

Kagan laughs loudly. "I prefer gimlito."

Hazel is relieved that she and her brother are not sniping at each other. Working together has softened their sharp elbows. She is leery that he is getting too relaxed as he downs the liquid in his glass, amounting to what Hazel counts as his third beverage since she arrived. Evidently, he is completely sidestepping his outrage and going headfirst into oblivion.

Kagan waits eagerly like a cat about to jump into Ava's lap. Ava brings the drink to her lips. She looks surprised.

"This is delicious," she says.

Kagan leans in. "I had a feeling you'd like it," he says suggestively. She cracks a small smile and turns her attention to Hazel. "What did you find out?"

"Perry was seeing Iris before Mom died." Hazel pauses for Ava's outrage, but her face remains neutral.

"That doesn't surprise me."

"You should have heard Iris describe their meeting and how sad the grieving widower was, all while Janice was still alive. Can you fucking imagine? I keep thinking about everything he was doing right under her nose," Hazel laments.

"And his new bird is clueless. She thinks *Walt* is the second coming." When he gestures, some liquid from Kagan's glass splashes onto the bedspread.

"K! Watch it," Hazel gripes, and turns back to Ava. "When she talks about him, it's like Iris is describing a completely different person." Hazel scrolls through the comments from her last video while recounting the day; she needs a boost.

"Walt *is* completely different from Perry. Did she say anything else? Details about the wedding or honeymoon?"

Kagan shakes his head.

"Hazel?"

She looks up from a comment by someone calling her a whore. No context, just one word. "Whore."

"What's the matter?" Kagan asks. "You look like you just got punched."

"I'm fucking pissed about Perry. What do you expect my face to look like?"

Kagan and Ava glance at each other, further infuriating Hazel.

"Whoa, mood swings, much?" Kagan mutters.

"What mood should I be in right now?! Iris was wearing our mother's engagement ring—the ring that Perry claimed she gave away to charity. I almost lunged for her finger when I saw it," Hazel yells.

Seeing something so familiar worn by a stranger broke her heart. Hazel's great-grandmother had passed down the five-karat emerald-cut diamond to the oldest daughter in each generation. Her mother shifted it to her right hand when Charles died. The piece had far more significance as a family heirloom than a symbol of her first marriage.

"We'll get it back," Ava says.

"Iris said that she would reach out to make plans."

"That's good news. Let's hope she wasn't just saying it to be polite."

"Iris seemed lonely. I think she was really happy for the attention."

"Makes sense. Leaving her alone right before their big day is all part of his design."

"Did you see him?" Kagan asks.

Ava nods.

Hazel considers asking her what it was like to see her father but holds off—something for later if they get some time alone.

"I followed him to a marina today, among other places. Looks like he's in the market for a boat."

"With our money?" Kagan asks heatedly.

"More likely Iris's, given the size."

A loud, tinny ringing draws everyone's attention to the bedside table. Kagan snaps the receiver up before Hazel even moves.

"Hello?"

Kagan winks at Ava.

"We were just talking about you."

Hazel shakes her head.

"Well, we were saying what a pleasure it was to spend time with you."

Hazel feels Ava's gaze on her while they watch Kagan.

"That would be lovely. Count us in . . . stop it, no, you are . . . great. We can't wait to meet him. See you then. Have a wonderful night."

He hangs up and turns to the women triumphantly. "We've just been invited to dinner with Walt and Iris tomorrow night in the Flybridge dining room at six thirty."

"Good. I'm sure the news of Iris befriending people is driving him crazy. While you guys are at dinner, I'll get into their room."

Kagan clears his throat. "As much as I love the idea of ruining this guy's night, what do we do when he goes ballistic on us?" Hazel is surprised to see a brief glimmer of her brother's vulnerability shine through.

"He won't," Ava replies. "He's invested too much time in Iris. Just act like it's the first time you're meeting him, and he'll realize that doing the same is the path of least resistance. He's good under pressure, but you'll have the upper hand. You guys will do great."

Ava's vote of confidence emboldens Hazel. As does the prospect of finally having some control over Perry.

"Once the shock wears off, he'll go on the defensive. So you'll need to be ready."

"Ready how?"

"He'll try to humiliate you or trip you up. It is fun for him and keeps you from asking too many questions." Hazel and Kagan watch Ava pace and unconsciously touch her neck. "Kagan, you'll need to come on pretty strong," she says. "Matt Devlin has a significant business opportunity percolating. In addition to celebrating your anniversary, you are in town building your next investment raise. It needs to be something Iris can persuade Walt they need to be a part of."

"Why can't I be the one with the business opportunity?" Hazel asks. She was the only one of them who even had a real business at all.

Ava sighs. "He's old school, and he doesn't do business with women."

"Right, he just kills them and steals all their children's money." Hazel pouts.

"Dinner tomorrow should drag on for a while; I need time in their room and to not get interrupted by them returning early. Kagan, you're on Walt like glue; the same goes for you and Iris." She holds Hazel's eyes for a beat. "You guys need to text me if anyone leaves the restaurant.

"Ask Walt the same questions you've asked Iris about their relationship and more. He'll have less time to devise excuses to end dinner early or turn things around on you two if he's trying to focus on keeping the details straight. We want him destabilized."

CHAPTER 36

You must be Walt." Approaching the table inside the Flybridge, Kagan finds himself momentarily transfixed by the sight of his former stepfather. For a whisper of a second the mask slips, and Kagan can make out the real Perry—or Walt, as the situation dictates. Rage, vulnerability, fear, and hatred swirl through his countenance like a tempest before the guy manages to twist the lid back onto the jar and return Kagan's cordial smile. "Matt Devlin," he continues, extending a hand. "And this is my wife, Patricia."

The shake Walt Pierson returns is both clammy and too tight, and Kagan clings to the burst of satisfaction he feels in catching the son of a bitch off-balance. Iris stands beside her husband-to-be, blissfully unaware of the undercurrent bubbling beneath their exchange.

"Oh," she gushes, "I'm so happy you're all meeting." She busies herself ushering everyone to their respective seat, then beams across the table at the siblings. "Thank you so much for coming. We've been so excited for tonight."

"We certainly have," Walt agrees, and like that, he's slipped seamlessly back into character. "And thank you both for keeping my Iris company while I've been shoring up the final details for our ceremony. I can't tell you how excited I am to make an honest woman out of this gal."

As Walt speaks, Kagan is reminded of the transformation his friend Vincent described while overhearing that fateful exchange inside Le Croquette months ago. The man who'd been married to their mother was now speaking to his wife-to-be in a sultry drawl an octave lower than Kagan was used to. The entire scenario feels maddeningly disorienting.

"You're a very lucky man," offers Hazel. "We just hope you're deserving of our girl here. Matt and I were commenting on our way down from the room that we've become very fond of your fiancée. Even a little protective."

"She inspires that in people, I think." Walt grasps Iris's hand and proceeds to moon over her. "And she's certainly taken a shine to the pair of you. I look forward to learning more about Matt and Patricia Devlin." He cracks open the wine list and begins to peruse. "Let's start with an easy one: red or white?"

"We'll trust ourselves in your capable hands." Kagan relaxes into his chair and stares directly at Walt. "You're a fan of the grape, I take it?"

"I'd like to think I know my way around a list, Matt." He traces his finger down the page, stops on a selection, and waves the sommelier over. After placing an order with the young woman, Walt arranges the napkin on his lap and returns his attention to the table. "You're visiting from Manhattan, Iris tells me?"

"We are, yes." Hazel keeps her tone bright. "Celebrating our five-year anniversary." She grins at her brother, and Kagan's impressed with how natural she seems leaning into the lie. "You spent some years there yourself, we understand."

"I did indeed. Wonderful years at that. But my sweetheart and I were ready to slow down and kick back. Enjoy our time in the sun."

Kagan tags back in. "The great outdoors. Speaking of which, Iris tells us you're an avid bird-watcher."

"I've been known to spend my days in the park. Are you a birder yourself, Matt?"

"Oh no. Nothing like that. But I remember learning a bit about them in science class as a kid. Some fascinating stuff there." Kagan had actually gleaned all the information he knew about avian behavior from the internet in preparation for this very conversation. Among those fun facts, he found one in particular he's been itching to share. Kagan takes a long sip of water, never diverting his eyes from Walt. "I wonder if you're familiar with the brown-headed cowbird?"

"I've come across a few in my time."

"Such an interesting species." Kagan sweeps his gaze across the table to bring the ladies into the conversation. "Cowbirds make no nest of their own. Instead, they lay eggs in the nests of other types of birds and then leave those birds to raise the babies. 'Nuisance birds,' I believe they're called. 'Hatch parasites.' Is that right, Walt?"

"'Brood parasites,' yes."

"That's the one. Also, they're a nonmonogamous species. Cowbirds are known to have several different mates within the *same season*. Isn't that wild? I mean, imagine the sort of destruction that combination of behaviors is capable of inflicting."

"Mmm." Walt reflects on the observation. "The animal kingdom can be a very volatile ecosystem."

"Gosh, you can say that again."

"Boys and their birds," quips Hazel, which elicits a giggle from Iris.

The sommelier returns to the table and presents the bottle with the label turned for Walt's approval. "The Louis Latour Puligny-Montrachet 2021, sir." A taste is poured. Walt swirls the selection in his glass before taking a deliberate sip. He gives the wine a few seconds to make an impression, then nods approvingly to the sommelier. She pours a glass for each member of the party, sets the bottle in a tableside ice bucket, and glides gracefully away.

"A toast," announces Kagan. "To the happy couple. May you experience many healthy and prosperous years together." They all clink glasses and enjoy sips of the wine.

"And if I might add," says Walt, "a very happy anniversary to the Devlins. You make a lovely couple. So natural with each other. It's as if you've known each other all your lives."

"Walt, this is simply divine." A blush blooms on Iris's cheeks. "Bravo."

"Thank you, darling. Matt, you approve, I hope?"

"Very charming." Kagan calibrates his tone carefully, in an attempt to sound patronizing to Walt while not tipping Iris off to the slight. "Quite drinkable."

"Glad you like it." He sets the glass on the table. "So, Matt, tell me how you keep yourself busy back in New York."

"Oh, honey." Hazel has mustered some excitement for this part of the show. "Tell him about the app."

"I'm sure Walt and Iris don't want to discuss business at the table, sweetie."

"No, no. I asked, after all." Walt's curiosity is evident. "What's this about an app?"

Kagan takes a sip of wine, making sure to screw up his face as he swallows it down. "Are you a big tech guy?"

Walt winces at Iris's guffaw. "Can't say that's the case, Matt. I'm more old school, as your generation likes to say."

"Does our generation still say that?" Kagan consults Hazel. "Anyway, I totally understand. Have to imagine it's difficult to keep up, once you reach a certain point in life."

Walt rebounds quickly from the slight. "You were explaining your business venture to us?"

"Right." Kagan leans his elbows against the edge of the table and steeples his fingers. "How familiar are you with the art world?"

"Oh," says Iris, "my Walt's a real art lover. Such wonderful taste!"

"So I'm speaking to the right man. Do you collect?"

"I did, for some time." There's a catch in Walt's voice. "My former wife and I put a nice collection together, full of pieces we both really responded to. But after she passed, the associations to the paintings were just too strong. So I sold off the lot, and now I'm looking forward to starting fresh with my new bride." He lets his gaze linger on the siblings as he grasps Iris's arm and gives it a squeeze.

It takes Kagan a moment to realize that his hands have balled into fists. He sets them in his lap and lets out a breath. "Well, with the stratospheric climb of the art market overall, forgeries have become much more commonplace. Even the so-called experts are proving less dependable, owing to the fact that there's so much financial incentive for institutions and private collectors to authenticate the provenance of a newly discovered piece by a hot artist or an artist whose known output is scarce. Increasing desperation results in a lowering of standards, I suppose.

"Further complicating matters is the fact that fine art is increasingly treated as an investment market, and oftentimes a tax haven, where people hide assets through dubious channels. Collectors routinely stash the real paintings in storage and then hire forgers to reproduce the work. They stick those on the wall while the actual masterpieces live in a crate inside a vault somewhere. So now you have a whole new batch of sanctioned forgeries out in the world." Kagan takes a sip of wine. "Can you imagine such a cynical approach as that, Walt? Reducing these timeless works to a revenue stream?"

"It's an outrage, if you ask me. Sadly, some people are unable to appreciate the beautiful things in life." He makes a show of taking Iris's hand, to put a finer point on the statement.

"Couldn't agree more. Now, this is where our app comes in. Essentially what we provide is an interface to help interested buyers authenticate a prospective purchase. We aggregate art databases from around the world—museums, galleries, dealers, and auction houses—to check against sales histories, incidents of theft, and inclusion in private and permanent collections, in order to help protect patrons from unwittingly purchasing forgeries."

"We mentioned we're here celebrating our anniversary," adds Hazel. "As it happens, we're also in the midst of an investment raise, so there's a business component to the trip as well."

"Ooh, Walt." Iris practically thrums. "Doesn't that sound like an exciting venture?"

"Sure, sure." He pats her hand dismissively. "It *does* seem to be a worthwhile endeavor, Matt. As I mentioned, I'm really not very keyed into the tech world, so I'm afraid the logistics would just go over my head."

"Oh, no worries." Kagan nonchalantly waves away Walt's hollow apology. "Didn't mean to mix business and pleasure. Anyhow, we're actually getting to the point where we're going to have to start turning investors away."

"Sounds like it's going very well," says Iris.

"We knew we were onto something big," explains Hazel, "but the response has surpassed our expectations. People are really excited to get in on this thing on the ground floor. It's going to provide such an innovative solution to a really pervasive issue."

"I'm so impressed with the two of you." Iris turns her attention to Walt. "Think of all the good the Devlins will be doing for the art world."

"Of course, honey. As you said, very impressive stuff."

"Matt," asks Iris, "did you say that you had *all* your investors in place?"

"Everyone's more or less lined up, yeah." Kagan consults wordlessly with his sister. "Though I suppose we could still find a spot for a couple of interested friends."

"Iris, honey," her fiancé manages through clenched teeth. "We'll discuss this later."

"Walt, if I may." Hazel sets her wineglass down and plants her palms on the table. "You mentioned being excited about building a collection with your bride-to-be. Imagine how you'd feel if you found out that this thing you'd bought into, that you'd put your faith in, turned out to be a lie."

"Patricia, forgive me for—"

"Also, you could look at it as a way to honor your late wife." Her eyes bore into his. "Seems like a fitting tribute, wouldn't you say?"

Iris is so rapt by Hazel's speech that she misses the tacit agreement passing between the men. Kagan reclines in his chair, feeling the self-satisfaction bleed into his grin.

CHAPTER 37

They're here.

Ava's pulse races with purpose as she replies to Hazel's text with a thumbs-up emoji and approaches the check-in desk. She wraps her arms around the luxe resort bathrobe she's wearing as a bright-eyed young man greets her with a smile. She feels the coolness of the marble floor under her bare feet as she makes her way.

"Good evening. How can I help you?" His teeth are as bright as his eyes, and his hair is the color of margarine. Ava guesses he isn't more than twenty-one years old.

"I'm such an idiot." She plants a palm over her face and shakes her head.

"I highly doubt that," he replies.

"I locked myself out of my room." Ava lays the practiced, subtle distress into her voice, adjusting the towel turban around her head. Luckily, it's dinnertime, and there aren't too many people milling around the lobby.

"Oh no!" he says a little too boisterously. "Happens to the best of us."

"I just stepped outside, and the door shut behind me before I realized that I had absolutely nothing on me"—she leans in—"or nothing on," she says sotto voce.

"Well, no worries. I can help with that."

His gold nameplate says Stanton on it, and she isn't sure if that is his first or last name, but his enthusiasm is wafting as potently as the Hawaiian Tropic in the air. He looks like he hails from some Midwestern plain.

"I just need your room number and the name on the reservation."

"Sure, Walt Pierson is the name on the reservation, and we are in suite two thirty-seven."

"Ah, the cloisters, excellent." Stanton's countenance changes slightly. Ava doesn't mind pretending to be a higher-caliber guest for a while; everything is more accessible when people think you have a lot of money.

"So how are you enjoying your stay?" He meets her eyes.

"Um, great, until I locked myself out." Ava gestures to her ensemble. "Since I'm not wearing anything under here," she whispers, "if I could get that key card quickly, I would be *so* grateful."

Stanton swallows and reddens.

"Of course." He types quickly, focusing on the screen and barely looking below her hairline as he swipes the card and hands it to her.

"Hey, Stanton?"

"Yes, Ms. Garrett?"

Ava nearly smarts at the moniker but fights the urge. "Can you do me a favor and not tell my fiancé I locked myself out? We have a running argument that I'm always doing stupid things like this when we travel, and I'd love it if he didn't have more ammo for that particular subject."

Stanton nods conspiratorially. "Of course. Your secret's safe with me."

/ / /

In Walt and Iris's room, Ava beelines for the phone and dials security. A deep voice answers on the first ring.

"Boca Raton security, how may we help you?"

"Yes, hello, I've locked myself out of my safe. My fiancé will kill me if he can't get into it when he returns. I think I messed up the code."

"No problem, Ms. Garrett. We'll send someone up soon."

"Oh, thank you. Can you have someone up here in the next ten minutes?"

"I'll personally make sure of it," the voice replies.

Ava returns the handset to its cradle and checks her phone. There are no more messages from Hazel, which is good. She instructed Kagan and Hazel not to send texts other than SOS if Iris or Walt left the restaurant for any reason. She hopes they won't drop the ball.

They were understandably nervous as they got ready for dinner. Ava was surprised by how seriously they took their roles and prepared. Kagan stayed sober, and Hazel hadn't looked at her phone for hours. They rehearsed possible exchanges between their former stepfather and themselves, coaching each other and developing hand signals and code words. She was almost proud of how far they'd come in working together. They clearly needed some purpose and direction to save them from themselves. Unfortunately, it took their mother's death to get them to that point.

Once he recovers from the reveal of Patricia and Matt Devlin's real identities, her father will want to keep them within reach for as long as it takes to assess the situation. Making a scene, confronting them, or bolting from the dinner will only decimate his hard work, so Ava isn't concerned about an early return. Meanwhile, she's at a safe distance, allowing her a sense of control she's never had in dealing with him. It is undeniable that as she got closer to him geographically, her ability to think like him became stronger. Like a homing device of deception, Ava has found herself pulled closer into the mindset she learned from him. Sam was right; her father had his own orbit.

In the time she has before hotel security arrives, Ava scans the suite. She moves to set the scene. She uncaps a bottle of red nail polish as the shower runs on extra hot for a few steamy minutes. She paints two toenails with the small brush before leaving the bottle slightly un-screwed on the coffee table, careful not to drip anything on the sand-colored carpet or the beige silk couch. She turns on the flat-screen, scrolls to a pay-per-view movie, buys *Furious 7,* and fast-forwards it an hour into the film. She'll wipe the purchase from the room folio long before Iris or Walt sees it. Ava retrieves a bag of half-eaten minibar peanut M&M's from the pocket of her robe and a slim bottle of Topo Chico seltzer from the other pocket. She unscrews the bottle and takes a few long-needed sips. Next, Ava goes to the closet and finds the cen-tral safe in the suite. There are three: one in the entryway closet, one in the main bedroom, and another in the common area closet. She's hedg-ing her bets that her father has utilized the bedroom safe since it's the roomiest. She enters a few purposefully wrong code attempts until the machine beeps angrily and flashes a red light. She loosens the tie around her waist and opens the robe slightly to reveal a few inches of her bare shoulder.

A baritone utterance of "Security" follows a knock at the door. Ava glides to the vestibule and catches sight of her still-turbaned head in the entry mirror. She unfurls the towel and places it behind an oversize flower arrangement. Ava shakes her head, letting the still-saturated hair cascade around her shoulders before pulling open the double doors. Standing before her is a man who could double as the professional wrestler Eddie Guerrero, a problematic but entertaining character from her teen years introduced by Sam while they were living together. She hopes he doesn't sense her scam and body-slam her into oblivion.

"Evening, ma'am. We got a call about an issue with your safe?" the man says in a gentler voice than Ava expects.

"Yes, thank God. My fiancé isn't back yet."

She steps aside to allow his large frame to enter. Even in his lack of visual wandering, Ava can tell that he is taking every detail in as he steps through the threshold. She would expect nothing less; security at a high-end resort like this one is well-trained to spot hustles whenever a new person enters the property. She figures him for a former law-enforcement or military officer. Ava watches him take in the nail polish, the candy, the paused movie, and her half-drunk water.

"I realized that I forgot to remove my wedding present." She touches the necklace around her neck. "I must return it to the safe before Walt returns, which will be any minute."

She lingers on his name, banking that the security guy has done his homework before coming up. If there is any chance that hotel security communicated with the resort restaurants about dinner reservations, this whole charade could go south quickly, but she doubts it.

"The thing is," she prattles on, wanting to distract him as much as possible, "I don't want my fiancé to know that I took it out of the safe in the first place. The necklace isn't technically mine until we get married. I just had to try it on."

Ava cups the emerald charm knockoff and shows it to the man. She'd picked it up at an exceptionally seedy pawnshop on the way back from her second trip to the marina, this time without her father on the premises, earlier today. The pawnshop owner tried to convince her that the fake was authentic, mistaking Ava for a tourist off the beaten path. So she repaid him by convincing him the fake Rolex in her possession was genuine. The smarmy owner professed to know his watches but revealed himself to be as phony as the necklace she traded the watch for.

"Which safe was giving you trouble, ma'am?" asks the guard, his eyeline already trained on the bedroom where Ava had purposely left the door open. The door to the walk-in closet housing the safe was ajar, as was the en suite bathroom's door, where the fogged-up mirror came into view as they walked in. If he doubted that Ava was the room occupant when he rode up the elevator, he now appears satisfied that she belongs here.

"I'm just so bad at working these things. I never seem to be able to get the code entered right! Anything remotely technological, and I'm useless. You should see me on a computer, disaster." She giggles.

She sits on the bed and crosses her bare legs while the man walks a few feet to the safe and uses a master key to open the metal box. The door clicks open, and she notices a document folder inside. The guard turns to her.

"Voilà." He hits a few keys, which beep while the door remains open.

"Thank you so much! You are a lifesaver."

"No problem at all. And if you have any more problems, please ask for me when you call." He points to his nameplate.

"Thank you so much, Sam." She thinks about her stepbrother with a trace of sadness.

He cracks the first smile since he's arrived. "Just doing my job."

"I hate to ask, but can you keep this little snafu between us? My fiancé—"

He cuts her off gently. "I was never here."

Ava nods gratefully, follows him into the entryway, and closes the door behind him after giving him a wave. She prays he doesn't see her hand shaking.

She rechecks her phone before retracing her steps back to the open safe. Inside, she finds a flat, slim, fireproof sheath and feels heavy dread as she flips through its contents.

The front door beeping and opening echoes through the suite, and adrenaline courses through Ava. She swiftly places the documents back in the carrier, her movements deliberate and silent. The door clicks shut, and the approaching footfalls on the marble entryway are heart-stopping as they draw nearer. Scanning the room, Ava slips behind the floor-to-ceiling blackout curtains flanking the grand oceanfront windows.

"It's me," his voice says from the main room, and Ava shuts her eyes when she remembers her props, still scattered on the table. She holds her breath.

"You'll never guess who showed up to dinner tonight—your girl-friend and her brother." Her father's tone is even but subtly rattled. He's furious.

Ava realizes he's alone and talking to someone on the phone, and it doesn't sound like he's moving toward her hiding spot.

"Why would I step out in the middle of my dinner to call you with a dumb joke like that? They're shaking me down. The son thinks he's a player. He has no idea." Ava's father laughs dryly. "Not a chance in hell. Now listen, the plan needs to change to account for this new development . . . yeah. Let's just say your bonus for the extra work will cover you for the rest of your life. . . . I need to get back to you; they think I'm in the john. I had to shake that asshole off. . . . I sent him to the bar for some Louis the thirteenth shots. . . . I knew that souser couldn't pass that up."

Ava takes a small breath to prevent passing out. She can hear the fear in his voice; he knows that Kagan and Hazel could ruin everything for him. But she can hear something else that makes her very sorry she ever agreed to do this.

Things are much worse than she imagined.

CHAPTER 38

"Wonderful." The server at the Flybridge offers the four-some an easy smile. "I'll go ahead and put that order right in." As the kid retreats toward the kitchen, Iris plucks the napkin from her lap and sets it next to the place setting.

"Won't you please excuse me for a moment? I need to powder my nose."

Walt's immediate impulse is to redirect the comment into a dig at Kagan, but he quashes the thought and instead stands up to see his lady off.

"I'll join you." Hazel seems in a hurry to accompany Iris. "I need to use the little girls' room myself."

The ladies cross in the direction of the washrooms, leaving the men alone at the table. As soon as Iris and Hazel are out of view, the smug son of a bitch makes his move.

"So, Perry . . . sorry, sorry. *Walt*. What a fun surprise to find you in the Sunshine State. You seem to be getting along extremely well, for a grieving widower."

"How'd you sniff me out, Kagan? I can make myself pretty hard to locate."

The shrug is overly charged and a little jerky. "Maybe you're not quite as slick as you think."

"Uh-huh." Walt begins to mentally cycle through the various tactics he could use to wipe the smirk off this pest's face as he lets a look of supreme boredom settle over his own. "What are we doing here, Kagan?"

"Oh no, no, no." His mouth slips into a depraved grin. "I'm afraid you're talking to the wrong guy."

Walt nearly laughs at the disconnect playing out before his eyes. This imbecile fancies himself some sort of savvy operator, clearly mistaking cocaine confidence and liquid courage for suavity and tact. It would almost be funny if it weren't threatening to derail Walt's current operation.

He lets out an exasperated sigh. "And whom exactly am I speaking with, then?"

"Why, Matt Devlin, of course. The guy who's bringing you an exciting investment opportunity."

"Go on."

"Seems like a pretty easy sell to me. Iris looks as if she's already on board with our app concept. So you let her know that you're interested in being an early investor. Then you go ahead and write out a check to me for the ten million that you grifted from our mother. Your fiancée will think you're on the up and up, just making a prudent and generous investment in an upstart company that's dedicated to helping the world become a fairer, more equitable place. And we won't have to inform our dear Iris of any of your . . . less charitable past. Sounds like a win-win, no?"

Walt eyes the door to the ladies' room, to make sure the coast is still clear. "You want to know the tragedy behind all of this, Kagan?"

His expression bends sourly at the unexpected comment. "Huh?"

"You've obviously got half a brain in that head of yours. Just look at this little plot you've managed to cook up. I can't imagine your sister's been much help in that regard, what with her face constantly buried in her phone and checked out from the world around her. So you've got the smarts and the potential, and yet you fritter it all away on these shortcuts and schemes, instead of just leaning in to hard work." His former stepson had always been painfully and obviously jealous of his sister. Janice had attributed it to her late husband's favoritism, which she had bored Perry about at length, but it's proving useful now to keep the young man off-balance.

Kagan's mouth hangs open stupidly until he manages to get it working again. "I'm sorry; did *you* just accuse *me* of being a schemer?"

"I have to say, as someone who once took a passing interest in your life, that it's a real shame you'll never know the satisfaction that comes from an earned sense of accomplishment. There was a time when you could have really made something of yourself. Then again, maybe it's not too late. You managed to track me down, which is no small feat."

"Okay, now look here." It takes Kagan a moment to land on the authoritative tone he's scrabbling after. "The girls are going to be back from the bathroom in a minute, and if we don't get this all sorted out before then, your dear fiancée is going to get an earful about Perry Walters and his unsavory exploits."

"Not exactly holding my breath there, Kagan. That broad's bladder is like a leaky garden hose. It'll take a while to stem the trickle." Walt stretches and casually sets an elbow atop his chairback. "The thing of it is, I don't have Janice's money on hand to give back to you, even if I wanted to."

"Bullshit."

"Keep your voice down, son. This isn't doing you any favors." Walt taps the side of his own wineglass. "And I'm giving it to you straight. At the moment, your mother's money is tied up with Iris's and my own. I won't bore you with the details, but in order for me to pull all this off, I needed to fold the finances in together, for appearances' sake. But here's what I'm willing to do. I can cut you a check for one point five million dollars, as a down payment. That's a nice round number, and a believable amount for my investment in your company. After the wedding, I'll have unfettered access to the whole nut, at which point I'll get you back the full amount I got from Janice."

"Stole."

"What's that?"

"The full amount you *stole* from our mother."

Walt cracks a grin in spite of himself. "You're going to pick now to lean in to semantics?"

"God, you're an asshole." Kagan apparently can't bring himself to make eye contact. Instead, he stares hazily into the distance.

"First rule of the game is to keep emotions out of it." Walt savors a slow sip of wine. "This is what all that life experience you missed out on should have taught you."

At once, Kagan's focus snaps to Walt. "Plus twenty percent."

"I'm sorry?"

"You'll give Hazel and me back the money you stole from our mother, plus twenty percent of the take from Iris."

"Now, that's a boy." A feeling akin to pride lights up in Walt. "Finally throwing your hat on the mat. Okay." He considers the demand for a moment. "I'm afraid I hustled too hard laying the groundwork on this one for you to swoop in and take that big of a chunk, but for the sake of fairness, I'll slide you ten. Believe me, it's a nice bit of change."

Kagan mulls over the counteroffer. Walt can tell he's starting to enjoy this. "Let's call it fifteen and call it a day."

"Deal." Out of the corner of his eye, Walt spies the ladies returning from the bathroom. "Okay, here come our blushing brides. Why don't you go ahead and remind your face how happy it should be."

As Iris and Hazel approach the table, Walt and Kagan stand, smiles in place. They all settle into their seats, the bride-to-be lazily waving the cloth napkin in an attempt to cool herself off.

"What did we miss, boys?"

"It seems Matt here is quite the pitchman. He's convinced me of the validity of this new business venture. I think it would make a sound investment."

"Oh, how wonderful!" Iris sets a hand on Walt's shoulder and gives it a squeeze. "I just knew you would hit it off, and now we'll have a great reason to stay in touch."

"I know a good deal when I see it, darlin'." Walt reaches across the table and puts as much as he can behind the handshake he gives Kagan. "And I have a feeling that Matt and Patricia Devlin are really going places."

CHAPTER 39

He was eating out of my fucking hand!" Kagan shouts triumphantly as soon as Ava is three steps into the room.

"KAGAN!" Hazel says his name in a tone used only by
their late father. He stops in his tracks and stares at her with angry
confusion. His eyes are spidery crimson veins laced around enlarged
pupils.

"What?" he asks, alternately grinning and jaw grinding.

"Can you bring it down a couple of notches, please?"

His luminous grin dims a few watts. "I put him in such a tight
spot. He had no choice but to promise me some money I know he'll
never hand over."

Despite Kagan's intense delivery, Ava appears calm, and Hazel
puts in effort to mirror her mood. The outcome of their dinner is de-
batable, and she's finding her brother's erratic energy irritating and
delusional. His grandiosity heightened the evening's stress, and Hazel
couldn't rein him in. Despite her attempts during dinner, he was riding

too high to catch her glances and rehearsed signals. The two-hour meal felt interminable, and Hazel endured insufferable small talk and forced laughter while steaming on the inside. Sitting at the same table as Perry unleashed a torrent of repressed fury toward him and his absent accomplice.

Kagan, on the other hand, exuded extra exuberance and intoxicated verbosity. He was vibrating on the walk back to the room, eager to boast to Ava. On the elevator ride, Hazel confronted Kagan about his behavior, which he justified as simply adopting Matt Devlin's personality. Hazel tried to evade memories of Janice's concerns about Kagan's "lifestyle," but they kept floating to the surface during the dinner. In the past, Hazel hadn't been in the headspace to think about her brother's well-being amid her anger at Janice for cutting her off. Now, observing Kagan struggle to control himself, Hazel knew his unpredictable volatility over the past week was a by-product of Kagan self-medicating himself off the rails.

While the thrill of screwing over Perry during the surprise reveal was delectable, the ongoing balancing act of double-speaking, following Iris's vacuous stream of consciousness, and keeping aliases straight left Hazel's head spinning. Each emptied wineglass and bathroom break filled her with anxious worry. The more engrossed she's become in her real-life drama, the less control she has over her online persona.

"I'm glad the dinner went well, in spite of Perry getting away from you, apparently," Ava says to Kagan sternly.

Kagan blanches and glances at Hazel, who is now fuming. She realizes that when Kagan followed Perry to the men's room early in the dinner, her brother must have lost track of Perry without her realizing. "What did I miss?" Hazel asks testily.

"It is fine; he came back to the room but didn't see me," Ava says. "I'll fill you in after you tell me about the meal."

Kagan looks shamed, but he doesn't respond and Ava turns her attention to Hazel. Her soulful eyes warm when Hazel meets them. Hazel feels her agitation lessening.

"Tell me everything," Ava says.

"Perry was definitely sweating. He's smooth, but I could sense his panic."

Ava pats her arm. "I wish I could have seen it."

"Perry claims he's going to give us the money back with interest." Hazel laughs.

Kagan snorts. "He promised he'd give us fifteen percent on top of the inheritance principal. And a check for one and a half million bucks this week as a show of good faith. How dumb does that asshole think we are?"

"I'm glad you both realize that he'll never hand you a dime. Have you guys thought about what you want to do about Iris?"

Hazel looks at her brother; his expression is blank.

"We've got plans to hang out at the pool tomorrow with her," Hazel replies while clicking hearts and thumbs-ups on comments she likes, hiding the ones she doesn't.

"That poor woman, she's oblivious," Kagan adds.

"I meant, once we get your money back, will you warn Iris?" Ava asks.

"Iris will be fine; she had two rich husbands before this. We should just take what is ours, tip off Calabrese that he's down here, and walk away. It's cleaner that way," Kagan says, thick-tongued.

"Are you forgetting our mothers are dead? He's dangerous." Ava's usual steadiness falters.

"This is the easier way, Ava," Hazel says, putting her phone aside.

Kagan sits on the side of Ava's chair and drapes his arm around her shoulders.

"Ava, babe, we've got this all under control."

Ava shakes Kagan's arm off and stands up, a serious expression eclipsing her earlier serenity. "Well, I can tell you from what I found out tonight, you most definitely do not."

CHAPTER 40

"All is right with the world."

Despite a dull ache that refuses to unlatch itself from Kagan's temples, he feels invigorated by the morning pick-me-up he indulged in on his way out the door. At Iris's insistence, he and Hazel have joined the bride-to-be for an informal poolside lunch. He figures that the toot, a bite to eat, and a couple of drinks ought to level him off just right. The heat abates slightly as an ocean breeze skims the deck. Kagan yawns and stretches catlike along the lounger.

"It certainly is." Iris is nicely put together for the casual meetup, a palm leaf–printed caftan covering her one-piece swimsuit. "Thank you so much for joining me."

"Our pleasure." Hazel looks up from her phone and offers the older woman a bleary-eyed smile. "It was such a thoughtful invite." She sets the device onto the table and uses her toes to unbunch the corner of the towel lining her deck chair.

A kid working the pool area approaches the group, a grin blooming on his face. "Good afternoon. May I bring you folks anything at the moment?"

The ladies order salads and glasses of prosecco. When the young man turns his attention to Kagan, an idea pops into his head. Kagan stifles a chuckle to avoid ruining the bit.

"I'll have a Bloody Mary and a steak sandwich and . . . a steak sandwich." Kagan's always wanted to drop the *Fletch* reference into an actual order request, though the kid's vacant stare suggests the movie quote is lost on this particular audience. Hey, no accounting for taste. Or age, supposes Kagan.

"I'm very sorry, sir, but we don't feature that item on our poolside menu. Could I interest you in one of our delicious burgers instead?"

"That'll be fine," he answers, slightly deflated. "Medium rare."

"Very good, sir. And your room number."

Iris opens her mouth to answer, but Kagan beats her to it. "Twelve thirteen," he blurts.

"Oh, now, Matt." Her mouth crinkles into a frown. "I invited *you two* to lunch."

He waves the kid off and returns his attention to Iris. "This is our treat, my dear. You and Walt were so generous at dinner last night." Kagan catches a concerned look on his sister's face and feels a flicker of annoyance. Whatever it's about this time—whether the money spending, his drinking, or something else—it's like his sister's dead set on suffocating any bit of fun that dares to rear its head. He remembers when she used to be more carefree, less tightfisted and anxious. It's embarrassing, frankly, and clearly Ava is noticing too. She got so weird at the end of last night, and when Kagan sneaked out late to knock on her door, there was no answer. *Strange.*

"Well, thank you both," says Iris. "It's very kind."

"It's nothing," demurs Kagan. "Hey, speaking of Walt, where is the old dog today? He wasn't overserved at dinner last night, was he?"

"Oh no, no." Iris's expression drops for a beat before she recovers, fixing a smile in place. "He's just out taking care of a few last-minute things ahead of the wedding tomorrow." Judging from the look on her face, Kagan doubts the woman believes her own story, but she clings to it just the same.

"So we get you all to ourselves this afternoon," says Hazel. "Lucky us!" Her enthusiasm helps give Iris's smile a little more buoyancy, and Kagan decides to grab the baton from his sister and run with it.

"What would you like to do after lunch?" he asks.

"I hadn't even thought about that." Iris's eyes light up as if they've handed her the keys to a car she's been forbidden to get behind the wheel of. "I mean, what are our options?"

"They've got tennis and golf," answers Hazel. "Or we could take a dip in the ocean, maybe sign up for a boat ride."

Iris lets out a yelp and takes a moment to collect herself. "I'm so sorry, I just . . . This is embarrassing, but I have a big fear of open water."

"Boat ride is off the list." Kagan mimes slashing a pencil across an imaginary slip of paper. "There's some great shopping around here, if you're in the mood for a more low-key afternoon."

Iris peers past the siblings, a look of utter contentment lighting up her features. "Do they have horses, down there on the beach?"

"I'm sorry?" Kagan feels he's missing something. "Horses?"

"Yes. Horseback rides."

Kagan looks to his sister, then back to Iris, who appears to have floated off to a different moment, a different setting, a different life. After a short spell, she snaps back into the here and now and her cheeks color.

"Oh, silly me. Just reminiscing. Forget I said anything."

"Did you used to ride?" asks Hazel.

"When I was a girl growing up on the ranch. It was the freest I ever felt." She lets out a bittersweet sigh. "Of course, I doubt I could even get my leg over anymore." She laughs, but the sound is tinged with a melancholy air.

"So hey," says Hazel, "are you excited for the big day tomorrow?"

"Oh, yes." A brightness returns to the woman's expression. "I'm glad you brought it up, in fact. There's something I wanted to ask you both."

The kid returns with a tray of drinks and deposits them onto the table. "Your food will be out in just a few minutes," he explains. Iris thanks the young man before he bops over to a neighboring group and she shifts her focus back to the siblings.

"Matt, Patricia, I've come to grow quite fond of you both over these last few days. Walt and I have a very modest ceremony planned, but it would really mean a lot to me if you'd do us the honor of acting as our witnesses tomorrow."

Kagan's thrown by the sheer absurdity of the request but manages to keep a reverential expression in place. He looks to his sister, who seems similarly at sea. They exchange a subtle nod.

"Wow," says Hazel, her smile masking the laugh Kagan knows she's suppressing. "We're so honored. We'd, uh, love to be there on your special day."

"The honor is mine." Iris flicks a tear from the corner of her eye. "I'd always dreamed about having kids of my own but was never able to. So it's . . . well, it's just wonderful to have you both here." She picks up her glass, and the siblings follow suit.

"To you and Walt," proclaims Kagan, who finds himself unexpectedly stirred by her comment. "May you enjoy a long and fruitful life together." The trio clinks glasses and sips their drinks.

"Thank you, Matt. Thank you, Patricia. I feel so lucky to have found you two. I'm touched that you've agreed to be there for us tomorrow. And thank you so much for lunch today." She can barely contain the smile spreading across her face.

"It's our absolute pleasure," says Kagan.

You'll pay for it all, he thinks, a bit ruefully.

CHAPTER 41

How lonely do you have to be to invite strangers to your wedding? I know we're good company, but it's just sad," Hazel says.

"That's exactly his type," Ava replies from her seat across the room. She watches Hazel lying on the bed, scrolling absently on her phone.

Kagan's voice belts "Bitch Better Have My Money" through the closed bathroom door, and Hazel rolls her eyes. They are both hoping the shower sobers Kagan up after another blurry day by the pool. Before going to rinse off, he gathered Ava into his arms and planted a full open-mouth kiss on her. She'd taken it in stride, pulling away after a second and cracking a joke, but her discomfort was hard to play off completely.

"I'm sorry that my brother keeps touching you," Hazel says, sitting up and focusing her attention on Ava.

"He's mostly harmless, and I can handle myself."

"That's generous of you, but I don't know how harmless he is," Hazel replies.

"Is there something I should know?"

Ava observes Hazel considering her answer deeply before responding. "My brother thinks he means well, even when he's being manipulative, which is fairly constant. And clearly, he has trouble with basic boundaries."

Ava takes this in, sensing there is more that Hazel wants to reveal and unsure if she wants to hear it.

"It's pretty obvious that he is infatuated with you, and correct me if I'm wrong, but I don't gather your feelings are mutual," Hazel says.

Ava looks at the door and back at Hazel awkwardly but doesn't respond.

Hazel looks disappointed but continues, "I wouldn't feel right if I didn't tell you"—she sighs dramatically—"Kagan originally wanted to use you as bait to get our money back."

"I can't tell if you're joking right now," Ava says lightly.

"I wish I were," Hazel says. "But he thought we could offer to tell your dad where you were in exchange for money."

"That would be pretty hard to do since you guys needed me to find him in the first place, not to mention I'm worth nothing as far as he's concerned." Ava can't hold her laughter in while Hazel watches her. Based on her vexed expression, it's clear to Ava that she didn't expect this reaction.

"I'm relieved that you aren't upset at him; I just thought you should know," Hazel says, clearly annoyed. "Honestly, I thought you'd be pissed. It was pretty screwed up for him to consider you collateral."

Ava joins her on the bed. "I'm laughing because it's absurd to think that my father would ever part with any money, especially where I'm concerned. He cares about me as much as he cares about you, or Kagan, or anyone else other than himself. Not even a little bit."

"That doesn't bother you? He's your father," Hazel presses.

"No, it doesn't. I moved on from that disappointment a long time ago. I know what he is, so I don't expect anything. I spent the past five years carrying around that head garbage before I realized I could just throw it away. I highly recommend it." Ava lays her hand on Hazel's arm and watches her soften.

"I want to be where you are. I think once we get everything settled with Perry, I can finally grieve my mom." Hazel's face crumples.

"I'm sorry. I know how hard it is to lose your mother. It's a relation- ship you can never have with anyone else," Ava says softly.

"I can't stop thinking about her," Hazel says miserably.

"Tell me something about your mom."

"She used to sound so happy when I called every day; we were so close. And she really wanted me to pursue my dreams, which is why I knew that Perry manipulated her into cutting us out. This is why help- ing us is going to be so healing."

Ava feels a dull cramping deep in her gut and moves to stand. "So what will you do after all this?" she asks while walking off the aching.

"I'll head back to New York." Hazel shrugs. "I don't exactly have a lot of options."

"I think you have infinite options. Nothing is holding you back from doing whatever you want. No spouse, kids, job, health issues, or financial limitations. Ultimate freedom."

"I have to film more videos for my channel; I'm behind. My follow- ers depend on me."

"I think you're better than your content."

Hazel looks like she's been sucker punched. "Jesus. Don't sugar- coat it."

"I just meant that you are so smart and creative; why be another voice in the crowd?"

"So what would you do if you were me?" Hazel props her back against the headboard and lifts her iPhone.

"I would throw my devices into the ocean."

Hazel shudders. "Pass. What are you going to do after this?"

"Sail away. Read a hundred books and learn some new shit. Say goodbye to the stuff I don't want or need."

"That sounds amazing," Hazel replies dreamily, before frowning. "I don't want to say goodbye to you, though. I've gotten really used to seeing you every day."

"Me too." Ava sits beside her.

"I wish I could come with you," Hazel says.

"Who says you can't?"

/ / /

Alone in her room, Ava washes away the day's events in the shower. Relationships have never been Ava's strong suit—computers have always felt easier. If the commands she enters don't yield the result she wants, she can figure out how to make it work. With people, she is regularly confounded, disappointed, and mystified. She wants to be better at being human, to not feel so out of place. To fall in love and have friends who are chosen family. She sees people having these things all around her, but it feels removed. Still buried in her is the sense that she is faulty.

Once she's dried off and thrown on a hotel robe, she cracks open her laptop and starts typing away when a knock interrupts her flow. A text from Kagan appears, asking if she's awake. He's waiting outside her room. Her chest tightens, reluctant to answer the door. She feels drained from the day.

As she moves to let him in, Ava chastises herself. Each time she allows this, it becomes another affirmation to Kagan that something is developing between them. Despite her self-admonishments, her hand twists the doorknob.

He's wobbly crossing the threshold and smiling widely.

"I wanted to see how you were doing," he tells her as he crosses to the bed and pats the space next to him and Ava tentatively sits beside him.

"I'm not really in a talkative mood," she says.

"What mood are you in?" he asks coyly, and rubs her shoulder.

"Tired," she says wearily.

"You know, I'm really glad you decided to come with us. Hazel thought we'd lost you that day you walked out, but I knew things between you and me were too strong."

"This has been quite an experience. I can honestly say that I've never met anyone like you and Hazel."

"Hazel's a little intense, but I love her like a sister." He laughs. "Sometimes she takes things too far. She definitely likes you *a lot*."

Déjà vu from her conversation with Hazel seeps into her unease. "Well, I like her too."

Kagan's eyes darken slightly, and the corners of his mouth slope downward. Ava can see him working something out. "You know, something has been weighing on me, and I think I need to be honest with you," he says.

"Oh?" Ava replies.

He places a firm hand over hers and dons a grave expression. "Hazel wanted to kidnap you, but I told her what a bad idea that was."

Ava withdraws her hand and smacks her knee, laughing even harder than at Hazel's confession earlier. Kagan looks confused but laughs along with her.

"Well, my father wouldn't have cared, but I understand Hazel's desperation," she says, catching her breath. Kagan moves closer to her.

"You are such an enigma, Ava." Kagan shifts his position and tactic. "Can I ask you something personal?"

Ava braces herself. "Okay."

"Why did you get locked up?"

Ava knew she'd have to get into this eventually. "Remember the website Swingset?"

Kagan's eyes widen. "The swingers app?"

Ava nods. "It was a cheater dating site, but three-quarters of the members were bots."

He nods. "And what were you doing on there?" Kagan asks suggestively.

"I offered the CEO the opportunity to take down the site in exchange for my not leaking all his members' info to the public. When he declined my offer, I kept my word. The fallout was not in my favor."

"Holy shit! That was you? What do you have against swingers?" Kagan asks, astonished.

"Nothing. What people do in their private lives makes no difference to me."

"Why, then?"

"I got involved with a radical hacker group. I was trying to prove myself and was immature, angry, and on a downward spiral."

"It doesn't seem that bad to me. So you exposed a bunch of scumbags, sounds like vigilante justice," he says.

"I did a lot of damage, but I hope I can make up for it in other ways. I want to help people." Ava is tired of falsely justifying her actions. She knows her leak caused harm to the people exposed. She had a lot of time to ponder this after the fact.

"I know one person you can help right about now." Kagan cups Ava's face and moves his mouth toward her.

Ava slips out of range a few feet to the left. "I don't think this is a good idea, not with everything going on at the moment."

He nods thoughtfully and rubs her shoulder again.

"Ava, you don't have to put walls up with me. I understand you."

A dull pain radiates behind her eyes. "Do you?"

He places his hand on what Ava assumes is meant to be his heart but lands on his shoulder. "I do. You remind me of my mother a lot. She didn't want to be taken care of when she was feeling vulnerable, but I was always there for her."

Ava's stomach aches again.

He puckers his lips, and Ava puts her hand over his mouth. "This will be better if we wait. We should both get some sleep."

Kagan rises slowly, and she sees how loaded he really is. "Ava, I like you. I don't want you to think I'm a creep."

Ava lays a firm hand on his back to guide him to the door. "I don't."

He looks disappointed but relieved. He steps into the hallway, and she keeps a few feet between them. Before the door closes, he leans back in.

"You do feel this thing between us, though, don't you?"

Ava looks at him and sees an exhaustion deeper than a lack of sleep.

"I do, and it's got me pretty turned around," she says, moving her head aside and kissing him on the cheek when he comes in close again.

"It is really simple," he says confidently. "You are a prize, Ava, the coin-toss prize," he garbles.

"Huh. Thanks, I guess?" Ava half laughs.

He continues proudly, "Hazel thought she would win you, but I did."

CHAPTER 42

How lucky can one man be?

Walt has to mask his glee as he stands inside the Dunes Ballroom, his fiancée fussing over the knot in his necktie. It's all coming together even better than he anticipated only a few days ago, before Janice's meddling kids reappeared in his life. He'd spent months painstakingly researching and laying the groundwork for this latest job, the last of his illustrious career if all went to plan. And she invited these two dolts to the ceremony as he'd subtly urged her to, laying the groundwork for him to tie up a couple of loose ends in the process.

Three for the price of one.

He was proud of how it all came together with Iris. In recent years, Walt had become familiar with the philanthropic divorcée from afar, her name popping up regularly in the society pages when she attended this or that benefit for whatever organization she sat on the board of or donated obscene gobs of money to.

Something about Iris in those photos had caught his eye. She'd ticked off the obvious prerequisites, of course: no ring, never arm in arm with a date, clearly plenty of financial security to go around. But there was something deeper—a loneliness behind the eyes and slight awkwardness to her bearing, a thirst to connect and forge a meaningful bond, that suggested to Walt that a gentleman such as himself might have something to offer this worldly woman.

And then, one weekend morning, the final piece clicked into place.

As custom dictated, he was sitting alone at the kitchen table reading the Sunday edition of the *New York Times* over a cup of coffee. Janice had lately been grating his nerves, and he'd taken advantage of any available opportunity to get a breather from the woman. Flipping through the metropolitan section of the paper, he landed on the Sunday Routine column, and there—in all her befrocked glory—was a photo of Iris Garrett.

He could never understand how otherwise savvy, successful people managed to sail through life with such naivete. He found himself constantly amazed at the trusting natures of folks who should have every reason to know better openly broadcasting their personal information for anyone who took an interest. It was as if, in some subconscious way, they were asking for it.

Didn't these people understand how the world worked?

And there was Iris, laying bare her routine for the world to see. In between name-dropping the fair-trade coffee she brewed in her French press and mentioning the nonprofits she worked with, Iris let slip the fact that she'd recently taken up bird-watching as a hobby, on the advice of a friend. She admitted to being a novice and provided enough geographical detail about her preferred spot in Central Park to give him a generous head start in locating her.

Something about the timing felt serendipitous. Here was this attractive, accomplished woman who needed saving from herself, and

who better to step in and step up to the task? A couple of genuine ro-
mantics, finding each other among the rubble of an ugly, unfeeling
world—or so he'd soon convince her. Walt can still remember the ecstatic rush he felt as he set about orchestrating an encounter.

Spring had recently sprung, and what could be more enchanting
than a seemingly fated meet-cute among the fresh seasonal blooms? He
made a run to the local bookstore that afternoon and spent the next
week locked in his office, boning up on avian behavior and migratory
patterns. The following Sunday, Walt Pierson came on the scene, ready
to make magic happen. And make magic he did, promptly wooing this
woman to within an inch of her singlehood. Iris was designed to provide an escape from the family Bailey, and yet here stand his insufferable former stepchildren, no doubt feeling as smug and clever as can be.

Perfection.

As far as they believe, these rotten, good-for-nothing brats have as
much riding on this day going smoothly as he does. No, *even more*.
Neither of them can hang on to a job worth a shit, and years of their
pitiful mother's indulgence has left them unable to function in society.
If these overgrown infants foil his current plot, they'll be left with
nothing.

Walt himself would be put out, sure. Supremely inconvenienced,
even. But he'd still be sitting on a pile of Janice's money, a more-than-
comfortable operating budget if he had to pivot from here and embark
on a different endeavor. The kids, meanwhile, would be absolutely
screwed. How many more years can Hazel get away with making
these ridiculous conspiracy-nut stroke videos before she ages out? And
are there any restaurants left in the city of New York that would even
entertain the thought of hiring her brain-dead, coked-out laboratory
ape of a brother at this point? God, what a complete waste of oxygen
these two are.

And then, it hits Walt: the pièce de résistance of the whole day, still waiting to gloriously unfurl before his eyes. He was so tickled by the kids' presence in the ballroom when he first arrived that this devilish detail slipped his attention. He'd announced to Iris just last night about the surprise, last-minute arrival of his "adopted son," to the woman's utter delight. Reflecting on the moment now, he can't help but crack a grin. Oh, how surprised the siblings will be—Hazel especially—when they realize they've known the young man all along. And they'll be forced to hold it together for fear of blowing their pitiful little scheme sky-high.

Walt could not have planned this better.

As Iris finishes fiddling with the necktie, she catches the smile on her soon-to-be-husband's face and reciprocates. Walt takes in the details of the scene: the gargantuan chandelier, brilliant in its opulent glimmer; Kagan, fidgeting uncomfortably in a seersucker suit, looking like some understudy who wandered in from a dinner-theater production of a Tennessee Williams play; the vases set around the ballroom, brimming with crisp calla lilies in shades of white, orange, and aubergine; Hazel, wearing a dress of a blue so similar to the shade of the carpet that it appears she's sprung from it, staring off into space with a vacant sulk; and Iris, the woman who would finally provide Walt with the sort of life he'd worked so tirelessly to attain, and certainly the one he deserves.

Just then, Adam enters the ballroom. Walt tries to contain his glee as he studies the faces of each member of the group registering the young man's presence: Hazel's ashen pallor and look of utter shock; Kagan's slow, addled realization; and the sheer bliss of Iris's delight coupled with her magnificent ignorance. They deserve one another, the lot of them.

And they certainly deserve the surprise Walt has in store.

CHAPTER 43

Hazel feels like she's been shot in the chest. She's having trouble catching her breath and feels like the floor of the ballroom is swiftly tilting as the seconds tick by. She grabs onto Kagan to steady herself. She was fine being in the room with Perry again, playing along with their charade, even taking some pleasure in the situation's absurdity. She'd been daydreaming about the money and Ava and her possible new perfect life. And it all came to a screeching halt when Adam walked into the room, glanced at her, and looked away with no discernible reaction. Like she didn't even exist.

She nearly lunges for him, but Kagan has a firm grip on her arm. Hazel sees her brother connect the face to Hazel's reaction, and a murderous expression overtakes his face too.

"I can't believe he's here," Hazel whispers aggressively. "We have to call the police. We have to restrain him."

"Not now," Kagan whispers without alerting Iris that chaos is nearly unfolding behind her. Adam hesitates for a split second, looks at the door, and returns to Perry, who nods and subtly gestures "everything is cool."

Hazel faces forward, concerned about the speed of her heart. All the moisture from her mouth has migrated to her palms. Kagan keeps a strong arm around her until the officiant motions for them to be seated, then guides her into the chair. She feels catatonic, unable to turn her neck the mere inches required to get Adam back in her periphery, but his lurking presence behind her is deeply unsettling.

Though Hazel hears only a series of murmurs of varying cadence and volume, the ceremony carries forward. Walt and Iris stand a row away from them, grinning at each other, clasping hands under an arch adorned with brightly colored hibiscus and coreopsis. A man stands before them, the officiant, and speaks in what sounds like gibberish to Hazel's panicked brain. All the moments she'd fantasized about what she'd say to Adam if she saw him again are gone. Her mind keeps spinning, the centrifugal force of her confusion pinning any logic or reason to the walls of her skull.

After a short while or an eternity, Kagan puts a heavy hand on her back and guides her to standing. He's clapping and motions for her to do the same. The blurry couple is kissing, and the officiant exits through a side door. Hazel finds her feet on the floor and strength in her brother's calm.

"Keep it together, *Patricia*," Kagan says softly.

"Why is Adam here?" she says through gritted teeth.

Kagan looks behind her. "He's gone."

Hazel forces her body to turn, and she sees that nobody is in the ballroom now except for Walt and Iris, who are holding hands and speaking closely at the front of the room. The siblings huddle. "We need to call Calabrese. We need to let Ava know he's here!"

Kagan frowns. "We can text her soon. Walt will bolt if we involve the authorities, and we'll never see a penny. Once Ava transfers the cash into our accounts, we'll drop the dime on these assholes."

Hazel is impressed with her brother's calm. The promise of solvency has focused him in a way she hasn't seen in a while. She's just realizing that Kagan appears sober for the first time in weeks.

"I'm so happy you came!" Iris squeals in their direction.

They snap into character quickly.

"You are a vision!" Kagan croons, and kisses Iris on each cheek. She beams.

"Congratulations," Hazel forces.

"Oh dear, you look stricken," Iris says, putting a comforting arm around Hazel.

"Sorry. I'm bad at weddings." She sniffles, realizing she's been crying. "I guess I was thinking about my mom."

Iris's face drops a little.

"Patricia's mom died before we got married," Kagan adds.

"Oh, you poor thing." Iris embraces her.

"It was a beautiful ceremony," Hazel recovers.

"No more dwelling on the past," Walt chimes in from a few feet away. "Today is about our bright futures."

"Well, I desperately need the bathroom before I move into my future." Iris nuzzles up to Walt. "You gave me too much champagne," she says, suddenly seeming much looser than she'd appeared at the altar. "Excuse me for a minute."

"Hurry back, dear; I've got a surprise for you."

"Oh, hubby, what are you up to now?"

Walt consults his watch. "It's a surprise. But be quick; we're losing daylight."

"Are Matt and Patricia coming?"

Walt grins, his veneered teeth catching the light of the grand chandelier above them. "You beat me to it, dear. I was about to invite our new friends. We have much to celebrate now that we're business partners."

/ / /

Walt sweeps them into an SUV just as Iris rejoins the group. The siblings stay quiet during the short ride while Iris blathers on. Hazel is fighting to keep her facade up while suppressing the primal scream rising in her. Kagan keeps the small talk going with Iris as Walt remains pensively quiet as they pull into a marina. Given the opportunity, Hazel is worried about what her brother might do to Adam.

"What are we doing here?" Iris laughs lightly. Hazel senses trepidation in her voice.

"Just a little longer, darling; your wedding gift is yonder." He guides her out of the Escalade and takes her by the hand down the dock without waiting for them. Hazel's phone vibrates, and she sees a text from Ava, one of a handful she's missed since the ceremony. She responds to the numerous inquiries about where they are with one word: marina. And then: ADAM IS HERE.

"Patricia, Matt! Join us," Walt calls, craning his neck as they disembark from the SUV and approach. As they follow Iris and Walt to the end of the dock, Hazel notices Iris's shoulders tensing with each step. Walt halts in front of a large sailboat draped with a white sheet over the bow. Adam stands on the deck, holding a bottle of champagne, pointedly avoiding eye contact with Hazel and Kagan. Hazel's blood runs cold, and Kagan's entire posture stiffens.

"Now!" Walt yells up to Adam.

Adam lifts the sheet, revealing "Iris" emblazoned across the bow.

Hazel observes Iris's facial expression progress from confused to worried and shocked before landing on feigned happiness.

"Walt, you really shouldn't have," she forces.

Hazel observes the hidden dismay lurking behind the forced smile and her meticulously applied makeup.

Walt puts an arm around her waist and walks her toward the gangway.

"My love, I know you aren't a boat person, but you've never been aboard with me. I'd never let anything happen to you. This is a worthy sea vessel, and Adam is a skilled captain. I taught him everything he knows."

She's dumbstruck as he guides her up the boarding ramp. She turns to the siblings, who are still standing on the dock. Hazel can see fear in her eyes.

"Matthew, Patricia! Join us," Walt commands again.

Kagan mutters "fuck" under his breath.

"Oh no, we couldn't impose on your romantic evening. We'll ride back to the resort and catch up with you guys tomorrow before you leave," Hazel says, straining.

"Oh, please!" Iris pleads.

"I insist," Walt says, calmly gesturing them over. "You're practically family now."

Kagan turns to Hazel and, without saying anything, says everything.

CHAPTER 44

"This is just the best day ever!"

Kagan can't square the words coming out of Iris's mouth with the look on her face. She's doing her darndest to summon some enthusiasm but is coming up woefully short. The look of unease is palpable. Anxious energy radiates off the woman as she tries to orient herself on the deck of the boat the group members now stand aboard. Walt helps to steady her, but his display of confidence isn't quite doing the trick.

Kagan can't afford to worry too much about Iris at the moment. His sister is of more immediate concern. Hazel's practically seething with hatred for the man she once dated. For the time being they are trapped on a sailboat with the same man who likely pushed their mother to her death, and who's shown up for the ceremony posing as some lost soul Walt supposedly adopted as part of a do-gooder program through his former church. And Kagan gets it. If not for the current circumstances, he'd tear the guy's head off himself. But this isn't the time. What they need to stay focused on is the pot of gold at the end of this shit show. He and Hazel can plot their revenge later.

Adam approaches with a tray of champagne-filled flutes. He's wearing a yacht cap, which has the effect of making him look like a first-class dickhead. Kagan steps forward and retrieves two glasses, in order to provide his sister a physical buffer. He'll need to do his best to keep the two separated for the duration of this cruise. The siblings are so close to finally getting some closure, the stability of their inheritance, and some sense of justice.

Captain Asshole finishes distributing the flutes, then takes one for himself. He sets the tray on the deck and raises his glass. "To the happy couple. May your life together be nothing but clear skies and smooth sailing." *Jesus. Seriously?*

The group raises their glasses and downs sips of the bubbly. The happy couple appear delighted by the trite toast. Walt grasps Iris's hands and stares lovingly into her eyes, a tear materializing from the corner of his own.

"Iris, you've shown me the greatest happiness I've ever known. Before I met you, I only thought I knew what real love was. But now I get to experience it with you, every day for the rest of our lives."

Good God, thinks Kagan. *These guys need speechwriters, stat.*

Iris begins sobbing, whether from the swirl of emotions or her crippling fear of the water, Kagan can't be sure. "Oh, Walty," she manages between heaving gasps. "You're a dream come true." She turns her attention to Adam. "And what a marvelous surprise to find out about your son! I've always dreamed of truly being part of a family."

Hazel squeezes her brother's forearm with such intensity that her nails threaten to break the skin. He slips her grip in such a way that their arms interlace, and Kagan steers his sister forward toward Iris. Of the people aboard, he reasons that the old lady will have the most calming effect on her. If they're to make it through the last leg of this ordeal without blowing everything up, using Iris to distract Hazel seems like the most sound strategy.

As expected, the new bride effuses emotion, hugging the siblings as she thanks them for sharing this most special of days and weeping about how much their friendship has come to mean to her. She grasps Hazel's hands and expresses sorrow over the fictional dead mother Kagan had drummed up earlier to cover for his pretend wife's mess of emotions. Iris goes on to commiserate by sharing her own heartbreak at the loss of her loving parents.

While his sister is swept up in conversation, Kagan notices Walt approach Adam and whisper something in the guy's ear before disappearing below deck. A moment later, the de facto captain joins the conversation that Iris is steering, careful to give Hazel a wide berth.

"Hope you're all enjoying this spectacular view," begins Adam. "Can I top up anyone's glasses?"

"We're fine," Kagan answers for himself and Hazel. He doesn't want to run the risk of his sister loosening up enough on the booze to cause a scene. "You know, sea legs and all."

Iris holds out her flute eagerly but frowns as she reconsiders the idea. "You know, Matt's right. I'm not the most stable boater to begin with." There's a trace of embarrassment in her expression as she hands the empty glass to Adam.

"Very well then." He adjusts the yacht cap and looks out toward the horizon. "We'll set sail in just a few minutes, but first let me tell you all a bit of fun history about Boca Raton. In the early 1900s, this charming little town became a modest agricultural hub, specializing in the cultivation of pineapples. . . ."

He blathers on for several minutes about Ponce de León and a safari park and numerous shipwrecks. As he name-checks various flora indigenous to the Florida coastline, Kagan notices Iris scanning the deck. Gilligan finally wraps up his spiel and consults his wristwatch.

"Ah, the moment has arrived. Matt, would you do me a favor and untie the line from the cleat at the bow of the boat?"

"Um, excuse me." There's mild agitation in Iris's tone. "Did you see where Walt ran off to?"

"Oh, not to worry." Adam slips an arm around Iris's shoulder in an effort to calm her nerves. "Dad was just feeling a little lightheaded. He'll join us on deck as soon as we get going. But we should leave now if we're going to catch the sunset. I promise it'll be fabulous!"

The explanation has the effect of calming Iris. Adam invites the ladies to have a seat as he instructs Kagan on how to help with the lines. After a few minutes, they push off from the dock and set sail.

"Oh, boy!" Adam gasps, pointing toward a cluster of clouds. "We'll be enjoying an especially picturesque scene this evening, that's for sure."

He proceeds to put some distance between them and the dock. As Kagan eyes the shore, he finds it harder to discern the fishing piers that dot the coast. He and the ladies continue their discussion as Walt's fake surrogate son maneuvers the vessel into increasingly deeper water, the chop of the sea becoming more agitated. In spite of this, Iris has settled in and is making a real effort to enjoy the adventure. Except for the occasional glance toward the cabin, she's fully present in the conversation with the siblings.

As Adam points out a lighthouse in the distance, Kagan finds himself distracted by a muffled whooshing sound that seems to be originating from below. He excuses himself and walks carefully along the deck to the cabin door. As he yanks it open, Kagan's greeted by a torrent of water ripping through the space.

"Adam! We've got a problem here."

The captain abandons his post and trots back toward Kagan, the ladies in tow. They all let out yelps and panicked gasps at the sight of the flooding.

"Walty!" yells Iris, bereft. Adam barrels down the steps, the other three hot on his heels. The water comes up to their calves. Adam flings open the door to the stateroom to find a perfectly made bed, unrumpled and unslept in.

Walt Pierson is nowhere to be found.

Iris's panic takes on a trace of confusion. She looks around the cabin and hollers desperately for Walt as Hazel screams Perry's name, blind rage animating her tone. The unfamiliar name stops Iris midyell. She stares at the siblings, dumbstruck. The water is flooding the cabin at such a rapid clip that Kagan barely has a moment to marvel at Walt's Houdini routine.

Just then, he eyes a small envelope set atop the pillow on the bed as if it were a mint left by housekeeping in a hotel suite. He hops across the room, feet sloshing water every which way, and plucks the envelope from the pillow. He hops back to the others and tugs a rectangle of textured card stock from the envelope. On it, written in elegant cursive, is a simple two-word message:

Bon Voyage

Kagan feels his stomach drop like a trapdoor built into a stage.

Hazel's face is a swirl of shock, fury, and desperation.

Adam falls back against the ladder with a whimper, his body gone limp.

Iris wears the disbelieving look of a woman who's been betrayed before.

And all the while, the rushing water, undaunted and unyielding, laps at them hungrily.

CHAPTER 45

Ava hadn't been given a say in her mother's death notice. When she'd been able to track down the newspaper archives many years later, the tribute she read had little about who her mother was and plenty about the heroic husband she left behind. Sometimes, she'd mentally rewrite the obituary, mentioning her mom's sweet singing voice or how she always smelled like the beach. Those sentimental tributes helped her sleep at night and were only for her.

This one was for them.

Ava had spent much of her childhood reading obituaries out loud for her father during their many diner sessions. The tributes were a gold mine, rich with information and opportunity to be exploited. He taught her how to spot the most desirable recently dead, the obits that included more personal info than most people share about themselves with their best friend. He instructed her on how to select which deceased stranger's family members to call upon, intuiting who would be the most desperate to talk about their loved one. These heartfelt homages were his bottomless wishing wells if he needed a new identity, quick cash and lines of credit, or a wealthy mark.

It was morbid work for a tween, but Ava liked reading about people's lives. She could imagine having a hundred different fates, better than the one she'd found herself in.

Some of the families included shades of their loved one's personalities that set their tributes apart: "In memory of Fran, who hated people but loved *Jeopardy!*"; "In tribute to Keith, who couldn't carry a tune but didn't let that stop him from weekly karaoke." The levity in these notices lifted her despite the morose context. Her father avoided those people; if the family was thoughtful enough to add a little extra to their obit, they probably paid more attention than was worth his time.

Sometimes the tributes struck memento mori in her, leaving her in an existential tailspin. She remembered a girl around her age who'd died: "In loving memory of Athena, who lived by the motto 'Why walk when you can dance; why cry when you can laugh?' Now she laughs and dances in heaven." Ava had kept that one folded in her pocket for a few weeks until the newsprint disintegrated in the wash.

She reflects on how sideways her existence has become since the siblings brought her father back into her life. For all the obits she had picked apart for deeper understanding, Ava felt clear on this one.

CHAPTER 46

Walt practically tiptoes down the staircase to the front door of his sister's cavernous old wreck of a home, a duffel bag slung over his shoulder. Since returning to the mansion on Hilton Head before the sun came up this morning, he's been accosted by Constance at every turn. He'd driven through the night, the adrenaline from the execution of his retirement score propelling him the entire way. To Walt's great surprise, Constance had been awake and shuffling around the living room when he let himself in. She was at first startled by his presence, then relieved at the familiar sound of his voice. That was followed in short order by elation, confusion, fear, and suspicion.

He wonders if she's onto him, if a sixth sense is cutting through the fog of her addled brain and tipping Constance off to the fact that today will be the last time she ever sees her brother in the flesh. He'd barely gotten a wink of sleep before she was down his throat with nosy questions, following him around the house as if he were there to rob the place. There's a whiff of desperation to her clinginess, and Walt figures a clean exit is best for both of them.

He approaches the front door and does his best to ease it open gingerly, but the protest of the squeaky hinge foils his plan. He suddenly feels like a teenager trying to sneak out past curfew.

"Harmon?" The screech of Constance's voice carrying down the hallway rankles him.

"He's dead, you old bat," Walt mutters.

"What?"

"Just running to town," he responds at an audible volume.

"Oh. Harmon, would you be a dear and pick me up a package of Vienna Fingers?"

"Certainly, darling." He winces.

"Toodle-oo."

Walt shuts the door behind him and hustles down the porch stairs as quickly as his cramping legs will carry him. He stows the duffel in the trunk of the Alfa Romeo, then lowers himself into the driver's seat. He keys the ignition and lets out a breath. Freedom is so close he can practically hear it ringing. Just this one last thing to check on, to confirm he's in the clear.

/ / /

Walt enters the internet café in town and promptly bristles at the sea of cold technology surrounding him. It's just as unsexy as he imagined. He'd have much preferred to consult an actual newspaper, but the *Miami Herald* apparently doesn't make the trip to newsstands in Hilton Head. Walt approaches the counter and orders an espresso, hoping the concentrated jolt of caffeine will provide him some much-needed energy. The space is nearly empty, and so he doesn't hesitate to ask the young lady behind the counter for some help logging on.

She gets him set up at one of the monitors, efficiently but politely, before returning to her station. Walt types the words "boating accident Boca Raton" into the search bar and hits the Return key, per the barista's instructions. The first thing to pop up on screen is a headline with today's date:

**REMAINS OF SAILBOAT RECOVERED
OFF BOCA RATON COAST. ONE CONFIRMED DEAD.**

One? Walt begins reading.

> Tragedy struck yesterday evening as a recreational vessel carrying members of a wedding party sank off the coast of Boca Raton during a sunset cruise. All but one of the members of the group were rescued and made it safely to shore. The remains of Walter Pierson, 76, were recovered along with the . . .

Walt doesn't realize he's slammed his fist against the table until the uneasy looks of the staff and trio of patrons alert him to the disturbance. He apologizes distractedly and returns his attention to the computer screen. Something is very wrong here. Very, very wrong.

Flummoxed, Walt types "*Miami Herald* obituaries" into the search bar and punches the Return key. At the top of the queue, he sees it. He can feel the vein in his temple begin to throb as he tries to make sense of the words on the screen and the photo of his younger self that accompanies them.

WALTER PIERSON, FLIMFLAM MAN, DIES AT 76

> Walter Pierson, an accomplished con man and unscrupulous death dealer, died at sea on July 14 amid the wreckage of a boat he'd purchased with the intention of using the craft to orchestrate multiple homicides. He was 76.

The death was confirmed by Mr. Pierson's daughter, whom he schooled in the ways of the grift a little too well. He is survived by his latest wife, who managed to escape his clutches, as well as a sister, Constance Danforth, née Leslie. Mr. Pierson died penniless and alone.

In lieu of flowers, donations can be made to the National Women's Coalition Against Violence & Exploitation (NWCAVE).

Confusion, disbelief, fear, and rage jockey for position as the realization clicks into place. Ava. His daughter's been manipulating the strings on this puppet show the entire time. Of course she has. Walt knew those idiot stepkids could never have managed all of this on their own. He sees now that the inkling of pride he'd felt for Kagan was misplaced. It had been his daughter, his own flesh and blood, this whole time.

Just below the last line of the obituary he notices a bit of scripture:

Ecclesiastes 5:13

There is a grievous evil which I have seen under the sun: riches being hoarded by their owner to his hurt.

The biblical reference throws Walt. He didn't raise Ava to be religious. If anything, he tried to alert his daughter to the inherent vulnerability of those who sought a higher power. People of faith were people who could be easily exploited. He's shocked that she . . .

And then it hits him, square in the gut. The word "hoarded" jumps out from the text on the screen, and he realizes where the photo of him must have been dug up. *No,* he thinks. *She wouldn't.*

Walt hustles out of the café, slips into the Alfa, and peels off toward the Hoard and Seek storage lot. The few-miles-long drive to the facility feels like an eternity. He rips into the lot and leaves the engine running as he gets out and fumbles frantically for the key in his pocket. Walt manages to calm his ping-ponging nerves enough to work the key into the lock and pull open the roll-up door.

The echoing emptiness hits his eardrums like the crack of a gunshot. The sunlight illuminates the space, bare but for a piece of paper set atop a lone chair in the middle of the unit. His wardrobe: gone. Filing cabinets full of ID cards and forms and bank-account information for his various aliases: gone. Folders full of research on his marks over the years: all gone. Every one of his existences has been stripped away. He thinks of Ava, and there is the briefest burst of pride, of regret, of fury, of hatred, of acceptance.

He has nothing.

As he approaches the chair, his legs falter. At the top of the official form, he deciphers the words "Certificate of Live Birth." Below that, he reads a name he hasn't thought about in as long as he can remember. "Jenson Leslie." No middle name. Between the booze and the men and the laughing fits and crying jags and all the other displays of self-absorption, his mother simply couldn't be bothered.

Jenson can't help but chuckle at the bitter irony of the situation. He'd schooled his only daughter a little too well indeed. Ava knew about the storage unit, and by holding on to the space for all this time, he left a loose thread for the quick study to tug on. Provided her the shovel with which to bury her dear old dad.

It all seems suddenly inevitable. After years of dedicated, selfless tutelage, Ava paid him back by abandoning him, like every other female in his bloodline. Of course she had. Only ever looking out for their own interests, these women.

Jenson eyes the birth certificate, a profound rage crackling inside him. Decades of hustle and hard work, and the identity he spent his entire life running from is the only thing he has left.

CHAPTER 47

The backdrop of Hazel's final video is appropriately bleak: cracked tile in a heavily mildewed bathtub; a suspicious, dark rust-colored ring around the drain; and a cheap opaque shower curtain that screams crime scene.

She sits on the tub's edge, watching the views quadruple, exhilarated by the virality of her unvarnished truth. As the shares and likes rapidly multiply, she's already reconsidered her claim that it will be her last. She never thought about a path in true crime, but evidently, she's a natural. The silver lining in all this drama shimmers; Hazel has finally found her true calling.

In the latest segment, she unpacked Janice's relationship with Perry and her murder. She dissected her situationship with Adam. She showed clear photos of both men she'd taken on the sailboat, and listed Perry's various aliases. She hoped the internet would do what it does best and storm the virtual castle by connecting Perry's and Adam's victims and defrosting all the cold cases. Hazel ended the segment with an in memoriam montage of Janice that rivaled the Oscars and would doubtlessly pressure authorities (and Hollywood producers) to take notice.

Hazel included a link to the video in a draft email to Detective Calabrese sharing Adam's next destination. He was bound for a check-cashing joint in the Florida Keys where Ava told him to pick up his compensation in exchange for not going after Walt for abandoning him and alerting him of the group's rescue in the process. This wasn't a hard sell, since Walt leaving him to drown with the rest of them had swiftly reversed Adam's loyalty. Hazel scheduled the message to be sent tomorrow morning, when they'd be out of the country and unreachable for further questioning. She's happy to be done with all that drama and has so much to look forward to.

When Hazel emerges from the dingy bathroom, Kagan is noticeably absent. His bed is empty, his bag is gone, and the car keys are no longer on the table by the door. There's a handwritten note on the bedside table.

Running out. Not sure when I'll be back.

Assuming Kagan is off copping more party favors, she represses the familiar anxiety reserved for him. This isn't her problem any longer. She's trying to cultivate a mindset of self-focus, not Kagan-focus. Hazel is ready to let someone take care of her, Ava specifically. She's unsure about the shape of their relationship, but Ava's attentiveness has piqued her interest in a way she hasn't experienced before.

Hazel is exhilarated by the image of Ava waiting for her at their meeting spot, ready to jump on a plane and fly to their financially secure future. It wasn't the relationship she'd imagined for herself, but Ava surprised Hazel. She's all in for reinvention, and although she's never felt fully part of the LGBTQ community, there's no denying the vast untapped demographic for Hazel. Her mind reels with crossover influencer possibilities. Hazel knows that Ava may be opposed to her keeping an online presence, but she will promise to be moderate and not let it affect their relationship. Though, maybe she won't mention it right away.

Relieved by Kagan's absence, the restlessness and irritability of the motel exile begins to lift. She navigated each eggshell moment with anticipatory excitement, mostly immune to his snippiness. While a hint of guilt lingers, it's merely a trace. It aligned with Janice's wishes and would steer him toward the option their mother had desired for him. A dying wish she believed he would one day appreciate.

The past forty-eight hours had been so ludicrous she wasn't sure if the ordeal would ever fully situate itself in the reality-discerning part of her brain. Yet, the near-death experience injected the perfect amount of existential jolt she needed.

After Ava had overheard her father conspiring with Adam on the phone the night of the dinner, she prepped Hazel and Kagan when they returned to the room. The invitation to the wedding confirmed what Ava laid out for them: the inclusion was calculated, as was the one for the sunset sail that followed.

"Four birds, one sinking. Nice and clean, just the way Perry likes it."

Even though they'd expected that Walt would desert them on board and Ava would retrieve them, things got dicey in the lead-up to the rescue. The boat took on seawater much faster than anyone had expected, and they found themselves waist-deep when Adam reported that Walt had sabotaged the water pump system and dismantled the ship's radio. With no phone service and a missing lifeboat, it dawned on Hazel that Ava might not be their hero after all. There was a terrifying moment when she looked at her brother with real fear, and he returned it.

But, of course, Ava was true to her word. Before the water got any higher, she rescued them in a boat she'd borrowed for a test drive from a hopeful seller earlier that day. Devastated by the truth about her new husband, Iris was inconsolable. With the revelation that Patricia and Matt Devlin were as fictitious as Walt Pierson and his adopted son, Adam, Iris turned against everyone except Ava, who received more leeway for saving her life. Things went from awkward to heated quickly, and Ava practically had to tackle Hazel and Kagan to keep them from attacking Adam until they'd reached the safety of land.

Ava brought the group to a secluded inlet, avoiding the marina, as it would jeopardize her plan. Ava assigned each member their tasks upon reaching dry land. Adam eventually conceded when presented with his options. Undetected, they scattered as advised—Hazel and Kagan to the Dime a Dream motel on the outskirts of the Everglades, Iris to a posher establishment in Boca, and Adam to the Florida Keys. No wistful farewells were exchanged.

Two days later, Hazel is ready to take Ava's advice and leave all of this behind her. She hastily packs her belongings into a carry-on. Plugging her destination into the Uber app, she impatiently waits by the window, hoping her ride arrives before her brother. When her phone alerts her that her driver is coming, Hazel steps into the muggy morning air, pulling the motel door closed behind her. A twinge of shame creeps in as she scans the parking lot for any sign of Kagan before sliding into the getaway car.

/ / /

The Olympus Diner is a facsimile of every other prefab eatery along the Eastern Seaboard. Despite passing such establishments countless times, Hazel can't recall ever dining in one until this week. They've always seemed like breeding grounds for mediocrity, a sentiment confirmed by the handful of diners at the counter. A few patrons glance her way over their coffees, but Hazel's glare sends them back to their conversations with the dour woman behind the counter.

A waitress wafts past, leaving the scent of smoke and drugstore perfume in her wake. "Just one, hon?" she asks.

"I'm meeting someone," Hazel replies, scanning the booths for Ava. They're all empty, except one with a half-drunk beer bottle atop the table. She'd intentionally arrived fifteen minutes late for their meeting, and is surprised and slightly miffed that Ava isn't already there. Hazel had wanted to make an entrance.

"Sit anywhere you want," the server calls over her shoulder, disappearing through the swinging doors into the kitchen.

Hazel heads to the booth farthest from the riffraff and takes a seat. She immediately checks her phone and doesn't see anything from Ava. She switches to her MeTube channel and reads through the responses. People relating to stories of being scammed flood the comment section. Unlike her previous posts, there's no negative commentary. And her user engagement is off the charts. She's ecstatic.

"Hazel?"

Kagan hovers nervously a few feet from the booth with the abandoned beer, likely returning from the bathroom. He grabs the half-full bottle and quickly walks over to where Hazel is sitting.

"What are you doing here?" she asks, flustered.

"What are *you* doing here?" he replies, remaining squirrelly and hovering next to the booth. Hazel realizes someone in the kitchen likely had what he was after. The coincidence of Kagan's drug hookup is just her luck.

He slides in across from her, glancing over his shoulder at the door. "Did you follow me?" Kagan accuses.

"No!"

"Then why are you here?"

"I'm meeting Ava," she says, looking out the window.

"Bullshit," Kagan retorts. He rubs his face with his hands and groans. "I'm meeting Ava."

Hazel's cheeks flame. "Seriously, K, why are you here?"

"I am being serious. And so are Ava and I."

Hazel snorts.

"Why are you so surprised?" Kagan looks hurt. "We kept things on the level out of respect for you until the operation was over."

She attempts composure, but her brimming eyes betray that effort. "I don't believe you."

"I don't understand why Ava asked you to come here too," he says.

"Same reason as you, apparently." She pats her overnight bag.

"Oh, God, Hazel. Not again."

"What?"

"It isn't what you think it is," Kagan says gently. "You're just fixated on her because she gave you attention."

"Evidently, neither of us thought correctly." The siblings sit in stunned silence until a server sidles up.

"What can I get you?" she asks.

"Another beer," Kagan replies.

"Nothing for me," Hazel says.

The server walks away. Hazel blows her hair out of her face. Waves of realization pummel her. "Were you going to run away with her?" Hazel asks quietly. He nods. "I feel so stupid."

"I can't believe you were going to leave without telling me," Kagan says.

"I can believe you would," Hazel mutters while staring at her phone screen.

"Is this conversation not interesting enough?" he snaps.

Hazel slams her phone down hard onto the table and immediately checks it for damage. "I'm trying to reach Ava."

"I don't get it. This isn't like her," Kagan mumbles.

"Obviously, neither of us really knows what Ava is like since we're both sitting here staring at each other," Hazel says miserably. Her phone vibrates with a text notification, and the siblings lock eyes. Hazel snatches the phone off the table and sees a number she doesn't recognize. She opens the message, and her heart drops again when she reads it.

> I've really missed you and our chats. I was very moved by your recent post. I hope my information contributed positively to the outcome. If there is ever anything you need, please don't hesitate to reach out. I am your biggest fan and would be honored to devote all of my time to your happiness. -Dick Vidocq

"Is it Ava? What did she say?" Kagan whines.

Crestfallen, she hands the phone to Kagan, who huffs when he reads the message. He checks his phone and frowns. "She's not coming, is she?"

"You were going to take my share," Hazel says angrily.

"Weren't you?" he counters.

"I would have given your share back when you pulled your shit together."

Kagan taps his phone screen frantically.

"What?" Hazel asks, doing the same.

"I'm trying to find out where our money is."

Hazel texts Ava again. She assumes Kagan does the same as he jams away on his screen.

A return text appears.

Not delivered.

"NO. WHAT? WOW," Kagan hollers. The counter crew all turn to stare at them. He throws his phone down and gawks at it, baffled. "That is just fucking unbelievable."

"K, *calm down*," Hazel hisses.

"Check your email."

"Why?"

"I just received a reservation confirmation for a bed at Hope's Crossroads; check-in *today*."

He flicks the phone toward Hazel. She's already scrolling through a reservation for the same facility under her name.

"I don't understand. A month of 'Digital dependency detox and rehabilitation'? Paid in full," Hazel whispers until she sees the total. "Seventy-five thousand fucking dollars?!"

Kagan laughs dryly and shakes his head disbelievingly.

Hazel is scanning the search results for Hope's Crossroads, twenty miles away.

"Ava's sending us to rehab?"

"With our money." Kagan accepts the beer from the waitress, his eyes wild.

"How did we not see this coming?" Hazel puts her head in her hands.

"She's a pro. She probably planned to do this the entire time, and Perry was probably in on it. The whole family is fucked." He hits the table hard, and their waitress warns them with a death look from across the diner.

"This is your fault. You were trying to turn her against me from the outset, Kagan. You wanted her all to yourself. You can't ever let me be the one who gets what they want."

"Bullshit. You don't even know what you want, Haze, besides validation."

"Did you actually care about her? Or did you just want to beat me?" Hazel asks, angry tears cascading down her cheeks.

"Yes, I liked her. Maybe I could have even loved her. I've been so twisted since Bethany and then Mom. I don't know anymore." Hazel's startled to see him well up.

"Hey, it is going to be okay," Hazel says, her chest hurting at the sight of her brother's pain.

"I'm so tired, Haze. I feel like the walls are closing in on me," he says.

Hazel holds her head in her hands and tries to catch her breath. She wants to scream, but she settles for silent, gutted shock. She checks her bank account in the hope that the overdrawn amount has been transformed into seven figures since this morning. Maybe Ava got delayed after she moved the money around. But it was never part of the plan to deposit the funds into their personal accounts; that was what the offshore accounts she'd set up for them were for.

"We handed her our money," Kagan says before downing his entire beer in one long swig.

"What are we going to do?" Hazel asks. "We have nothing. We have no one."

The siblings stare at each other, waiting. Hazel silently urges her brother to speak first, hoping he will take the lead as the older sibling and guide them toward the right decision.

"You know what Mom would have wanted us to do," Hazel finally says. "Apparently, Ava knew too."

He smiles sadly. "We'll go to Hope's Crossroads."

Hazel senses a new emotion welling up inside her—perhaps relief or a newfound respect for her brother, tinged with hope. This wasn't the ending she'd expected when she woke up today, but she's ready to surrender. And at least she's still with Kagan.

"Really?"

"Absolutely." His eyes darken, and he pounds the table with a closed fist. "We'll demand full refunds, and if they refuse, we'll tell them to take it up with our lawyer. And when we finish there, we get your boyfriend Dick Vidocq to find Ava again, and this time, we'll take her down. She has no idea who she's messed with."

EPILOGUE

Ava steers the boat into the vast expanse of the Caribbean as the cluster of islands making up the Keys dissolve into specks behind her. The gentle waves lapping against the hull provide a soothing soundtrack. It feels good to be on her own again; her only travel companions are the seabirds catching the updraft and the rising sun, a palette of brighter things ahead.

A south wind pulls the boat swiftly away from the mainland as the keel slices through the glassy water. The color morphs from aquamarine into darker blues, reflecting the changing depth beneath her, a reminder that she is leaving the safety of land and heading farther into the uncharted open water. Soon, nothing will be behind or before her, making her vessel utterly insignificant against the blue expanse.

The 1982 Valiant had seen better days, but Ava quickly paid the eager seller sixty grand in cash for the swift transaction and a half-day loan of a Sea Ray speedboat, which she used to rescue the panicked wedding crew from drowning.

The Valiant is charming in its weather-beaten appearance, and all forty feet will take her as far as Nassau, where she plans to upgrade with some of the money from Walt Pierson's account, transferred into the offshore shell corporation Trust in Hope, LLC.

Ava knew the day she followed her father to the marina that he was planning to sink the large sailboat that he was buying with Iris's money. This was confirmed by the multiple insurance policies she discovered in the hotel safe and what she overheard during her father's conversation with Adam in his hotel room the night of the dinner.

The night after breaking into their room, Ava returned to the marina. She learned that the boat was a lemon with a flashy new nav system when she talked her way onto it. The owner explained it was no longer for sale as he'd just taken a cash deposit for it, but he'd let her take a gander if she'd agree to have a sunset cocktail with him on board. She spotted several things wrong with the pump system, and the hull was shoddily patched in several places, but to the novice, all of that was eclipsed by the flashy technology.

As the sun set, she sipped a glass of champagne with the pervy skipper and got the Wi-Fi for the boat, enabling her to hack into the nav back at the hotel that night. That was how she'd located the group in the rapidly sinking ship on the wedding day; her father hadn't known the first thing about digital, so he destroyed the radio, not realizing the much more modern system would be a problem if anyone left on the boat, or off, knew how to use it.

Ava wonders how Hazel and Kagan have processed her nonintervention intervention and if they've given in. She hopes so. They lost a lot, and regardless of her conflicted feelings about them, she wishes them the best. Though the image of the siblings miserably sitting in group therapy was amusing.

This outcome wasn't what she had anticipated when they cornered her in Hell. As she immersed herself deeper, the opportunities to honor her mother, Hope; Sam's mother, Alison; and Janice multiplied, presenting a chance to make significant amends in her life by helping Kagan and Hazel and ending her father's cycle.

However, spending more time with them revealed that Kagan and Hazel were not the victims they portrayed, and things quickly veered.

Her reversal came when Ava hacked their mother's email account a few days into their trip. Janice had been very organized and saved a cache of Hazel's and Kagan's emails, which revealed them to be money-grubbers who regularly manipulated their mother with little regard for the woman's emotional well-being. Ava discovered a significantly different spin on Hazel and Kagan's claims about Perry being the cause of their relationship rifts. Janice had cut them out of their inheritance six months before Perry Walters came on the scene. Hazel depleted her trust fund in four years through a series of frivolous expenses, ranging from months-long vacations to handbags that cost more than Ava's monthly income. Hazel burned through almost two million dollars in six months. Her appeals for financial assistance were typically guilt-ridden, often invoking her troubled childhood due to their father and Janice.

By the time Perry entered the picture, Janice had already cut Hazel off. The only change, as far as Ava could see, was that Hazel blocked Janice's emails and phone calls, missing a year's worth of messages. These messages included Janice's attempts to rebuild their relationship, her concerns about Kagan's addictions, updates about her new job at the Cloisters, and praises for Hazel's growing fan base on MeTube. Ava discovered Janice's confirmation email from the video platform, revealing her username, JanArt54, and the hundreds of positive comments she had made on Hazel's videos. Janice had been watching and supporting her daughter the entire time.

As for Kagan, Janice had stopped giving him any money after the fourth time she'd had to post bail for him. Kagan had asked his mother for money with the same frequency as his sister after he, too, squandered his trust. He'd appeared to make an effort to get to know Janice's new husband, until Janice realized that Kagan was simply hitting Perry up for money. She'd put her foot down, and Kagan rarely responded to any of the concerned emails when he missed several family events and birthdays. In a reply to one email she'd sent, he wrote that she needed to "stop smothering and let go" of him, which is what she finally did.

Ava also accessed Janice's Google documents, which she had written to Perry Walters after their meeting in the support group. Janice had typed her notes and printed them out due to severe arthritis that made writing by hand difficult. In the first letter, she expressed her appreciation for Perry's old-fashioned ways, noting how refreshing it was that he avoided email and how much she enjoyed receiving his handwritten cards.

Ava got to know and like Janice; she was sharing all the parts of herself that people do when they are newly smitten. She'd given Perry all the information he needed to initially manipulate her. In her early letters to Perry, she expressed her desire to mend things with her adult children, especially after learning about the daughter he had lost and the profound impact it had on him.

In an unsent email draft to Hazel and Kagan a month before her murder, Janice had become suspicious of Perry, noting a change in his behavior. He would disappear for extended periods, move money around without telling her, and become defensively evasive when questioned. Janice expressed her desire to reconnect with the kids and hoped they would visit her at the Cloisters one day.

The more she learned, the more conflicted Ava became. Rather than solely fixating on teaching her father a long overdue lesson, she turned her attention toward the siblings. At every juncture, Ava hadn't intended to deceive Hazel and Kagan, but their betrayal, manipulation, and tendency to treat her as a pawn made them irresistible targets.

When they each tattled on the other about using her as leverage with her father, she was angry, but it was their callousness about Iris's fate that pushed her over the edge. They needed a severe wake-up call.

Ava was haunted by her hypocrisy: raging against becoming like her father while actively plotting alongside him. The night before the wedding, Ava gave them the opportunity to be honest with her. But when they each completely fabricated versions of their loyalty and closeness with their mother, she was clear on their true natures. If Ava was given the chance to have five more minutes with her own mom, she'd have sacrificed anything. But Hazel and Kagan revised their mother's memory in an attempt to get everything.

After returning Iris's money in exchange for her delaying her police report and omitting Ava from her statement, she reached out to the famous private investigator whom Sam wanted to work with to finally solve his mother's case. Ava wired a hefty deposit along with Sam's contact information and all the digitized files she could extract from the local precinct in Virginia, along with the evidence she and Sam had found when they cleaned out Perry's Hoard and Seek storage space the day after the attempted sinking. There was so much she owed to Sam. It felt amazing when she opened an account for Sam and funded it with all the money she owed him from the yellow house on Peace Road. The remaining cash from her father's Hoard and Seek retirement fund was sufficient to ensure Sam would be taken care of for a while, at least until he got his life back on track. It was a small restitution for what he'd lost, but Ava was glad to reroute her father's ill-gotten nest egg to him.

A courier service had been arranged to deliver a package containing Janice's engagement and wedding rings to the rehabilitation facility with instructions to release them when they completed treatment. Alongside the rings was an envelope filled with cash, ensuring they could return to New York and sustain themselves until they secured jobs.

Her final hack had been to plant the fake shipwreck story and Walter Pierson's obituary. She hoped her father would force himself online to read both before they were taken down. If not, she knew the storage space was enough to get her point across.

The cool breeze refocuses her on the serene surroundings. She takes in the absence of everything. The open water reminds her that she can control only how she lives her life, not much else. She is but a tiny part of something so much more significant.

As clearly as she sees the uninterrupted horizon, Ava recalls what her father said to her when she threatened to leave him: "You can run, but you will never escape who you are."

Before, his words always made her feel trapped by her legacy. Now, surrounded by a vast expanse, she feels the opposite. Ava pictures her father's birth certificate and feels completely free knowing he's the one who can't escape who he truly is.

ACKNOWLEDGMENTS

This book draws inspiration from the personal stories of friends and loved ones who have shared their experiences dealing with con artists and the impact those encounters have had on their lives. We are deeply grateful for the strength, courage, and healing we've witnessed in these individuals, and we are honored to find inspiration in their experiences within these pages. Abuse, coercion, and fraud are unfortunately pervasive in our society, but support and awareness are also on the rise. There are some fantastic organizations we recommend for learning more about what to do if you've been scammed, conned, or victimized, and we've included them here.

Creating a book takes a village of talented individuals, and we are fortunate to have an incredible team at Dutton. Numerous gifted people, including our editors, John Parsley, Lexy Cassola, and Lashanda Anakwah, brought this book to life. Your collective guidance and vision made the writing experience and this book our favorite to date.

We sincerely appreciate our publicity and marketing whizzes: Amanda Walker, Jamie Knapp, Stephanie Cooper, Lauren Morrow, and Diamond Bridges. Special thanks to Christine Ball, Alison Dobson, Lauren Monaco, and the PRH sales team for their enthusiasm for our books.

We are also grateful to David Litman for another stunning jacket design, art director Christopher Lin, and our production dynamos: LeeAnn Pemberton, Gaelyn Galbreath, Lorie Pagnozzi, Laura Corless, Clare Shearer, and Melissa Solis.

To our remarkable agent, Christopher Schelling. His unwavering support for our careers and enduring friendship mean the world to us.

To our incredible families, thank you for your early reading, steadfast encouragement, and support on this unconventional storytelling journey. Your support means everything to us.

Thank you to the authors of these books for their fascinating and inspiring content, which was invaluable in the writing of this book: *Hype* by Gabrielle Bluestone, *The Confidence Game* by Maria Konnikova, *The Big Con* by David W. Maurer, *Confident Women* by Tori Telfer, *The Art of the Con: How to Think Like a Real Hustler and Avoid Being Scammed* by R. Paul Wilson, *The Duke of Deception* by Geoffrey Wolff, and *Without Conscience* by Robert D. Hare.

We are deeply grateful for all our dear friends' inspiration, motivation, and unwavering encouragement. Many of you are writers, artists, performers, and creators, and your passion and creativity continually inspire and energize us. We couldn't write these books without your invaluable influence and encouragement. Thank you from the bottom of our hearts.

Huge thanks to all the authors, readers, bloggers, bookstagrammers, booksellers, and librarians who make this wonderful literary community what it is. Your passion and enthusiasm have been instrumental in our journey, and we are deeply grateful for your role in making this book a reality. Your talent, perseverance, and generosity inspire us daily.

And special thanks to Brian and Quinn for the love, giggles, and daily adventures. You keep me grounded, humble, and constantly inspired.

And huge thanks and love to Fiona. None of this would be nearly as special without you.

The after-school program Kagan references in the text is 826NYC, a chapter of 826 National, an organization that provides students from under-resourced communities with high-quality writing and publishing programs in inspiring, creative spaces. Anyone looking to volunteer with or donate to this wonderful organization can find more information here: 826national.org

SUPPORT ORGANIZATION RESOURCES

National Domestic Violence Hotline (USA): Provides crisis intervention, information, and referral services for victims of domestic violence. (thehotline.org)

VictimConnect Resource Center (USA): Offers support and information for victims of all types of crime, including scams and fraud. (victimconnect.org)

Safe Horizon (USA): Provides support, prevents violence, and promotes justice for victims of crime and abuse, including scams and fraud. (safehorizon.org)

Elder Abuse (USA): Assists older adults who are victims of financial exploitation or other forms of abuse. (Information varies by state.)

National Women's Coalition Against Violence & Exploitation (NWCAVE) (USA): Helps to inform, educate, and prevent violence while advocating for justice and accountability. (nwcave.org)

ABOUT THE AUTHORS

Elizabeth McCullough Keenan and **Greg Wands** are internationally bestselling co-authors of three novels under the pen name E. G. Scott: *The Woman Inside*, *In Case of Emergency*, and *The Rule of Three*. Their books have been translated into a dozen languages and featured in *Entertainment Weekly*, *BuzzFeed*, *Real Simple*, and *InStyle*. They are the creators and cohosts of the podcast *Imposter Hour with Liz and Greg*. They are based in Pennsylvania and New York City.